GAIA'S GIFT

BY

FRAN ORENSTEIN

World Castle Publishing
http://www.worldcastlepublishing.com

FRAN ORENSTEIN

This is a work of fiction. Names, characters, places, and incidents are products of the author's imagination or are used factiously and are not to be construed as real. Any resemblance to actual events, locations, organizations, or person, living or dead, is entirely coincidental.

World Castle Publishing
Pensacola, Florida

Copyright © by Fran Orenstein 2012
ISBN: 9781937593827
First Edition World Castle Publishing January 12, 2012
http://www.worldcastlepublishing.com

License Notes
This book is licensed for your personal enjoyment only. This book may not be re-sold or given away to other people. If you would like to share this book with another person, please purchase an additional copy for each recipient. If you're reading this book and did not purchase it, or it was not purchased for your use only, then please purchase your own copy. Thank you respecting the hard work of this author.

Cover Artist: Karen Fuller
Editor: Beth Price

GAIA'S GIFT

DEDICATION

For Rachel Claire Orenstein, my special muse. At age nine, you suggested a children's story of a little girl named Abigail. It blossomed to become this novel.

Thank you, my dear.

Thank you to my readers, Anne Keller, Ellen George, Fran Beiman, and Malca Chall. Your input was invaluable.

Special thanks to L. Stern and Carol Oschmann for your expert advice on boats and boating. All the errors belong to me.

FRAN ORENSTEIN

Books by Fran Orenstein

Young adult historical romance novels
The Spice Merchant's Daughter
The Calling of the Flute

'Tween Books
The Mystery of Under Third Base
The Mystery of the Green Goblin
A Huby mystery series

The Wizard of Balalac
The Gargoyles of Blackthorne
A fantasy series from The Book of Mysteries

Fat Girls From Outer Space

FRAN ORENSTEIN

THE CORNER OF FREE WILL

Choices shape the journey of one's life
moving on from birth to death.
Every crossroad displays a sign
clearly marked in vibrant colors.

This is The Corner of Free Will.
You have the choice to stop or go,
to turn or move ahead, or not;
options taken at your own risk.

The Corner of Free Will takes no responsibility
for selections made by logical reflection,
or hasty, rash, emotion-driven thought.
The decisions belong to the traveler.

To go back and relive is not an option,
only forward steps or stagnation is allowed,
confronting us every minute of our lives,
as we cross the Corner of Free Will, or not.

Fran Orenstein, 2011

FRAN ORENSTEIN

CHAPTER ONE

Off the southwest coast of Florida, a cabin cruiser bobbed on the placid water of the Gulf of Mexico. To the east, the darkening, silvery light of a gathering storm filled the skies over central Florida. Thunder clouds sent intermittent shards of lightning into the earth, illuminating the fantasy worlds built from man's imagination. Seen from above, the exodus of people resembled ants scurrying from a hill beset by invading anteaters, and the gods laughed.

Innocent at this moment in time, Rachel Wells lay on the sun-drenched deck of the boat, drifting in blissful unawareness, lulled by the rocking sea. She absently tucked an errant, tickling curl, blown astray by the ocean breeze, behind her ear. A believer in the natural spirits of the world, Rachel silently thanked Gaia, goddess of the earth who had outdone herself today. Cotton clouds dotted the blue sky and the breeze carried the scent of sea salt. Arching her back, she lifted her chin into the salty spray that caressed her sun-kissed cheek.

"You are so beautiful," a deep voice sang from the cockpit.

Rachel laughed and arched her back further, seductively, full breasts rising in the sparse bikini bra.

"Watch it, lady...women have been ravished for less."

She laughed. "Anytime big fella, anytime."

"I'll get you later," he called.

"My door is always open," Rachel vamped.

She settled back on the mat. Life was perfect. The universe had given her all the blessings a woman could ask for: a wonderful husband, loving and kind, and an amazing, adorable little daughter. They had even discussed trying for a second child, perhaps a boy this time, but it didn't really matter, because another daughter would always be welcome. The organic herbs she grew and marketed had developed into a thriving business with orders from shops and herbalists across the country and Jack's veterinary practice was growing. He was even considering bringing on another vet or expanding it to include veterinarians who specialized in ophthalmology and oncology.

Jack, the rock of her existence, was her bulwark against the ragged memories of a lonely childhood spent shuttling between foster homes and children's shelters until she was finally adopted at age six. For a moment, a frisson of fear rushed down her spine and Rachel shuddered. Shaking it off, she silently thanked the universe for her blessings. The warm sun lulled her into a half-sleep, although her subconscious was always alert for her napping daughter's cry from the cabin below.

In this twilight time, between consciousness and sleep, thoughts of the past surfaced and Rachel's memory drifted to her own long-dead parents, shadowy figures with no substance; a figment of the foggy memories of a four-year-old. Sometimes she saw another, a toddler, but other than a halo of blonde curls, she too lived in the lost and faded past. As an adult, Rachel had tried to resurrect her without success from uncaring bureaucrats guarding closed files. "Rules," they said, sending her back into the harsh reality of non-existence where she remained a numbered file in a locked drawer that never saw the light of the sun. Who was the tiny child trapped in her memory? Sometimes, she could still feel the chubby hand in hers and see the worshipful blue eyes gazing up at her. Rachel loved her adoptive parents and her childhood had been happy, except for the missing pieces, the never-answered questions.

"Let it go," whispered the pragmatist.

"Easy for you to say, figment of her mind," the idealist retorted.

"Oh, and just what are you?" the pragmatist continued.

Rachel shook off the invading dialogue and let her body relax into the gentle rocking of the boat.

"Honey, I think you should go below."

The voice of her husband slowly penetrated her mind and she stretched, like a languid cat. Rolling over, she looked up at the bridge. "What did you have in mind, lover?"

"No, seriously! Look over there to the east."

Rachel looked back over her shoulder. A large black bank of storm clouds rolled over the horizon toward them. She could see the lines of rain and faint flashes of lightning. "Where did that come from?"

"Typical Florida storm, you know how they suddenly appear and disappear. I'm not worried, I just think you should go below, the baby might get scared."

She rose on long slim legs and climbed up to the bridge. She kissed her husband and nuzzled his neck. "I love you so much, Skipper Jack."

He reached out and caressed her breast. "I love you, too, Skipper's wife. I'm going to look for a safe inlet to ride out the storm. Now go below before something else steers the boat besides my hands."

Rachel giggled and crossed the now rolling deck. Suddenly frowning, she shivered under the hot Florida sun. A thought flashed like heat lightning and was gone in an instant; *this joke would be the last words Jack ever spoke.* Resolutely shaking the words from her mind, she descended the few steps to the cabin below.

FRAN ORENSTEIN

CHAPTER TWO

Inside the cabin, Rachel looked down at her sleeping daughter, curled in a fetal position, body wrapped around a Raggedy Ann doll. Her thumb hung loosely in her mouth and every so often she would suck on it. One of these days they would have to get her to stop sucking before her teeth were pushed out. She stroked the child's back and murmured in her ear, "Wake up, sleepy head. Time to get up."

The little girl opened her blue eyes and reached up. Immediately she was enveloped in her mother's arms, wrapped in a cocoon of warmth, feeling secure and safe. She sighed and burrowed into her mother's shoulder, her tousled blonde curls blending with Rachel's hair.

"Come on, baby girl. You have to put on your life vest."

"No!"

"Come on, sweetheart, there's a big storm coming and you know what that means."

"No! Hate it, arms stick out." Emma crossed her arms, pouting.

"I know, but it's only for a little while, until the nasty clouds pass by."

Thunder rumbled in the distance and the boat rocked.

"Emma, now!"

"You first," the child stubbornly insisted crossing her arms.

Rachel sighed; this was not the time for a lesson in obedience. She reached under the bunk and pulled out the two orange life vests. She quickly shrugged her arms into hers and tied the strings. "Okay? Now it's your turn."

The little girl reluctantly stood and allowed the tiny hated vest to be pulled around her torso. Rachel tied the strings and double knotted the bows. The child had been known to pull open the ties in the past.

"Hate it." The child screwed up her face.

"I know, baby girl. Me, too, but it will keep you safe in the water."

"No go in the water."

"That won't happen. This is just in case, to be safe."

The boat rocked like a wild child bouncing up and down on a rocking horse on springs.

The child pressed against her mother. "I scared, Mommy."

"It's okay, honey. Daddy is finding us a nice island where we can walk on the beach and look for pretty pink shells. Then we'll have a picnic lunch and wade in the water."

Rachel continued to drone on about the mythical island as the boat rocked harder and rain pounded on the deck above, like spring hail on a tin roof. She looked up at the ceiling and wished she knew what was happening on deck, if Jack was safe. She felt trapped down here in the cabin. She always hated tight, enclosed spaces and a claustrophobic fear threatened to engulf her. Focusing on her child's safety, she fought it back like a boxer pounding his opponent into the ropes. She couldn't lose it now, for her baby and her beloved husband.

"You can do it, be strong," the pragmatic voice echoed in her head. *"Don't give in."*

The boat shuddered suddenly and came to a jarring stop *"Rocks, we hit the rocks."* The panicky words tumbled around in her brain as she fell to the bunk.

"Mommeeee…."

"Climb on my back and hold on to me, Em. Whatever you do, don't let go."

"Piggy back?"

"That's right; we're taking a piggy back ride."

The child closed her legs around Rachel's waist and wrapped her arms tightly around her neck, nearly cutting off the air supply. The boat listed to one side and Rachel struggled to stand and balance the child on her back. She fought her way up the few steps to the door. It took her entire body weight to push open the cabin door.

The world had gone mad. Thunderous black clouds roiled and crashed overhead. Jagged flashes of lightning seared the water line through the deluge of rain. At once, they were soaked through.

"Jack!" Rachel screamed into the shrieking wind, her voice carried away as soon as the name was uttered.

The boat had foundered on a barrier of rocks just short of landfall. The cockpit was empty.

"NO!" she yelled. "Jaaaack!"

Clutching the child, she plowed through the howling deluge toward the small life preserver hanging on the side of the cockpit. Rachel pulled it down and fighting the blinding rain, she pushed the screaming child into the middle of the ring and dropped it into the water, jumping in after it. But a powerful wave pulled the ring out of her grip, breaking her wrist. "Emmaaaaaa!" she cried, ignoring the agony in her wrist. Rachel tried to swim toward the preserver, only to be swept backward with each stroke. The ring pulled further away toward the damnable rocks.

"Mommeeeee." The small voice disappeared in the din of the maelstrom. Through the torrential downpour, she watched helplessly as the ring hit the sharp rocks and began to deflate. A tiny orange life vest bobbed and rocked, teasing her, as the little child's body bounced among the jagged rocks and disappeared into the vast sea.

"Oh, Gaia, why us?" Her last thought before she blessedly fainted, held afloat by her orange vest. The storm moved off into the vast firmament to wreak more havoc and misery along the line of Keys that dotted the Florida Gulf Coast. A final flash of lightning, like the taunting finger of God, pierced the line of black at the edge of the now blue and tranquil sky.

FRAN ORENSTEIN

CHAPTER THREE

A plane, patrolling the Gulf after the particularly severe and sudden storm, spotted the wreckage early the next morning, on the shoreline of an isolated island. A rescue boat set out from the mainland. They found the woman, bruised and battered, lying half in the water.

"She's still breathing, but just barely," the rescuer said to his partner.

He shook his head. "Unbelievable! Somehow she survived."

"Oh yeah! The next tide would have washed her out to sea and probably back onto the rocks. Any other survivors?"

"Not that I can see, but we'll still search."

"Okay, got to get her back and to a hospital."

Two days later, Rachel awoke in great pain. She moaned and fell back into drug-induced, welcome oblivion. The next time she awoke, someone was seated by her bed.

"Ma'am, I'm Officer Carpenter, Harbor Police. Can you answer some questions?"

Rachel saw an earnest, somber young man, brown hair standing straight up in a short military cut. Her eyes blurred and he faded away, leaving her in a heavy fog bank, unable to wade through to the light.

"Ma'am, please. It's important," he insisted.

Rachel tried to focus on the voice and eventually the figure reappeared, although blurred around the edges.

"Em, Em, Em…," she moaned.

"Ma'am, please, can you say your name?"

Rachel strained against the fog, "Em," she whispered.

"Your name is Em?" he asked.

She wanted to shake her head and scream, but the effort and pain were beyond her brain's ability to obey the order. *"No, you stupid... Where's Em? Jack...Jack."* her mind screamed silently.

"Your name, please, ma'am?"

Rachel licked her lips. Finally, the officer woke up to the fact that she needed a drink. He picked up the glass and moved the straw to her lips. She sipped and swallowed, sighing. The cool water felt like silk against her parched throat.

Finally she croaked, "Rachel...Wells."

The policeman looked so happy, she wanted to kiss him and kill him at the same time.

"Em, Jack," she whispered.

"What is going on here?" a brusque voice interrupted. "What are you doing here, young man?"

The officer leapt to his feet and practically saluted. "Sorry, ma'am, just trying to find out her identity and who was with her on the boat."

The nurse pointed to the door. "Out, now. No visitors."

He backed out of the room, nearly bowing in the wake of her anger.

She waited until the door shut and then turned to the pathetic figure on the bed. "I'm so sorry, my dear, he must have sneaked in when no one was on the desk."

Rachel made a huge effort and whispered, "Please, my baby, my husband, help..." Then she fell into blessed oblivion again.

The nurse clasped her hand to her mouth, turned and rushed out after the policeman.

They searched and searched, but never found the tiny body in the hated orange life vest that hadn't saved her after all. No trace was found of Jack Wells, either. Perhaps his decimated body would wash up on some beach one day, but it was doubtful that he would ever be found.

Days later, Rachel railed at Gaia and her progeny, Poseidon, the god of the oceans for taking away her family. Slowly, she slipped into an alternate world, drifting in a fog bank that obscured reality. The times she swam through the thick mist into consciousness, Rachel heard the beeping of the monitors and the hush-hush of the nurse's shoes, but refused to open her mind to reality.

Finally, one evening, Rachel awoke and stared into the loving brown eyes of her friend, Mary Cross. Mary's pale face looked down at her. The dark hair that normally framed her face in a shiny, sleek bob, now hung in untidy clumps around her ears, uncombed and unwashed. Mary perched on the edge of a chair, her tall, thin body hunched over the bed.

Rachel opened her hand and Mary clasped it tightly. Tears flowed freely from Mary's swollen eyes and she whispered, "Stay with me, Rachel, please. Stay awake."

"They're gone, aren't they?" Rachel murmured.

Mary nodded and sniffed. "I'm so sorry, Rachel."

Rachel turned her head away and crawled inside herself.

FRAN ORENSTEIN

CHAPTER FOUR

During the year of insanity that followed the tragedy, Rachel ate little and shrank to a gaunt, pale specter. Black circles rimmed her eyes from sleepless nights and when she did sleep, black dreams invaded the peaceful, healing slumber and drove jagged knives through her brain. She woke screaming from repeated nightmares of a tiny skeleton caught in a ragged orange life vest bobbing on the endless sea, while she reached out helplessly from the rocky shore.

Her once shiny, golden hair hung in lifeless clots of greasy, tangled knots. Morning and evening, Rachel wandered the beach barefoot, in unwashed clothes, stopping now and then to reach out her arms to the sea and fall to her knees in supplication. Her eyes continually searched the waves for a tiny speck of orange to come floating toward her outstretched arms. On days of darkest despair, she willed herself to walk into the sea, further and further until the rip tide could suck her under, but never summoned enough courage to go further than the lapping wavelets a few feet offshore.

Wandering the beach, she raged in a silent voice to herself or castigated Gaia in unspoken curses. She constantly rubbed the angry scar on her cheek where the rocks had cut her face, the only visible vestige of her ordeal. She vaguely saw people crossing the street when they saw her ambling toward the beach, but they were mere shadows with no substance. Those who knew her shook their heads in pity or averted their eyes so they wouldn't witness the agony she projected, or worse, feel the nagging guilt of avoidance. Parents instinctively pulled their children close. Others clutched their companions arm, or simply sped up and hurried past. Rachel never saw them, or if their images intruded, she tossed them away like brushing at flies.

Eventually, caring people stopped calling and ringing the doorbell. When she bothered to think rationally at all, Rachel felt a tiny twinge of guilt about Mary Cross. At first, Mary came to the door, ringing the bell incessantly. When no one answered, she phoned daily, then weekly, then monthly, but recently, the calls had stopped. Actually, Rachel had lost count of the days, weeks and months. She had been as close as she could be to Mary Cross, the woman who supervised the veterinary technicians and managed the medical side of Jack's animal hospital. There was still a distance that had to be kept, professionally, but Mary had also been Emma's occasional baby sitter and the child had loved her. Now none of that mattered. The clinic was closed, forever. Emma was gone from her life, along with everything and everyone else who had mattered. Her heart closed with the finality of a door shutting on a once-loved house that no longer beat with life or joy.

Seated at the kitchen table, staring into space, Rachel heard the doorbell ring, and at first couldn't place the sound. It hadn't rung in months. She tentatively peered through the window and saw Gary Vaughn, ever the impeccably dressed attorney. Briefcase in hand, shoes polished and not a wrinkle in his pristine suit. He looked the same as ever, dark wavy hair, strong cleft chin and a straight thin nose. Only the v-shaped wrinkle between his eyebrows belied the worry behind his perfect exterior.

"Don't open the door," the voice of fear shouted in her head.

The voice of reason countered and won. *"Don't be stupid, it's just Gary, he's our attorney."* That forever 'our'; would it ever me just 'my'?

Why fear Gary? He and Jack had been best friends for years. He handled all their legal business so why this sudden revulsion toward the man? Rachel shook her head at the irrational reaction and opened the door.

Gary Vaughn gasped. "Oh, Rachel, what's happened to you?" Gary stopped his retreat mid-step and reached out. Then, he hesitated. "I'm sorry, I'm sorry, Rachel. Are you all right?"

Rachel grimaced at the stupid question and stepped back out of reach. She wondered at the inanities people said in times of disaster and misery. Of course she wasn't all right...she would never be all right again.

Pulling a vestige of ancient, unused manners out of her ravaged mind Rachel tried to speak, but she hadn't talked to anyone in so long her voice was hoarse. She cleared her throat and tried again. "I'm fine, Gary. What do you want?" It came out more like a growl.

Gary dropped his arms. "I was worried, Rachel. There are all kinds of rumors and I wanted to make sure you were okay."

"I don't care about rumors. People can just fuck off, for all I care."

Gary backtracked and bumped the door jamb. He couldn't remember Rachel ever using such a word. She looked disheveled and a sour odor came off her clothes. Rachel had always taken pride in her appearance and even when tending her herb garden, she always wore clean, neat clothes. She had a model's figure and anything she wore, from shorts to gowns, fit her with flair and panache, to the envy of his wife, Laura. Now soiled shorts and a tee shirt hung on her emaciated body. What happened to the shiny blonde curls, now dirty and matted and her once vibrant, healthy skin, sagging, pale and dry?

"For heaven's sake, Rachel, we've known each other since college; I was Jack's best friend and best man at your wedding. You know you can trust me."

"Can I? Where've you been these past months, Gary? Where's Laura been? I don't have leprosy," Rachel shouted, then began coughing from the strain.

The voice in her head whispered, *"Is that fair? Maybe they had called. Would you have even answered the phone?"*

Rachel shrugged it off. It didn't really matter, anyway. That part of her life ended on a pile of jagged rocks in the Gulf of Mexico.

Gary couldn't meet her eyes. "You're right Rachel, Laura and I haven't been here for you."

"It doesn't rub off, you know…death and destruction…it's not catching." Rachel felt the lump rising in her throat.

"I'm sorry, Rachel, I'm really sorry. I know there's no excuse, but Laura was pregnant and she was nervous. And, well, I guess we've been preoccupied, what with the new baby and everything. You know how it is at first…." His hand flew up to his face. "Oh, my God, Rachel, I'm so sorry. I shouldn't be telling you all this. I'm sorry, I'm sorry."

Rachel staggered and felt her way to the double chair, the womb where she cuddled with her baby and read books on rainy days. She fell into it and curled up in a tight ball, as tears rolled down her cheeks. Charm, her beloved cat, jumped down from the sill and leaped up onto Rachel's chair. She sat there glaring at Gary and hissing, guarding her mistress like a fearless knight in shining black armor.

Rachel wished Gary would just leave. She wasn't ready to share anything with the outside world, to begin to live again. She just wanted to stay wrapped in her cocoon of anguish and feel the intense pain and guilt of the survivor.

"Jesus, I can't do anything right today. I want to help you. Rachel, look at me, please let me help you."

Rachel lifted her head and growled, "Get the hell out of my house, Gary. Go back to your wife and baby, whatever. Just take care of my money and take your billable hours out of the interest. Just leave me alone."

Gary took a card out of his pocket. He put it gingerly on the side table. "This guy is a psychiatrist…he's really good. Please go see him, Rachel. Jack would have wanted you to go on."

"Get out!" Rachel screamed.

The door shut behind Jack's best friend, now relegated to the status of her attorney, only because she didn't have the energy to find someone else.

A month later, when she couldn't stand herself any more and wanted to die more than anything else, Rachel found the business card still waiting on the table for a moment of lucidity. With shaking hands she called and made an appointment that was forgotten on a day she couldn't get out of bed. A week later, the card called to her from the table and she tried again. This time she showered and dressed and kept the appointment.

The psychiatrist was a nice man, young with the requisite beard and gentle brown eyes. "I'm Doctor Breslin. Is it all right to call you Rachel or do you prefer Mrs. Wells?"

Rachel stared at him. "There is no Mrs. Wells," she whispered.

He nodded as if he understood.

"He's a liar. No one could understand. He would always be Dr., Mr., whoever...," said the pragmatist.

"He's only trying to help," reason countered.

Rachel pushed the thoughts away and pulled at her stringy hair.

"All right then, tell me about yourself, Rachel."

Silence! The doctor waited patiently, but she said nothing for 50 minutes, just crawled inside herself and built a wall, a solid, stone, un-penetrable wall. The pain and grief refused to rise to the surface to be plucked from the murky depths and deposited for anyone to see.

She missed the next appointment, but kept the one after; another silent session. The doctor prescribed an antidepressant that she didn't fill. She never went back.

Finally she disappeared into her house and waited for Death, burning the calendar and smashing the clocks, so she wouldn't have to watch time move on for everyone else. But Death, ever elusive until he was ready to appear, ignored her entreaties.

FRAN ORENSTEIN

CHAPTER FIVE

Time shifted. Spring's inevitable arrival brought the birth of life and a lessening of the sorrow that had engulfed Rachel like a deluge of black rain. The fog of grief that enshrouded her finally lifted with the burgeoning buds on the trees and shrubs. Perhaps somewhere in her muddled brain, Rachel realized that death required her active participation and she wasn't ready to go there. Anxiety twisted her intestines. Was something out there waiting to disturb the cocoon in which she had wrapped herself? Huge waves of overwhelming guilt engulfed her and she tried in vain to crawl back into the black cavern of despair, but the awakened sun relentlessly drilled a widening hole through the crack in the shutters.

On the momentous morning that heralded the enormous change in her life, Rachel's first awareness upon opening her eyes, was not the loss of Jack and Emma and her own unbearable pain, but the brightness of the sun and the raucous sound of ducks and gulls calling to each other. In the next moment, she smelled the sour odor emanating from her body and the bed that culminated a year of physical neglect and disregard of her surroundings. Then, she remembered.

"Oh, Jack, what have I done?" Tears welled, as she looked around at the filthy bedroom. She forced herself to the bathroom and peered in the mirror, jerking back in horror at the gaunt, wild woman facing her.

"This can't be me!" she cried.

A cool lemony breeze drifted around her bare legs, delicately caressing the skin. She whirled, but nothing was there and the window was shut. Still the breeze gently stroked her skin, now moving up to her shoulders.

"Jack?" she whispered. The breeze withdrew.

"Please come back, please," she pleaded.

A faint scent of lavender permeated the air.

"Emma? Is that you?" Rachel called to the empty room. "Come back, please, I'm sorry, I'll do better, I promise, please come back." In the next instance she deciphered the message and accepted her fate. She was to live on, but the reason eluded her muddled brain.

Angry with herself that she had fallen so low, Rachel pulled off her tee shirt and filthy underpants. She viciously brushed her tangled, dirty hair, pulling out whole strands in violent self-punishment. Then in frustration, she grabbed the scissors and chopped it off until it stood up in straggly spikes on her head. "Stupid woman, stupid, stupid woman," she shouted at the thin, ugly shell of her once pretty self, reflected in the mirror.

Rachel turned on the shower as hot as she could stand it. Then she rummaged in the linen closet for some clean towels. Kicking the disgusting bathmat into the corner she put one towel on the floor and hung the other carefully on the hook. She stepped into the shower, gasping at the heat. Soaping her body twice and shampooing her hair three times, she rinsed in an icy blast of cold water. After she dried, she shuffled on the towel to the closet.

There were plenty of clean clothes still on the shelves because she hadn't bothered to change very often in the past year. Putting on fresh underwear, she pulled on shorts and a tee shirt and stepped into sandals, reluctant to place her feet on the filthy floor. Walking into the kitchen, she surveyed the accumulation of dirty dishes and garbage. Beleaguered, she sat at the dirt-encrusted table and put her head in her hands. The initial energy quickly dissipated in the overwhelming confrontation of year's worth of debris.

A gentle breeze crossed her face, like the touch of a lover's fingers, Jack's fingers. Taking a deep breath, Rachel reached for the telephone and stared at it as though confronting an incomprehensible instrument on an alien space ship. She brushed her fingers over the number pad and sighing, pressed auto-dial and the number five. One called the police and two the pediatrician…well two would never be used again, nor would three or four, Jack's work number and Jack's cell phone.

The phone buzzed three times in her ear and a familiar voice sounded in her ear. "Hello?"

Rachel opened her mouth to speak, but only a croak emerged.

"Hello? I can't hear you, can you speak up?"

"Mary, help me," Rachel whispered.

"Rachel, is that you?"

"Please, help me Mary, I can't do this alone."

"Ten minutes, Rachel! Don't do anything, okay? Just wait for me. I'm coming!"

Tears rolled from Rachel's eyelids and streaked down her face. Her shoulders shuddered and heaved. Heavy sobs wracked her bony body as she released the tremendous anxiety of allowing someone else into her life; even someone like Mary Cross. Wonderful Mary, who mourned and grieved and reached out to Rachel in the early days, only to be rebuffed by Rachel's indifference and sorrowful anger. Mary, who still had never given up, but dropped everything when Rachel called.

Charm, sensing the arrival of a long-lost friend, leaped to the window sill in anticipation. Rachel raised her tear-streaked face at the sound of a car, crunching the gravel on the driveway. Charm leaped down and raced to the front door. Wiping her eyes, Rachel rose like an ancient crone and walked slowly to the door. When she opened it, there stood Mary Cross, arms outstretched. Rachel fell into the arms and folded into the strong embrace of her loyal friend. Charm wound herself around Mary's ankles and purred. Mary kicked the door shut behind her, locking Rachel's heaving sobs into the privacy of her house.

A large-boned, tall woman, Mary Cross commanded a room with her presence.

She wore her auburn hair in a long single braid down her back, its curly wisps escaping. Her freckled face and up-turned nose would have fit nicely into Dublin, the home of her ancestors. The commanding air and tone of her voice belied the gentle soul that lay beneath the exterior. Despite the shock of the sights that greeted her, Mary's sweet smile remained locked into place.

Arms around Rachel's shoulders, Mary led her into the kitchen. "I'm here now, Rachel. A cup of hot chamomile tea will calm you." Mary Cross was now in charge. After making sure Rachel would drink the tea, she called a cleaning service and offered an exorbitant extra fee for immediate response by a crew. By evening, the house was clean, the trash waiting at the curb for early morning pick-up, and the five loads of laundry folded neatly in their places. She shopped for food and even brought home a rotisserie chicken and coleslaw for dinner.

"Got to fatten you up, darlin'," Mary said cheerfully, as she set the table.

Rachel opened her mouth, but Mary cut her off. "I don't want to hear anything negative. I went to the natural foods market, so you don't have to worry about the food not being natural and organic. There are brownies and ice cream for dessert. And I even got a special treat for Charm."

She pulled a catnip mouse from the bag and dangled it before the cat. Charm rose on her hind legs and batted at the fake-fur creature. She snagged the mouse and took off into the other room.

"I just wanted to say thank you, Mary. You're an amazing woman."

"Yes, well, I've missed you, Rachel. I've missed the clinic."

Rachel sighed. "Did you find another job?"

Mary shook her head. "I go into the clinic three times a week to straighten up and check the mail."

"Oh, Mary, I didn't know. I'll call Gary and make sure he pays you for your time."

"I didn't do it for money, Rachel, although it would help, I did it because I miss you all and I didn't want to lose touch with a place I loved for so many years. I felt...well, I can't really explain.

It was like Jack was still there and the rest of the staff and the animals. It was like my going there kept everything alive."

Rachel swiped at her eyes and sniffed. "There was a letter from Gary a few months ago that somebody wanted to buy the clinic. I didn't answer it."

"Maybe you should, Rachel. The clinic needs to feel alive and useful again."

Rachel nodded. "Perhaps you're right. But there would be one stipulation. You have to be hired as the staff manager and vet assistant and stay as long as you wish."

"That would be wonderful. If I wasn't happy, I could always leave." She smiled.

"But the new vet couldn't fire you, either," Rachel added.

Mary grinned. "Now why on earth would anyone want to fire me? I'm a terrific employee."

"Absolutely! You have my highest recommendations."

"I'd like to stay over tonight, if it's all right with you. It's getting late and I'm really too tired to drive."

"You are always welcome, Mary." Although, Rachel suspected Mary was afraid to leave in case Rachel slipped back into her fugue state again.

Rachel lay down on the clean, cool sheets, relaxed and at peace knowing Mary was in the guest room. The scent of lavender permeated the air. "Emma," she whispered. Drawing the blanket over her, she smelled the musky animal scent of the past invading the room. The odor Jack could never seem to wash out of his hair even with the tea tree shampoo. At last, spooned in her mind by a familiar shape that held her, Rachel drifted off into her first full night of dreamless sleep in a year.

FRAN ORENSTEIN

CHAPTER SIX

Mary left the next morning and Rachel promised she would call Gary to see if the buyer was still interested in purchasing Jack's practice.

An hour later, she ventured into the herb garden to survey the weeds that grew wild in the neglected beds. Before, and there would always be that caveat…before, Rachel's herb garden was her business. Her husband, Jack, a sacrifice to Poseidon, had delighted in her success. But for the past year she had neglected the herbs and ignored the requests from shops and the herbalist for product. Instead she had lived inside a shell, much like a snail, burrowing deeper and deeper until all light disappeared. Darkness was a safe haven from reality.

She didn't need money now. In fact, once she had left the hospital over a year ago, Gary had happily given her good news that thanks to the insurance and Jack's frugal investments, she was now a wealthy woman. She looked at him with such pain, that he had dropped his eyes. "Thank you," she said finally, in a barely discernable voice. *Riches are relative when they come with an awful price*, she thought, with bitterness. She finally understood what tainted, dirty money meant.

Today, though, the warm sun pierced the cold fog of grief and Rachel, armed with her gardening tools, knelt in the herb garden, shielded from the street by a thick row of bougainvillea bordering the property. As she pulled weeds, Rachel heard a rustling sound and the whispering of childish voices.

"It's the witch's house."

"You think she's in there?"

"What's she doing?"

"You think she's really a witch?"

"My mom says she is; I heard her telling her reading club."

"Yeah?"

"Uh, huh. My mom says Mrs. Wells is weird and makes these potions from plants to maybe poison people."

"That's stupid. My mom buys her tea. We ain't poisoned."

"My mom thinks maybe she killed her family with the poison."

"That's so dumb, they got lost in a storm at sea."

"How do you know what happened?"

"My dad said so, and he's smart."

Rachel shivered against a sudden chill of their words and hugged herself. *Did people really believe she poisoned her family? Was everyone going insane or was she losing her mind?*

"Well, I think she's a witch. My mom says they should run her out of town."

"That's the stupidest thing I ever heard. She doesn't even look like a witch."

"Yeah she does, and she has that black cat and rides on a broomstick."

"You are so dumb…she don't ride a broomstick."

"Yeah, she does."

"No she don't."

Suddenly, Rachel stood up and the boys shrieked and ran away down the street. "Witch, witch," they screamed.

The voices faded with the sound of feet running down the street. Rachel sat back on her heels. *Witch*, she thought, shivering. *Are we in Salem?* She turned her head and looked toward the house. Charm sat inside on the window sill in the warm sun, watching a lizard crawling up the outside of the pane.

"Are you my familiar, Charm?" Rachel whispered. "Is this what I've become…an outcast to be feared by children, a witch to be hanged or burned?"

Maybe it was time to leave.

GAIA'S GIFT

Her decision was set in stone the next day when the police visited her house accompanied by Iris Janson, mother of one of the boys. Rachel looked out the window when the doorbell rang. She saw the police uniform and Iris, once her friend, now an angry mother, pacing on the porch.

She reluctantly opened the door and stepped outside. There was no way she was letting anyone into her house. She didn't say a word, just leaned against the door.

"Uh, sorry, Mrs. Wells, but, uh, Mrs. Janson says you scared her son Bobby and his friend Kit yesterday," the policeman said, refusing to meet her eyes.

"He should be ashamed," the idealist said.

"He's just doing his job," retorted the pragmatist.

Rachel turned from the police officer and tuned out the voices. She focused on Iris. Say it, she thought. Tell me I'm a witch to my face.

Iris Janson glanced away from Rachel's stare. "Bobby says you threatened them with a witch's spell," she said without much conviction.

"Ma'am, please let me do the talking," the officer said. His face was red and he couldn't meet Rachel's eyes.

"See, even he thinks this is dumb," the idealist ventured.

Rachel stared them down. Then she said to Iris, "Ten years of friendship, so think about that before you say or do something very, very stupid. Now, leave me alone. Maybe you should go home and hug your child...I can't do that anymore."

She opened the door behind her and slipped in, slamming it shut and locking it. There was silence for a minute, then the sound of footsteps faded away until she couldn't hear them anymore.

What would be next? Did this backward, redneck town burn witches at the stake or did they drown them? Maybe, drowning would be a good thing. Do you want me too, Gaia? The whole Wells family...what a coup.

FRAN ORENSTEIN

CHAPTER SEVEN

Over the next 12 months Rachel planned her escape from civilization. It took a year to learn survival techniques, using wind and generators for energy, animal husbandry, and carpentry skills. It was a time during which she sold her herb business and the veterinary practice.

Selling the house was the hardest thing she had to do. For days after signing the contract, she wandered from room to room, memories floating just beyond her grasp. Sometimes in the family room, she caught a mist-shrouded glimpse of a small blonde girl, dressed as Snow White serving tea to her teddy bears and Raggedy Ann. Sometimes she caught the whiff of lemon aftershave, Jack's aftershave, lingering in the bathroom. Once Rachel thought she saw an indentation in the pillow on his side of the bed, but it disappeared. She buried her face in the pillow and wept.

Rachel bought an 18 foot Boston Whaler, a reliable boat that could carry what she would need to create a new life and began her search for an oasis where she could heal. She found it on an isolated tip of another key, separated from the populated area by 30 or more miles of dense inland vegetation. Her sensible brain still functioned, and in an emergency she could follow the shoreline to civilization. Gentle waves from a lagoon kissed the sandy beach, safe and secure, secluded from prying eyes, far enough from her memories. She bought the uninhabited part of the island from a would-be developer who could not believe his good luck. He thought she was crazy, but decided that her offer benefited him in a shifting market. Perhaps she was crazy.

A contractor sworn to secrecy by the almighty dollar hired workers to clear the ground, build a small house, sheds and a dock. Finally, Rachel surveyed her tiny kingdom and found it livable, for as long as she remained too frightened to die.

She told Mary Cross.

"You're what?" Mary asked, horrified.

"You can't talk me out of it, Mary. I'm determined in this decision. I can't go on living here in this redneck town, with people calling me a witch and saying I sell poisonous herbs."

"People will get over that, once you show them you're...."

"Please, Mary, I've made my decision and it is mine to make. I love you for your kindness and friendship, but I need to leave this place and the memories that haunt me every day and night."

Mary argued. "You can't heal off by yourself, isolated, just thinking day and night."

"I have to do this, Mary. Please try to understand. I can't live around people any more. It hurts too much." Rachel knew that no one could comprehend the agony of watching other children, seeing couples holding hands, watching life go on without her.

Mary nodded, her face getting blotchy as tears fell. She threw her arms around Rachel and hugged her. "I'll miss you so much, Rachel Wells."

"I promise to call whenever I go to the mainland. You can write to me and give the letters to Gary Vaughn. He'll send them on to me. We won't lose touch, Mary."

Rachel finally sent Mary on her way and watched her friend's sagging shoulders as she walked slowly across the driveway to her car. Mary looked up one last time and held up her hand. Rachel blew her a kiss and closed the door.

Rachel told Gary, not as a friend, but as an attorney, sworn to secrecy by his position and even then, only for security and financial reasons. She made out a new will leaving everything in a trust to different charities that cared for animals, children and the Earth. As a gesture toward her husband, she endowed a chair at their alma mater in Jack's memory in the School of Veterinary Medicine. Then she set up a foundation for abused and abandoned children, called Emma's Place. Finally, she arranged for money to be placed in an investment account for Mary Cross, where she could access the principal or use the interest to live on. It was all she had to give the one person who stood by her, for emotionally, Rachel was bereft.

Rachel didn't need much money, not any more; certainly not filthy, death-defiled money.

"*So give it all away,*" the idealist whispered in her ear.

"*Keep some for yourself,*" the pragmatist countered.

"*Give it away.*"

"*Keep it.*"

"*Give.*"

"*Keep.*"

"Shut up." Rachel put her hands over her ears as if that would muffle their ever-present voices.

A week later, Rachel made arrangements with her attorney to deposit an obscene sum of money in an existing on-line investment account Jack had opened years before, and have traveler's checks and a money order delivered quarterly to a post office box in a tourist resort on the mainland. There would be no bank accounts to expose her to the world, besides there was nothing to buy on her end of the island. That satisfied the arguing voices in her head.

A week later, with aching heart, Rachel Wells shut the door of the house for the last time, leaving behind the memories of love and laughter, pain and sorrow, and disappeared.

FRAN ORENSTEIN

CHAPTER EIGHT

Five years later a cabin cruiser sailed on the calm waters of the Gulf of Mexico off the southwest Florida coast. Paul Stern, a tall, athletic man in his late twenties, hummed to himself as he deftly steered the boat toward a line of islands in the distance. He watched a bank of clouds rise above the horizon and felt the increased wind on his face.

Below in the cabin, tiny Abigail curled up in her mother's lap and rested her head against her soft breasts. She drifted with the gentle rocking of the boat and the familiar beat of her mother's heart. The sweet familiar voice sang:

"Hush little baby, don't say a word. Mama's gonna buy you a mocking bird...."

Abigail hugged her brown teddy bear to her cheek. The pink ribbon around the bear's neck tickled her chin. She reached up with a pudgy hand and brushed it away.

"...if that mocking bird don't sing...Mama's gonna buy you a diamond ring."

Three year-old Abigail drifted off into sleep, safe and secure, lulled by the motion of the waves. She fluttered her fingers as feathery white and gray birds flitted into her dream of sparkling ice-blue nests in leafy green swaying trees.

The next thing she knew the boat was tossing about on angry black waves. Thunder crashed overhead and lightning flashed onto the water. Fists clenched, Abigail screamed, "Mommeee!"

"I'm right here, darling. It's just a storm. A bad old storm," her mother said, rubbing Abigail's back. "Let me put on your life jacket, sweetheart."

Abby folded her arms. "No."

"Abigail Stern, hold out your arms, right now."

But when Abigail looked up at her mother, she saw fear. "Mommy, I scared."

"There's nothing to be scared about, Abigail. Daddy has found a beautiful island and we're going to stay there until the storm ends." Her mother smiled down at her and tied the ribbons on the life jacket.

Abigail was very afraid. She didn't like the boat rocking so hard on the water or the noise of the rain falling on the cabin roof. It sounded like a zillion billion woodpeckers. She cringed when a loud thunder boom echoed through the cabin. "Mommeee...."

"Ann, I need you up here, now." Abigail heard her father calling.

"Abigail, you stay down here, I have to go up to help Daddy."

"I scared. Don't leave me," she cried, tears welling in her eyes.

"Honey, you are safe here. I have to help Daddy." Her mother handed her the brown teddy bear. "Jon Bear will take care of you and I'll be right back."

She ran up the steps and turned around at the top. "I love you, Abigail baby." When her mother opened the hatch, rain poured in. Rachel heard her father yelling, "Mayday, mayday, mayday. Anyone! This is Yankee Tango Whisky 9737, Sweet Abigail out of Miami...." The rest was lost in the wind that slammed shut the hatch.

"I wuv you, too, Mommy," Abigail replied, but mommy was gone. Abigail rolled over on the bunk and curled up around the bear. Her tiny body shook and tears rolled down her cheeks. "I scared, Jon Bear, I scared." She stuck her thumb in her mouth and sucked frantically.

GAIA'S GIFT

The last sound Abigail heard was a loud crack. She felt her body bob up and down like she was bouncing on a trampoline. Then her world went black and silent.

FRAN ORENSTEIN

CHAPTER NINE

Abigail opened her eyes. She was lying on sand, shivering. Her clothes felt wet and sticky. Her head hurt. "Owie, owie." She rubbed her head and sticky red stuff clung to her hand. "Yucky, icky," she said, rubbing her hand on her shorts. The little girl sat up. "Mommy? Daddy?"

Silence!

"Where are you? Abby scared. Mommeee?" she screamed and screamed and screamed.

Then…blessed darkness…silence…

Abigail sat up and looked around. Her head hurt. She squinted against the bright sun shining on the gentle waves lapping against the edges of the beach, littered with planks of painted wood. She saw a round orange ring with a white rope hanging from one end. She knew she had seen it before, but could not remember where. There were letters painted on one side of the ring, but Abigail couldn't read yet. She thought she recognized the first letter of her name. Mommy called it an A and said it sounded like when Abby went to the doctor and he looked in her mouth and had her say 'aaaah'. The memory of a boat flicked across Abigail's three-year-old mind, but was instantly gone.

The sun dipped lower and the clouds turned pink. Abigail shivered so hard, her teeth rattled. "Mommy," she called again, but knew deep inside that no one was coming. She rubbed her head again. "Owie, Mommy." The only response was the wind rubbing the palm fronds together and the waves lapping against the shoreline.

House, she thought. The flash of a white house with green shutters appeared for an instant. Abigail looked around. *Need house.* She saw an intact piece of the hull near the tree line, with a tiny opening she could crawl through.

The child staggered to her feet, turned and tripped over a large palm branch and fell, landing on her bottom. Abigail began to cry. Full sentences deserted her. "Hurt, Mommy. Abby...owie kiss."

Mommy didn't come. Abigail hiccupped, then stood up and hit the branch "Bad, bad, hurt Abby." She tugged at the branch and dragged it over to the hull, pulling it over the top. It was hard work for a small girl. She couldn't put her arms down at her sides because of a funny orange jacket she was wearing. It was like her puffy blanky with the pink flowers. *What puffy blanky?* She struggled to bring home the memory, but it eluded her.

Abigail stood back and looked at the structure. Now she had a house. She dragged the orange ring to the 'house' and pushed it in through the opening.

"Abby need blanky," she said, looking around. The light was fading. Abigail didn't like the dark. Monsters lived in the dark. A piece of pink cloth fluttered from under a fragment of wood. Abigail went over and pulled on the cloth. She tugged and tugged, finally dislodging it. The memory of a pink towel crossed her mind and disappeared. The wood that was holding the cloth rolled over and there was Jon Bear.

Abigail grabbed the soggy bear and hugged him to her chest. "Oh, Jon Bear, now Abby not alone." Clutching the bear and dragging the cloth behind her, she toddled back to the 'house' and crawled inside. She curled up in the orange ring and pulled the pink 'blanky' over her tiny body. Thrusting her thumb in her mouth, Abigail curled up in a ball, clutching the tattered and stiff, sand-encrusted bear and drifting into a deep sleep, sinking into younger years, before she had the words that made sentences.

The moon fell below the horizon and Earth awakened to a blood-red sun. Droplets of rain hung like sparkling jewels from the palm fronds and tree branches. The scruffy, dirty, dog crept on its belly along the sand. Its throat throbbed with muted growls and whines. Slowly, it inched along, shifting to avoid the larger pieces of wood and debris that littered the beach.

Still in the puppy stage and not yet fully feral, it sniffed at a broken dish. It had a strange smell, not a food smell, not like the bowl in the corner of the warm room where all the good smells were. The dog was very hungry, and thirsty. The big water tasted terrible, like the pool he remembered from where he used to live. The dog did not drink it. He lapped instead at the small puddles on the ground, filled with water that had fallen from above when the world got dark.

The puppy remembered the loud booms and crackling light, and shivered. He was cold and scared. A pack of wild dogs had been stalking him since he had crawled under the fence and ran off into the woods after a rabbit. He lifted his nose and smelled something lurking in the far reaches of his memory. He followed his nose to a broken hull, sniffing at the familiar something. It smelled like his boy, but not quite the same. His boy would have food. He would hug him and throw the ball. Puppy wriggled inside and curled up beside the almost recognizable smell.

The little girl whimpered but remained asleep. She rolled over and put her arms around the dog. It shivered, then snuggled against the child's soft body, sighed and fell asleep.

FRAN ORENSTEIN

GAIA'S GIFT

CHAPTER TEN

The sun rose along the horizon spreading an orange and pink glaze across the white clouds. Rachel stood at the edge of the tiny inlet watching the whitecaps break along the crest of the gentle waves. A lazy breeze ruffled the short, dark blonde hair that capped her head. Although to the deceived eye, she appeared slight and slender; her body was well-toned and muscular, athletic and very strong.

Rachel unconsciously rubbed the white scar line along her right cheek and shivered despite the warming sun. Yesterday's storm was a spectacular, yet terrifying revolt by Mother Nature. Gaia was appeased for now and rested quietly, plotting her next insurgency against the humans who imposed atrocities upon her ravaged body.

Rachel had waited out the storm in a rocker on the deep front porch, holding Charm, the black short-haired cat, one of the salvaged remnants of her past. She had whispered in Charm's ear, calming her, praising her for her bravery. The cat had meowed and stretched her paw, gently kneading Rachel's sweater. Black waves swelled against the shoreline, sending shells and driftwood onto the sand, then reclaiming them in an endless cycle of give and take. Flashes of lightning had broken through the raging black clouds, pointing beckoning electric fingers at the roiling sea, an invitation to participate in a game of chaos. Thunderous crashes shook the windows of the small cabin Rachel had commissioned five years ago.

Rachel shivered, remembering the storm that had changed her life forever, the rage and fury of Gaia against humanity, taking the innocent along with the guilty, for the Goddess did not discriminate in her pain. She saw the faces of the innocents in the torrents of water that poured over the beach and heard the breaking of tree branches, so like the hull of a wooden boat cracking over rocks, tossed like flotsam and jetsam on the shore.

Angrily swiping at her eyes, Rachel pushed the memories into the black abyss. Now, with the storm abated, Rachel would search the beach in the morning for remnants of the sacrificial, broken boat that had soothed Gaia's battered breasts last night. In the darkness of the storm, she had watched the flickering lights bobbing like a demented dancer twirling on the rise and fall of the ocean's bosom. Memories had flooded her like the incoming tide. She sat in silence, helpless, imagining the panic of the crew, the rocks ripping into the bottom of the boat, tearing it apart. Rachel had lit a lantern and hung it from a hook on the porch roof. It swung in the wind like a welcoming hand, but she knew the fragile light couldn't penetrate the rain shrouded darkness to draw the boat to her safe inlet.

Swallowing the bile burning her throat, she bent down and hefted a small backpack filled with a bottle of water from the rain barrel, crackers, cheese and a first aid kit, over her shoulders. She fastened a tool belt around her waist and added a small folding shovel and a flashlight.

"Just in case," she muttered to Charm. "You wait here on the porch. I'll be back in time for dinner." Charm curled up on the rocker and with one green eye open, watched Rachel walk along the edge of the surf and disappear beyond the curving shoreline.

After walking about 2 miles, Rachel saw the debris stretching across the sand. She picked up a round orange life preserver. Brushing off the sand, she read, SWEET ABIGAIL, MIAMI, FL. Rachel grimaced and angrily tossed the life preserver back on the sand. She was about to turn and head home, when, out of the corner of her eye, she saw the body. It was a young woman, blonde and slim, lying on her back beside a pile of driftwood. The woman, or what was left of her, stared sightlessly at the blue sky, arms flung out from her sides. Strands of seaweed draped her body and a small starfish rested on her belly. Startled, Rachel stared at the woman who could have been a younger version of herself. Nightmare tendrils of memory reached from the abyss into her skull and wrapped themselves around her brain.

"That's not me," she told herself, grimly shaking off the initial reaction, although deeply imbedded in her mind, she wished it were. Rachel rubbed her sweaty hand along her shorts, then, reached out tentatively to check the woman's pulse, even though she knew death had claimed her hours ago. She closed the woman's eyes, now faded to milky white.

"Well, Gaia, did this appease your rage?" Rachel asked, clenching her fists.

A gust of wind rustled the fronds of palms leaves. "Hmm, perhaps not, but greed too is an evil," Rachel called to the wind. "Beware you don't become venal like us humans."

Turning in a half circle, Rachel surveyed the rest of the beach. She thought she saw a white sneaker poking out from under a broken black leather seat. Heaving the seat up and pushing it aside, Rachel looked down on a young man, probably the woman's partner or husband. A large gash had opened his forehead, but any blood had washed away in the deluge. He clasped a waterproof bag looped around his wrist.

"The skipper, I suppose" she muttered.

The man was dead, but Rachel checked anyway. Very dead. She pried open his fingers and pulled the bag from his hand. Inside, she found the ship's log and a wallet. She glanced at the name and picture on the driver's license, then at the battered face on the sand. "I'm sorry, Paul Stern," she whispered.

She pulled out three passports, one for Paul Stern and the other belonging to the dead woman, Ann Stern; husband and wife, then. The name, Ann niggled at the back of her skull, but refused to surface in recognition. Perhaps an Ann, existed in another life, but the memory eluded her. Annie! Where had the name Annie suddenly come from, she wondered? Rachel tucked the items inside the backpack without checking them further. Time enough for that later, if she felt like bothering.

Rachel opened the third passport. Her heart stopped when she saw the picture of a little girl with a cherubic round face, blue eyes and curly blonde hair. Emma! *"Wake up, Rachel,"* she thought. *"Emma is gone, forever. This is...."* Rachel read the name aloud, "Abigail Jane Stern." Rachel shut the passport and pushed it back into the pouch with a shaking hand.

Rachel sat down on the leather seat. She glanced around, seeing only the two adults. Another child lost to the sea gods, another sacrifice to their insatiable lust. She wiped away the tears. *What now*, she thought.

"Burying time, I guess," she said aloud, her voice heard only by the spirits silently observing.

Opening the shovel, Rachel dug one large grave. She dragged the bodies over and rolled them in, facing each other, their arms entwined. "At least you got to die together, whoever you are." Shaking off the shroud of despair that dropped over her shoulders, Rachel filled in the grave and placed some planks from the ship over it. Hammering a stick into the ground at the head of the grave, she hung the life preserver over it.

"Guess I should say something," she mumbled. "Well…hope you enjoy eternity together. Maybe your lives meant something, 'cause your deaths sure didn't mean a damn thing." Overhead, the palm fronds clacked in the rising wind.

Rachel looked up. "I know, Gaia, you're still not satisfied. I'm sorry for that. I wish it could be different. I don't know what these people did to harm you, but then you don't discriminate in your rage, do you?"

Rachel picked up the backpack, folded and tucked the shovel in her tool belt. As she turned toward home, a small mewling sound drifted in on the wind. "What the hell was that? Don't tell me these people had a cat on board the boat."

The mewling began again, then a whimper. "That's no cat," Rachel mumbled. She prowled through the debris until she spotted a small triangular piece of hull covered with palm fronds. "This isn't natural," she said, moving closer. She lifted the palm fronds and backed up, tripping over a tree root and sitting down hard on her butt. "Damn."

Rachel knelt and peered inside the makeshift lean-to. A little girl stared at her through giant blue eyes. She was filthy and covered with sand and blood. In one hand she clutched a matted teddy bear and a dirty pink towel. The other arm was wrapped around a mangy puppy that looked at Rachel and growled deep in its throat. The little girl pulled her arm from beneath the dog and reached up with both arms, "Mommy."

FRAN ORENSTEIN

CHAPTER ELEVEN

Rachel fell back on her heels as though punched in the face. Her chest constricted; she could barely breathe. Rushing, pulsing blood pounded in her ears. Images of another time, another place flew backward across the transparent screen separating dimensions. "Don't go there," she whispered. "Stay here in the now. This is not Emma."

Closing her mind to the flickering pictures, Rachel flipped over the hull, reached in and lifted the child. The little girl, still clutching the bear and towel put her thumb in her mouth and laid her head on Rachel's shoulder. Rachel could feel the tiny heart beating under her hand. Grief nearly overwhelmed her. She sat down hard in the sand, trying to breathe normally. All the feelings and emotions she had locked away five years ago pushed at the steel trap door, screaming to be released. She didn't even feel the salty tears that flowed from her eyes and fell in rivulets down her cheeks. Rachel gripped the baby tighter, until she squealed. Rachel willed her muscles to relax. Then she noticed the puppy. Where'd it come from, surely not the boat? It sat patiently to one side looking up at her with imploring brown eyes.

Rachel cleared her throat but the words still came out hoarse. "I won't leave you here, puppy. Thank you for keeping her warm and safe. You're a good puppy."

The puppy wagged its tail and lay down, its head on Rachel's shoe. Suddenly it raised its head and growled. Rachel stood and turned. Three small wild dogs, heads lowered, stared from the edge of the forest. Growls echoed across the beach. Rachel gripped the baby closer and said to the puppy. "Have they been bothering you, sweet, brave, puppy?"

The puppy whined and pressed against Rachel's leg. "Stay here and guard." She put the baby back down inside the shelter. The golden puppy stood before the opening, a stalwart sentinel, legs rigid, head raised, alert for whatever might result from this confrontation of the alpha female and the wild pack, for he had accepted her immediately as the alpha and would give his life to protect her pup.

Rachel removed the shovel from her belt, unfolded the handle and walked slowly toward the pack, speaking softly to them. They stopped growling and watched her. She hoped that her ability to deal with animals would surface because she did not want to hurt these dogs, wild and lost through no fault of their own. Picking out the leader, Rachel extended her free hand. He moved toward her and sniffed at her fingers. The dog lowered his head and Rachel nodded, then said softly but firmly, "Go now, go away. There is nothing for you here."

The dog hesitated, recognizing sounds and smells from a lost past, saw her alpha strength and with his tail between his legs, moved back into the woods. The other two dogs turned and followed him. Rachel let out a deep breath. She had been prepared to use the shovel as a weapon, but the leader of the pack still remembered human contact and had yielded to Rachel's command.

Rachel returned to the makeshift house. She fed the child and dog water, crackers and cheese. With their immediate needs sated, Rachel replaced the shovel, hoisted her pack and picked up the little girl. "Come along, brave puppy, we're going home."

She retraced her steps along the edge of the beach. Rachel let the waves lap against her sandaled feet. The puppy dodged in and out of the wavelets, shaking off the excess water every now and then. The child breathed softly against the Rachel's shoulder. Every so often, the tiny girl would suck loudly on her thumb, then satisfied and calm, she would resume the even breathing of baby sleep. Tiny breaths washed Rachel's neck in baby kisses. Tears welled, but Rachel mentally shook them off and plodded on.

GAIA'S GIFT

Charm saw them in the distance. She stood up and arched her back. New smells, strange creatures, yet familiar somehow. Charm leaped to the porch railing, then to the low overhanging roof. From her high safe perch, she peered down on the approaching trio.

Rachel stopped at the foot of the porch steps. She looked up at Charm. "I see you up there. Come down and meet your new family."

Rachel realized what she had just said. In less than a blink in time, she had made a momentous, life-altering decision. She looked at the child. "You are my gift from the sea," she whispered.

"Hmm," said the pragmatist.

"Shut up," growled the idealist.

Charm leaped down on the railing. The puppy barked and ran around in a circle. Then he stopped and stared at the cat. Charm arched her back and hissed. The puppy dropped to his belly and crawled toward the porch. Charm hissed again. The puppy rolled on his back, four legs in the air. Charm grinned her cat grin and proceeded to wash her paw.

"Well, that's been decided, too, I guess. Good choice, puppy. She's definitely the Queen of the Cabin." Rachel announced. "Now you wait right here on the porch until I tend to the child, then I'll take care of you. Meanwhile, Charm, do your thing."

The puppy stretched out on the porch. Charm jumped down and began to clean the dog, starting with his head. The puppy sighed and closed his eyes as the raspy cat tongue roughly massaged his fur. He knew he was home.

Rachel laid the sleeping child down on the well-worn sofa. She filled the sink with hot water. "Good, the hot water tank is working," she mumbled to herself.

Then she collected some worn towels and one of her tee shirts. She hoped the girl was toilet trained. "No diapers here, not anymore", she mumbled, rubbing the scar on her face, now faded to a white line.

From the other room the little girl whimpered. "Mommy, mommy, mommeeee!" The last a scream.

Rachel ran to her and folded her into her arms. "It's all right, baby. I'm right here."

The child pushed away and looked up at Rachel. "I not a baby, I, Abby. I twee," she announced, pulling up three fingers one at a time. "Silly Mommy!"

Rachel sat back on her heels and opened her mouth. A strange, foreign sound flew through her lips. The walls of the cabin resounded with never before heard laughter. More laughter filled her chest, verging on hysterical. Her throat choked closed. "Oh my God, oh my God." She hugged herself and rocked forward and back, head bowed.

"Ooh, Mommy, you have owie? Abby kiss." The little girl reached out and put her arms around Rachel. She planted a wet kiss on Rachel's scarred cheek. "Now, Mommy all better. No more owie."

Rachel raised her dripping eyes to the child. She sniffed and nodded. "No more owie, Abby, all better, thank you."

The little girl nodded.

"Would you like to take a nice warm bath?" Rachel asked.

Abigail nodded. She picked up the matted bear. "Jon Bear need bath. He vewy dirty."

"We'll give Jon Bear a bath, too."

"And my blanky." Abby gripped the torn towel in her other hand.

"And your blanket," Rachel said.

"No, Mommy, you amember, blanky."

Rachel smiled. "Of course, Abby, blanky. You need to take off those dirty clothes. Do you need help?"

"Mommeee! I can do it. I a big girl."

Rachel fell in love that instant. She was overwhelmed with passion for this feisty, brave, independent little girl named Abigail. She felt a dull ache in her womb and pressure in her breasts. The Goddess had looked down on her and nodded. At that moment she knew with certainty this child belonged to her. The sea took and the sea gave back; ebb and flow, ebb and flow.

GAIA'S GIFT

Gaia had circled around many times over the past five years and with the incoming tide had given her back what she had lost.
"Thank you Gaia, she whispered, fingering the scar again.

FRAN ORENSTEIN

CHAPTER TWELVE

Cleaned and fed, child and puppy slept intertwined on the sofa. Rachel rocked back and forth on the rocker and stared at them. For hours, her eyes feasted on this golden child wrapped around the golden puppy, the image imprinting like a tattoo upon the surface of her brain. The moon was high in the night sky when she finally lifted Charm from her lap and gently placed her on the rocker cushion.

Rachel went to the small back room she used for storage and sewing. She surveyed the space that would have a new occupant very soon. An old wood and leather ship's chest rested on the floor in one corner. Rachel stood before it, searching for enough courage to raise the lid. Finally, she sighed and knelt down, placing her hands on the lid, as if to feel any vibrations emanating from within. "I'm sorry, baby girl." she said, softly and lifted the lid.

Carefully wrapped in tissue paper were layers upon layers of tiny sets of dresses, shorts, pants, shirts and underwear. There were little shoes and sneakers in small brown boxes, hair ribbons and barrettes, and a small comb and brush and a yellow rubber ducky. A cloth Raggedy Ann doll stared sightlessly, entombed in a plastic bag.

Rachel took the doll out of the bag and held her. She pushed her face into the doll's hair and smelled…nothing; just a musty, aged smell of something locked away too long. "Is nothing left?" she whimpered. "Not even your scent."

Rachel closed the lid of the trunk. Her shoulders shook and sobs wracked her body. She curled up on the floor holding the cloth doll. Eventually, she fell asleep, and the moon watched through the window, finally giving up and slipping down toward the horizon. The faint odor of lavender permeated the room.

Like a tape on rewind, time moved rapidly backward, sucking Rachel into the nightmarish morass of grief and pain. In her dream-driven state, she pressed her fingers against the white jagged scar that cut into her cheek from eye to jaw line. Another storm, another boat, another sacrifice to Gaia twirled in concentric circles around her brain.

Disjointed images and sounds permeated Rachel's sleep and unfelt tears squeezed from the corners of her eyes. Swirling, whirling currents pulled at Rachel's strong arms as they fought frantically to hold onto her baby. Visions of a tiny body in an orange life jacket carried away on a giant wave to become another denizen of the sea. Then the separation, pain, disconnect, and finally blessed unconsciousness until she blasted back to reality in the stark white hospital room, alone with her memories.

Finally, her brain spent and exhausted by the flooding nightmares, Rachel slept unfettered by dreams, still clutching Raggedy Ann.

***

The bright sun woke Abigail. She sat up on the couch and looked around.

Something was wrong, but her memory failed her and she could not put words to her concerns. Why was she sleeping on a sofa? Where was her room? Her familiar world was gone. Panic rose in her chest, threatening to fly screaming from her mouth like bats from a dark cave. Her small body shook as if wracked with fever. The puppy licked the tears off her face and then nosed the stuffed bear towards her. Abigail pulled the bear to her and buried her face in the puppy's neck, resorting again to baby talk. "Not right, Puppy. Not right, Jon Bear. Abby scared."

The dog softly woofed, snuffled and wagged his tail.

"This not right, Puppy. Wrong, wrong, wrong! Bad, bad, bad!" her voice grew agitated and she shook her head.

The dog pushed his nose into Abigail's hand and woofed again.

The child tilted her head toward the puppy as if listening and nodded. "Okay, Puppy. Abby big girl. Okay!"

The dog sat back on its haunches and grinned, its tongue lolling.

Sucking her thumb and clutching the bear, Abigail slipped off the couch and padded into the next room, circumnavigating the rocker, the two end tables covered with books and the pair of wooden chairs with their striped cushions that filled the tiny space. In the far corner she saw a little kitchen with a small table, two chairs and an open door leading to a bathroom.

Seeing another door, she opened it. Crossing the threshold, she looked around. This room didn't seem right either, but she still couldn't bring familiar memories into focus. The world of the past was a vision blurred like a steam covered mirror after a hot shower. An empty bed with rumpled yellow covers nearly filled the small room. Shelves of folded clothes covered two of the walls and another rocker stood by the window next to a small round table. On the table were a small lamp, a candle in a brass holder and several books. "Not mine," she mumbled.

Abigail turned and went back across the living room and through the other open door. She saw a wooden chest and boxes. *Not Abby's room.* Then she saw Rachel lying on the floor and giggled. The yellow puppy peered around the little girl. Abigail vigorously sucked her thumb and clutched Jon Bear tightly to her chest. "Why mommy on the floor? Mommy funny. She take dolly to bed," she whispered to the still damp bear. "She fall down, Puppy?"

The puppy woofed and sat down.

The child knelt down and patted Rachel's hair. "Mommy wake up."

The woman stirred and Abigail jumped back. Rachel did not awaken.

"Silly mommy, floor hard." The little girl toddled off to find the toilet, the puppy her ever present shadow. This was different, too. Abigail put the bear on the floor and hauled herself up onto the toilet seat, holding onto the sides with both hands. "No potty. Abby not fall in, puppy." The small dog grinned, watching her with interest, its tongue lolling out of the side of its mouth. "Not funny, Puppy. Abby not want to fall in." The dog huffed.

Finished, she delicately wiped herself and slid down off the toilet bowl. "Abby good girl, not peepee in panties."

She flushed the toilet and looked at the sink. "Where Abby's bear bench? Abby can't reach water." She looked around the bathroom, no bench. The child considered the toilet, closed the lid and climbed up leaning over the sink. Stretching, she struggled for a minute with the lever until a trickle of water came from the spout. She ran her hands under the water then backed down off the toilet and wiped her hands on a towel.

Tucking the bear under her arm, she said, "Come, puppy. We get mommy."

CHAPTER THIRTEEN

Rachel opened her eyes and squinted at the sun streaming through the window. A small face framed with a mop of curly blonde hair peered down at her. "Mommy? You wake up?"

Rachel sat up and winced. The shooting pains in her back and shoulders reminded her that sleeping on the hard floor all night was a very bad idea. Disoriented, she stared at the golden child before her. Then reality rushed in on the tide and littered the beach with memories of yesterday's storm and its aftermath. Still wrapped in sleepy fog, Rachel cleared her throat. "Good morning, Em…uh, Abby," she rasped.

"You hurt, Mommy? Abby kiss the owie." The little girl leaned over and kissed Rachel's cheek. "All better!"

Rachel rubbed her cheek and felt the fine line of the scar. "Thank you, Abby. That feels much better."

Not to be outdone, the puppy stood up against Rachel's chest and licked her other cheek. Rachel's laughter echoed through the house, so long filled with silent anger and despair. "Thank you, puppy. Now I feel twice as good."

Abigail reached out for Rachel's hand to pull her up. Rachel's back protested at the abrupt change of alignment, but she managed to rise and unfold her cramped muscles.

"I a good girl," the child said.

"Of course you are, sweet girl," Rachel said.

"I peepee all by myself."

Rachel opened her mouth, then, closed it. She quelled a laugh. "Good job, Abby. I'm very proud of you."

"It was hard, Mommy. No potty. Abby not find bear bench."

Rachel had no clue what Abigail was talking about but the child seemed to have forgotten about it the next moment. So Rachel asked, "Are you hungry, baby?"

The little girl stopped and put her hands on her hips, pouting. She opened her mouth, but Rachel interrupted. "I'm sorry, Abby. I forget sometimes that you are a big girl of three." Rachel held up three fingers.

Abigail smiled and led the way into the kitchen. "We hungry," she said, pointing at the dog and the cat, who was grooming herself while she waited patiently beside her bowl. "Jon Bear hungry."

"Aha, I see. Let me see what I have for breakfast today." Rachel opened a small, chipped refrigerator and gazed inside. "Hmm, this morning, there are eggs, some goat cheese and cornbread. How does that sound?"

"I want corn pops and milk," Abigail said.

"Let me see." Rachel opened a long cabinet. "No corn pops. Just cornbread. Would you like French toast made from cornbread and goat's milk?"

"With lots of syrup?"

"I have strawberry jam," Rachel said.

Abigail made a face. "Okay, but you go to Super Foods, Mommy."

Rachel stopped breathing. She didn't know whether to laugh or cry or do both simultaneously. Her mind heard a different voice echoing similar words. Memories stabbed at her heart, penetrating like bullets punching holes in the fabric of time. Super Foods, the holy Mecca of colliding shopping carts, bins of insecticide-tainted produce from third-world countries, glass cases of antibiotic and hormone laced meat, little hands pulling cans off shelves, which she surreptitiously put back. Breathe, her brain ordered.

"We eat differently, now, little one. No more Super Foods, just good, healthy Mommy food."

"Why?"

Question and answer time. She had forgotten that part of mothering. *Because* just wouldn't do, not for this bright child.

GAIA'S GIFT

"Now we grow our own food. We catch fish in the ocean. We have chickens for eggs and sometimes meat. There is a goat for milk, cheese and butter."

Abigail didn't wait to hear more. She bounced up and down on her tiny pink feet, blonde curls bobbing in rhythm. "A goat? We have goat? Where? A goat and chickens. Abby see chickens?"

"I'll show you everything after breakfast," Rachel said. "You can even help me feed them."

"Okay." Abigail climbed up on a chair and put her hands in her lap. "Where food, Mommy?"

Rachel turned away so Abby wouldn't see the grin on her face. The child was so serious, she didn't want her thinking Rachel was laughing at her.

Everyone was fed and full. The cat showed the dog their special door to the back yard. Abigail jumped off the chair. "I help." She took her plate and fork to the sink. "Where my bench?"

"I'll have to make you a little bench so you can reach the sink," Rachel said.

"I want my bench. My red bench. With bears. Where's my bench?" Abigail wailed, tears falling.

Now, Rachel understood what Abigail had been talking about. She picked her up and held her. "Oh, Abby, we'll make another one, today. You can help me. You'll show me just what it looked like."

"No, my bench," the child persisted.

"This will be better because you helped me make it," Rachel said.

Abigail hiccupped. "Pwomise?"

Rachel nodded. "Come along; let's pick out what you are going to wear today."

They went into the spare room and Rachel opened the trunk. "These are for you, Abby."

The child reached in and pulled out a blue flowered sun dress. "Ooh, this is pretty."

"Wouldn't you rather wear shorts and a tee shirt, today?"

Abigail shook her head. "No! Today, Abby a princess."

Rachel smiled. So Cinderella and company were still in style. As long as Abigail didn't expect Prince Charming to ride in and carry her off to the nonexistent 'happily forever after' castle in the clouds. Life just didn't work that way. Nothing good lasts, she thought bitterly. Then she looked down at the blonde curls of the child kneeling in front of the trunk. But sometimes we get to do it over.

CHAPTER FOURTEEN

Rachel and Princess Abigail toured the farm. Rachel showed her how to feed grain to the chickens and put water out for the goat. Then Rachel milked the goat. Abigail stared, thumb in mouth. "Can I do it?" she asked.

"You have to have strong hands, so when you are older I'll teach you how," Rachel answered. "Right now, you need to stay out of the goat's pen. She might try to eat your dress. Goats like to eat everything."

"Even little girls?" Abigail hugged her bear.

"No, not little girls, but she might want your skirt, or Jon Bear."

"Then Abby wear shorts and shirt. Goat not eat shorts." Abby looked down at the tattered bear clutched in her hand. "I leave Jon Bear in the house."

"Well, I would rather have you promise me you won't go into the goat's pen until I tell you it's okay. Can you do that?"

Abigail considered this for a moment, then, nodded. "Will goat bite Abby?"

Questions and more questions. "I'll talk to her and tell her not to bother you."

"You talk to goat?" Abigail eyes opened wide.

"Oh, yes. I can talk to all the animals," Rachel replied.

"Can Abby talk to animals?" Abigail asked.

"I'll teach you."

"Now!"

"We can do it later. Come let me show you how to gather eggs."

Abigail stamped her foot. "Now!"

"Hmmm," Rachel said. Abigail had a stubborn streak. Reluctant to start a tantrum in the animal quarters, Rachel knelt down in front of the child. "First, you have to be very, very, calm and quiet. Stamping feet and shouting will only scare the animals."

Abigail hung her head. "I sorry. I be vewy quiet."

"That's fine. Now you have to listen very hard to the voices of the animals and watch their faces and bodies. When you talk to them, you need to be very gentle and calm. Tell them good things about themselves. Tell them you love them."

Abigail nodded vigorously. "I can do that, Mommy."

Rachel smiled, handed a basket to Abigail and led the child to the chicken coop. A large black and red rooster hopped down off the roof and confronted them. Rachel waved her hands at him, "Shoo, now, Rooster. We need eggs today."

The rooster and Abigail stared at each other, then, he crowed.

"His name is Charlie," Abigail announced.

Rachel knelt down in front of the child. "Charlie? What made you think of it?"

Abigail shrugged. "He say so."

Rachel looked from child to rooster. "He told you?"

The child's head flew up and down. "Uh huh! He's Charlie, not Rooster."

Rachel nodded and smiled. "Hmm! Okay, Charlie it is."

Abigail turned to the rooster. "Okay, Charlie?"

The rooster bobbed his head and flew back on the roof of the chicken coop. Rachel was amazed, yet not really surprised at the communication between Abigail and a bad-tempered rooster named Charlie. She had witnessed her interaction with the dog and the cat that loved and accepted this miracle child, the glorious gift from Gaia. What other powers did she possess, Rachel wondered?

Rachel left the door to the coop ajar to let in more light. They gathered the eggs, still warm, from the nests. Some of the chickens protested and ran squawking from the coop.

"Chickies mad," Abigail said.

"Yes, well, tomorrow they will lay more eggs."

They put away the eggs and Rachel took Abigail out to the garden. Rachel named each of the vegetables as they gathered them in a basket.

"Abby like carrots," Abigail announced.

"Good girl. I like carrots, too. Would you like carrots for dinner?"

"Okay. And peas. Abby like peas."

"Carrots and peas it is," Rachel said, smiling. "Do you know what color carrots are?"

"Owange and peas is gween," Abigail said proudly.

"You are very smart, Abby. You know your colors."

"Silly Mommy, you teach me colors. Don't you amember?" Abby asked.

"Of course, I remember. I was just checking to see if you remembered." Rachel hugged the little girl. She couldn't seem to stop hugging or touching her. Rachel feared she would disappear like a dream in the middle of the night, elusive and fading, then dying. Everything dies...eventually...disappearing into the mist. She held the child tighter.

Abigail giggled. "You silly, mommy. Abby squooshed like pancake."

Rachel released her. "I'm sorry. You are just so huggable."

Abigail danced away, spinning, her arms outstretched. "Huggable, huggable me," she sang. The golden puppy circled around her legs, yipping. Charm sat on the fence and watched the show with feline disdain. Her twitching tail and ears gave her away, though. Charm was enjoying the event as though it were staged just for her benefit. Abigail, dizzy, sat down on the grass. The puppy licked her face with relish.

"Ooh, yucky puppy. Ooey, phooey." The little girl put her arms around the puppy's neck and hugged him until he yelped and pulled away.

Rachel laughed until her sides hurt and tears poured like waterfalls from her eyes. All the stress accumulated during the years of grief and loneliness exploded from her head like a captive eagle, now released to the freedom of the cloudless sky.

Tiny hands patted her face. "Mommy okay? Need owie kiss?"

Rachel lifted her tee shirt and wiped her face. "No darlin' girl, Mommy is okay. I am just so happy to watch you dance and laugh, it made my eyes water."

Abigail nodded sagely. "Good. We make Abby's bench with bears?"

Rachel took Abigail's hand and picked up the vegetable basket. "First, I want to talk about your room. You need a bed to sleep on and some place to put your clothes."

"Yes, but Abby needs a bench with bears."

"That's right. A bench with bears is very important."

After lunch, Rachel made Abigail change into an old tee shirt of hers.

"Abby is a princess," Abigail insisted, shaking her head.

"Well, all right, Princess Abby, but then you can't help me because princesses don't like to dirty their beautiful dresses and I do need your help. So I guess you won't be getting a bed or a bench today."

Abigail thought for a minute. "Oh, okay." She pulled off her dress and carefully folded it and put it on the couch. Then she pulled the tee shirt over her head. Rachel tied a piece of rope around the waist to keep it from dragging on the ground and rolled up the sleeves.

Rachel studied the child. "Good. Now you look like a helper princess and you can get as dirty as you wish."

Abigail grinned and took Rachel's hand, pulling her toward the door. Rachel led her to a shed where she kept tools, wood, and paint. Rachel looked down at Abigail. She would have to put a lock on the shed.

She must have said it aloud because Abigail asked, "Why lock?"

Rachel ruffled Abigail's hair. "To keep little fingers from getting hurt from the dangerous things I keep inside."

"Oh, Abby no like dangewus things," Abigail said in a serious voice.

Rachel bit her lip to stop herself from laughing. "Smart girl."

The rest of that day, Rachel and Abigail built a bed and shelves from the scrap lumber stored in the sheds. Abigail sanded the wood and Rachel painted it red. Then Abigail helped pound the nails into a bench. Rachel drew three bears on the bench and helped Abigail paint them. Now covered with red paint and blue bears, the child stood back and surveyed the results. "Good job, Mommy," Abigail stated.

Rachel replied, "Good job, Abby."

"I sleep in the bed tonight." Abby announced.

Rachel thrilled to hear Abigail use a full sentence, answered, "The paint has to dry. Tomorrow morning I'll make a mattress for the bed. We'll hang the shelves and put your clothes on them. Tomorrow night you can sleep in your new room."

Abby nodded. "Jon Bear and Raggy Ann, too." She stopped and her brow puckered. "Ann, Ann help," she said in a very tiny voice.

Rachel's heart constricted. Was Abigail's memory returning? She remembered the passport and the name Ann. Ann must have been her mother. Should she ask, or....

Abigail shook her head as if to loosen a cobweb of thought sticking to her mind that would not surface to clarity. Rachel held her breath. The child looked up at Rachel and held up her hands. "Yucky paint, sticky fingers. I need a bath."

Rachel let out a whoosh of air. "Let's go swimming in the ocean."

FRAN ORENSTEIN

CHAPTER FIFTEEN

"Yes, yes," Abigail shouted jumping up and down. She grabbed Rachel's hand and pulled her toward the beach, the puppy dashing ahead.

"Whoa, not so fast Abby Dabby."

The little girl tossed her head and laughed. "Abby Dabby, Abby Dabby," she sang, dancing toward the water.

They took off their clothes and stepped into the water. The puppy splashed around their feet, then he ran down along the beach and back again. Rachel picked up Abigail and walked further into the surf. "Let me see you swim," Rachel said.

"I swim good. Daddy teach me." Abigail looked around. "Where's Daddy?"

A lump in Rachel's throat threatened to choke her. She swallowed. "Daddy went away for a while."

"Why?"

The inevitable interrogation of a three-year-old! "He had important business."

"What bidness?"

Rachel sighed. "Boat business."

"Where?"

Questions and lies, more questions and more lies, the circular destruction of deceit. Rachel hesitated. "Daddy went out to sea."

"When he come back?"

The circle tightened. "Soon."

"Oh, okay. Watch me." Abigail dog-paddled around Rachel.

"Good job, Abby. Good swimming." Rachel scooped her up and hugged her. "Promise me something?"

Abby pulled back and looked into Rachel's eyes. "What?"

"You will never come down to the water alone. Not even with puppy. Ever, ever, ever."

"I know. You told me." Abby wriggled out of her arms and began to paddle around again.

Rachel closed her eyes. Abigail's mother had already warned her once and the child remembered. What else would she remember, eventually? "Abby?"

The child stopped paddling and held on to Rachel's leg. She looked up. "What?"

"I may have told you before, but now I want you to promise again. Will you do that?" Rachel asked.

Abigail nodded, water spraying from her curls. "I pwomise."

"Why don't you climb on my back and hold on tight to my neck. We'll go for a swim together."

"Ooh, like dolphin ride. Fun."

Rachel wondered if Abigail had been to a dolphin preserve or theme park or had watched a movie about dolphins, but she couldn't ask. The secret silence of deceit, where questions and answers remained buried. She hoisted the child up and swam out into deeper water. Abigail shrieked with glee, and the puppy paddled behind until he got tired and headed back to shore, where he sat on the beach and watched, waiting for his family.

CHAPTER SIXTEEN

Six weeks later, Rachel considered what she had to do. Guilt and fear had gnawed at her soul to the point where she could no longer sleep or eat. The voices of the pragmatist and idealist argued night and day creating chaos in her brain. The idealist prevailed, but the pragmatist got the last word. Whatever happened, Rachel was not giving up this gift from Gaia, but she had to protect her. If something happened to her, the child would die. She considered her options and her throat closed at the realization that she would have to leave this place and travel with the child on the open sea, even if only for one day.

Four or five times a year she crossed the water with trepidation, to a tiny outpost of civilization where she would post letters to her attorney and retrieve the mail, which always included a letter from Mary Cross and the money order and traveler's checks with which to purchase necessities. No one knew her, except as a boater, so if she arrived with a child, it would not generate questions.

Now that she had Abigail, she needed toys and books for reading and schooling, clothing in different sizes, and more fabric. She also needed a good mattress and pillows for Abigail's new bed, and dog food, huge bags of Kibbles and some boxes of biscuits.

Finally, and most important, the very thing she had avoided all these years…a reliable form of communication, perhaps a satellite cell phone and a computer or perhaps both. She tried to tell herself that these were backups for emergencies and to protect Abigail should something happen. There was a radio in the boat, but that could be destroyed or swept out to sea in a storm. Storm....

"Move to the mainland," the pragmatist whispered in her ear. *The idealist kept silent.*

Rachel heard the pragmatic logic and for a moment considered such a possibility, then tossed it aside, at least for now. There were too many variables regarding Abigail, mainly proof of her existence. She was not giving up this gift.

"She isn't your child," the rational pragmatist said.

The idealist spoke up, "She is a gift sent by the goddess."

"No! She belongs to someone else. You have to find her family," the pragmatist insisted.

"Keep her," the idealist said.

"No!"

Rachel tuned out the voices and breathed in the delicate scent of lavender that swirled around her. *Oh Emma, I miss you, but I need Abigail."* "I know it's wrong, but cannot give her up," Rachel said to the hovering spirit. An icy finger of air touched her cheek and Rachel covered the spot with her hand, as if to trap it forever.

Abigail danced across the yard and jumped on her lap. "What you doing, Mommy?"

Rachel jumped, startled. "Oh, you scared me."

Abigail patted Rachel's cheek. "I sorry, Mommy."

Rachel smiled, noticing that Abigail's speech was improving. "It's okay, Abby. I am making a shopping list. Would you like to take a trip, tomorrow?"

"Ooh, I love twips. Can we go to Super Foods?" Abigail hugged her.

Rachel laughed at her enthusiasm. "There isn't any Super Foods, but there is a store like it. You can pick out new clothes and toys. We'll leave tomorrow if the sun is shining."

"Can we go now?"

"Tomorrow, Abby," Rachel said and Abigail skipped off around the yard chasing the puppy.

Rachel resumed her to-do list, which was growing larger by the minute. The most important item was a letter to the attorney to amend her will and create a healthy trust fund for…what name to use? She pictured the child's passport, Abigail Jane Stern. Should she use Abigail Jane Wells or Abigail Jane Stern-Wells? The third name would be best, so she would have no trouble in the future when she learned her true identity, for Rachel one day intended to tell her, far into the future.

No explanation to Gary was necessary. It was none of his business and anyway, he couldn't reach her to ask questions. Let him assume it was a new-born relative. She would have it notarized at the bank and mail it to Gary.

Satisfied with her decision, Rachel beckoned to Abigail. They walked down to the beach and turned left toward a dense clump of bushes overhanging the water. A long dock jutted out from the underbrush and at the far end, bobbing gently, the Boston Whaler floated on the calm sea. She kept it in pristine condition, along with the dingy, beached for now under the dock. The boat was her escape in an emergency. Buried in the sand in a waterproof bag inside a metal container, were three cans of gasoline and motor oil. Rachel started to lift Abigail onto the dock, but the child pulled back.

"It's okay, Abby. You sit right here on the sand and I'll be right back." Rachel turned to the dog, "Guard." The yellow dog lay down, his head on Abigail's lap; his eyes following Rachel as she walked down the dock toward the boat.

Turning every minute to check that the child was still sitting with the dog, Rachel went over the boat carefully and started the engine. It took a few tries, but it finally caught. She checked the gas level, but wasn't worried because she had checked it last month as was her habit. There were several empty cans in the boat that she would refill at the boat dock.

Turning off the engine, Rachel heard a whimper. She looked behind her at Abigail, watching her, thumb in mouth, shaking. The puppy was standing, now, alert. Rachel jumped from the boat and rushed down the dock to the child, lifting her up into her arms. "Oh, sweet baby, tell Mommy what's wrong."

"No boat. Abby scared. Big booms and rocks on roof, bad light. May Day, May Day, May Day, Ann, help," she repeated over and over.

Rachel held her and stroked her hair. "It's just a bad dream, Abby. You dreamed about a bad storm, that's all."

"No, no, noooooo!" she screamed. "Bad, bad, bad, Mommeeee!"

"It's all right, honey, I'm right here." Rachel held her at arms length. "Abby, look at me! I won't let anything happen to you."

Abigail sniffed and wiped her nose on her sleeve and hiccupped. "Abby scared, Mommy."

"I know. Storms can be scary. Come and see the boat. You can explore it with me. Okay?"

Abigail hesitated, then took Rachel's hand and walked with her to the boat. Rachel climbed in first and lifted Abigail up and over. The child was shaking again. Rachel picked her up and moved forward to the helm. She sat in the Captain's chair and set the frightened child on her lap. "See? This wheel steers the boat. Would you like to turn it?"

Abigail nodded and reached for the wheel. They spent an hour on the boat, until Rachel felt Abigail was calm. Then she told her everything they would buy tomorrow. At the end of the afternoon, the child was relaxed and smiling.

The puppy watched from the beach, his head on his paws, eyes sad, as though he knew they were leaving. Abigail saw him and ran over. "Don't be sad, Puppy, Abby get you toy." She turned to Rachel. "We get a puppy toy, and a kitty toy?"

"I think we can do that, Abby."

"And the goat and the chickens?"

"They don't play with toys."

"Goat sad," Abby said.

"I didn't know that, Abby. Why is the goat sad?" Rachel asked.

"She all alone. She tell Puppy."

"Well, maybe one day we can get her a brother."

Abby jumped up and down. "She like that. Abby get brother, too, at Super Foods?"

Rachel smothered a laugh. "They don't sell brothers there or goats."

"Oh. You tell them to sell brothers and goats. Come puppy, let's go tell goat." Abigail started to run down the beach.

"Wait, Abby. Let's surprise her," Rachel called.

"Okay, I love supwises." Abby continued running with the dog.

Rachel wondered if Abby was making up the story or if she could really talk to the dog, and did the dog talk to the goat. The goat had never told her anything and she was supposed to be able to communicate with animals. It might be a good idea to get a young Billy goat, to insure future generations of goats. The miracle child who could talk to the animals needed milk and cheese. But not tomorrow! There was too much to bring back tomorrow and she had Abby as a passenger now.

FRAN ORENSTEIN

CHAPTER SEVENTEEN

The morning sun reflected golden rays on the calm water. A few white puffs dotted the azure backdrop of the sky, but that could change in an instant. Rachel stood on the porch and stared at the ocean. She was having second thoughts about the trip across the water, but it was necessary. She hoped Gaia and her sons were calm and satisfied today and the weather would remain tranquil. She did not relish dealing with her own nightmares and a panicked child while fighting turbulent seas.

"Are we going now?" the small voice asked.

"After breakfast, Abby Dabby."

"Corn pops, Mommy?"

"I'll buy corn pops today. This morning we are having eggs and toast."

Abigail frowned, but brightened again. "Cwispy Cwunchies, too?"

Rachel smiled. "As long as they don't have sugar."

"Why?"

"It's bad for your teeth." Rachel made a mental note to find a dentist.

"Why?"

Rachel took a deep breath. "Sugar rots your teeth, then they will all fall out and you will look like this." Rachel sucked in her lips.

Abigail stuck out her tongue. "Oh, poopy. I don't want to look like that."

"So, no sugar."

Abigail sighed. "Oh all right."

Rachel smiled. Even the lisp was fading. They fed the animals and made quick work of breakfast. "Are you ready, sailor-girl?" Rachel asked.

Abigail saluted. "Aye, aye, Captain Paul...." She frowned and looked up at Rachel, eyes pleading for understanding.

Rachel's heart raced and she closed her eyes. More lies? "It's okay, Abby. You learned that from your Daddy. Don't worry; it's hard to remember everything when you are little."

Abigail hesitated, then asked, "Who is Captain Paul?"

Finally, a truthful answer. "He's your Daddy."

"Oh. He come home soon?"

Rachel bit her lip to keep the tears at bay. "One day, you'll see him again, Abby."

The little girl stuck her thumb in her mouth and crushed Jon Bear to her body. The puppy rubbed against her tiny legs. "I miss my Daddy."

Rachel picked her up and sat on the porch swing. The puppy jumped up and put his golden head on her lap. "I know, Abby. It's hard to miss somebody so much."

"My eyes want to cry, Mommy."

"You go ahead and cry, Abby. I'll hold you until you feel better."

The little girl's shoulders shook as she grieved for her father, not knowing he would never come home again. Rachel rubbed Abigail's back as tears slid silently down her own cheeks. A waft of lavender-laced air encircled her head. "Thank you, baby," she whispered. They sat like that in a tableau of darkness under the blazing sun, until Charlie Rooster crowed from the top of the chicken coop.

Abigail sat up and wiped her eyes, sniffing. "Charlie says it's time to go, Mommy."

Aha, Charlie the timekeeper. Rachel smiled, wiping her cheeks with the back of her hand and set Abigail down on the porch. "He's absolutely, positively, definitely right, Abby Dabby. It is time to go sailing."

"Aboluty, positily, definty, we go sailing, now!" Abigail exclaimed jumping up and down.

Rachel laughed and hefted the backpack. She leaned down and smoothed the dog's head. "You watch over everyone, Puppy. You're in charge."

"Bye, Puppy! Bye, Charm! See you later," Abigail shouted. "Bye, Charlie Rooster! Oh, and bye, bye Miss Goat and chickens!"

The child followed behind Rachel, then stopped when she saw the boat. Rachel turned and took her hand. "It's okay, sweetheart. Remember, there is nothing to be afraid of. You are very brave."

The voyage was uneventful. Well, almost. Abigail balked at wearing the life vest, so Rachel put on her own vest, then sat down holding out Abigail's vest and didn't say a word. It took a while, but finally with a deep sigh, the child relented and held out her arms.

That hurdle jumped, Abigail relaxed and sat up front asking Rachel non-stop questions. Rachel was grateful that the child was used to sailing. Once they reached the mainland and walked down the pier onto the main street, Abigail, with the boundless curiosity of a three-year-old, plied her with more questions. She wanted to know everything Rachel was doing, at the bank, the post office, and the electronics store, where Rachel purchased a satellite phone and a wireless computer, which she hoped would work on their end of the key. Wise to the vagaries of toddlers, Rachel left the food for last, stopping at the huge market with its kid friendly shopping cart cum auto that delighted Abigail.

"I want Cwispy Cwunchies," Abigail demanded.

"There aren't any in this store," Rachel said.

"I want Cwispy Cwunchies," Abigail's voice rose, her face scrunching.

Rachel, anticipating a melt-down moved quickly to the syrups, although she had hoped that honey would suffice. "Would you like to choose a syrup to go with pancakes and French toast?"

Abigail gnawed on her lip and sniffed. "Okay…maple bwown sugar."

Rachel relented even though there was sugar involved because she didn't want to attract attention with a screaming child. The rest of the food shopping proceeded without a tantrum, and Rachel sighed in relief as she wheeled the newly purchased folding shopping cart filled to the brim with food, down to the dock. Abigail sat on the dock, thumb in mouth, watching Rachel as she unloaded the packages onto the boat and placed the perishables in an ice cooler.

Rachel lifted Abigail onto the boat, then struggled once more to get the life vest onto the protesting child. Finally, an exhausted Abigail curled up on a blanket on the deck behind Rachel and fell asleep. She awoke just as Rachel dropped the anchor over the side in her secluded cove. Rachel lifted Abigail onto the dock. The puppy raced over and gave them both a rough tongue bath.

"Ooh, yucky Puppy," Abigail said, but she put her arms around his neck and hugged him. "We got you a toy, Puppy and a ball. We can play ball, you and me. Oh, and Mommy, too, and Charm and Charlie and the goat and the chickens...." Her voice dwindled as she ran after the dog toward the cabin, clutching a small bag of treats for the animals.

Rachel chuckled as she followed, pulling the new shopping cart filled with canvas bags of food, the ice chest resting on top. "Thank you, Gaia," she whispered. The faint scent of lavender tickled her nostrils.

CHAPTER EIGHTEEN

Two years passed and Abigail grew to love all the animals, but especially the puppy and Charlie the Rooster. Abigail thought he was funny as he strutted around the yard, puffing out his chest, bossing all the chickens. He was like a king when he flew up on the top of the roof of the coop and stretched his neck, opening his mouth with a cock-a-doodle-doo. Charlie told her all sorts of stories about the animals. He could see far into the woods and out into the ocean from the coop roof.

Abigail sat on the ground with puppy and listened to Charlie squawk about tales of the dolphins in the sea and the rabbit family that lived behind the chicken pen. She told the stories to the dog, the goat and the cat. "There are five baby rabbits." Abigail said. "And you mustn't be mean to them, Charm, because they are just babies. Promise you won't go near their nest."

The silky, black cat stretched and licked her paw.

"You didn't answer me," Abigail said sternly.

Charm looked up at Abigail, blinked, and flicked her tail.

"Okay, I guess that means yes."

The child looked doubtfully at the cat that could never really be trusted to pay attention. Mommy said cats were natural hunters, so it would be hard for her to change her nature. Besides, Charm survived by hunting her own food. Abigail just thought that baby rabbits should be kept safe. "Listen, Charm. If you leave them alone and their Mommy, and let them grow up, they'll be that much bigger and tastier next year." Secretly her stomach churned at the thought of eating any rabbits, but cats were carnivas or something…or so mommy said and had to eat meat to survive.

Abigail looked at the puppy, who was big now and very yellow. "Dogs, too, I guess," she said aloud. The dog grinned and swept its tail back and forth across the grass.

The child looked at the goat. "At least you don't eat rabbits."

The goat bleated and pulled a stalk of grass out of the ground in demonstration of her herbivorous habits.

Abigail wondered at the diversity of nature, but of course not in those terms. She was only five years old. Pictures flashed in her mind sometimes of a different kind of person, although she didn't phrase it that way. She had seen these persons when she and mommy went to the mainland in the boat. They were called men, but she sometimes recalled one man from the deepest recesses of her mind, although she had no understanding of him.

He was tall and had a tickly brush of brown hair on his lip and chin. He wasn't like mommy. His chest was flat where she had bumps. He had hair on his body. His voice was low and growly, but in a nice way. Sometimes she sat on his shoulders and he ran around with her. She bounced up and down, shrieking, reaching up to touch the clouds. But the memory was just a spark that faded like a burnt-out sparkler on Fourth of July. She had no name for this person, just a faint, whispy whisper, Daddy. She never told mommy about it. She wanted to keep it to herself, like a secret. Well, she did tell Puppy and Charm, but she could trust them not to tell mommy.

Memories, faint but familiar drifted into her consciousness. Sometimes these emerged from the depths of her memory like pieces of driftwood rising up from the sea; seaweed-clad monsters, to be cast upon the shore. She never questioned their existence, just feasted on their shapes as she passed by.

"Okay, listen now, I'm going to tell you a story…once upon a time there were three little bunnies…their names were Flopsy, Mopsy, and Peter Cottontail." Abigail never considered where the story had come from, it was just there in there, floating out of her head, a bedtime tale imbedded by a woman she would never know again.

The dog raised its head and listened intently. The cat stopped licking her paw and stared raptly at the child. The goat slowly chewed her grass, ears perked. A hush seemed to fall over a farmyard smothered in a sudden blanket of silence. Charlie peered down from the fence of the goat pen. Birds stopped twittering in the trees, frogs ceased to chirp, and the murmur of the surf faded into the distance as the Abigail version of the tale of a brave bunny evading a cruel fate in Farmer McGregor's cabbage patch unfolded. Even the goat, with visions of row after row of cabbages floating before her eyes, nibbled silently.

Abigail sighed, "The End. Did you like the story?"

The animals all looked up at Abigail and one by one made a special sound as if in answer to her question. Charlie Rooster crowed.

"I'm so glad you liked it, and no Goat, you may not eat the lettuce in Mommy's vegetable garden. But, if you behave, I might just bring you a few leaves of lettuce after dinner."

Charm meowed.

"I'm sorry, Charm. Peter Cottontail is not your dinner tonight. He's safe at home with his sister and brother. Besides, I told you not to eat baby bunnies."

Abigail looked at her animal friends with so much affection, it seemed to pour from her eyes and envelop them in a blanket of peace and love. Charm jumped into her lap and curled up, purring and kneading. Puppy pushed his head under her hand and wriggled his rear in ecstasy, as she tickled him behind his ear. The goat pressed her forehead against Abigail's back, drawing her share of loving kindness. Charlie, still on the fence of the goat pen, ruffled his feathers in dignified and aloof joy, while his harem of hens pecked at the ground below.

Abigail lay her head on the puppy's back and closed her eyes. Rachel found them all sleeping together an hour later. She returned to the cabin and retrieved the camera she had purchased a few years ago. More pictures for the Abigail collection she had amassed.

CHAPTER NINETEEN

They sat in the gently rocking rowboat waiting for an unsuspecting fish to make the ultimate sacrifice to the dinner god. This was their first fishing trip out on the water; before they just fished off the rocks. On their last trip to the mainland, she had bought a small fishing rod and reel for Abigail and now the lines were gently bobbing in the water just off shore.

Rachel watched the child wiggle the new fishing pole. She could not get enough of Abigail as she grew from toddler to child. Every accomplishment was a miracle; every new experience opened another level of awareness for Rachel.

Instead of a hook, which could prove dangerous for a young child, a safety pin held a worm that Abigail had impaled by herself. She had been so proud of that accomplishment. "See, Mommy. I can do it all by myself."

"Yes you can, Abby. Good job!"

Abigail beamed. Rachel couldn't inhale. There was no more room for the tiniest speck of air. She thought her chest would burst from love. Abigail filled her life with newness and zest. Every discovery Abigail made was another knot in the ribbon that tied their lives together. The few times in the past two years Rachel wondered about this glorious child who had washed up on the shore like some mysterious sea nymph, she roughly pushed the thought from her mind.

She had never opened the waterproof bag again, not wanting to know anything about the boat, Sweet Abigail or the young couple lost forever. It would change everything, an intrusion of reality. Instead, she buried it under the floorboards in the chicken coop, where it would never be found, at least not in her living years. After that, once she was reunited with the others, it wouldn't matter a damn. Not to her. Perhaps to Abigail, but she would be grown, hopefully with a family of her own to give her love and support.

"Mommy, wake up. Your fishing pole is jiggling," Abigail shouted.

Rachel sat up with a start and began reeling in the fish. It flopped over the side of the dingy. Rachel picked it up and removed the hook. Then she dropped the fish into a bucket of water. "Tonight, we eat grilled fish."

Abigail peered into the bucket. "Poor fishy. Do you think it had a family?"

Rachel bit her lip. "Fish eat other fish. We eat fish. It is the way of nature. It is how everything stays alive."

Abigail nodded. "Oh. But do you think it had a family? Maybe a mommy fish is looking for it."

Rachel rubbed her scar. "What do you want to do with the fish, Abby? We can grill it or we can throw it back into the water."

Abigail looked into the bucket, her face awash with serious contemplation. "Is it okay to send it back?"

"That's fine, Abby. Would you like to do it?"

The little girl reached into the bucket with both hands and lifted the squirming fish. She turned it so she could see one eye. Fish and child stared at each other. "Go home, fishy." She leaned over the side of the dingy and dropped the fish into the water. It swam a few feet, then turned and swam back just under the surface. The fish looked up at Abigail, slapped the water with its tail, then it dove and disappeared.

Rachel stared in wonder at this child who communicated with fish. "I guess we are eating vegetarian from now on," she said, think that it was a good thing Abigail didn't realize she had been eating fish these past few years.

"What is begetan?" Abigail asked.

Rachel laughed as she picked up the oars and turned the boat toward shore. "It's vege-tar-i-an, and it means we don't eat any meat."

"Vegetaran," Abigail repeated. "Okay. I like vegetables. Can we still eat eggs? I love eggs."

"Eggs it is. You know what, Abby Dabby? I love you."

"Silly Mommy, I'm not Abby Dabby. That's a baby name. I'm a big girl, now."

Rachel's heart clenched with so much love, she could barely breathe. She pushed aside the pragmatist whispering in her ear, *"She isn't yours."*

"Fool. Don't you know possession is nine tenths of the law," The idealist stated.

"Who are you calling a fool...."

Rachel pushed them both back into the furthest corners of her mind and tuned them out. "How about a vegetable omelet for dinner, Abby?"

FRAN ORENSTEIN

CHAPTER TWENTY

One evening, the sun sank, a fiery ball in a flaming sky against the black line of the horizon. Watching the spectacular display, Rachel and Abigail gently moved back and forth on the porch swing. Charm slept on the railing and the yellow lab lay at their feet.

"We should give the dog a name," Rachel said.

"Why?"

"Because we can't keep calling him Puppy."

"Why?" Abigail looked up at her.

"Because he's all grown up now and puppy is what he was when he was a baby, not his name."

"Why?"

Rachel sighed. "Well, supposing I called you girl. How would I know you from some other girl?"

Abigail looked around "There aren't any other girls here, Mommy."

Patience! "All right! We are in the supermarket and I need to call you. If I say girl, all the other girls in the store will turn around. But if I say Abby, only you will turn around."

The child nodded. "So he will know when you are calling him."

"Yes, that's why he needs a name."

"But we've been calling him Puppy and he knows who he is."

Rachel dropped her tense shoulders and said, "Why don't you ask him what he wants?"

Abigail slid off the swing and sat down on the ground by the dog. He raised his head and she looked at the dog. "What do you think? Do you want a name?"

Rachel waited and watched, enthralled by the invisible communication between child and dog.

She climbed back up on the "Okay, Mommy. He says yes."

"You choose a name, Abby."

Abigail concentrated on that idea, scrunching her forehead in what Rachel called her little old lady look. "Sandy," she announced.

"Why?" Rachel asked.

"Because he came from the sand."

Indeed, why not? He had sandy-colored fur and a young child, dazed and frightened might think he had come from the sand. "Why don't you ask him if he likes the name Sandy?" Rachel suggested.

Abigail slid off the chair and sat down in front of the puppy. He looked up at her, expectantly, with big brown eyes. She put her hands on either side of his head and said, "I want to call you Sandy. Do you like the name Sandy?"

The puppy wriggled his rear end and waved his tail wildly. Then he barked once.

Abigail patted his head and raised her eyes to Rachel. "He said yes."

Rachel nodded. "I believe you're right, Abby. Sandy it is."

That night, after Abigail had gone to sleep with Puppy, reborn as Sandy, Rachel rocked on the porch and watched the stars. Charm lay on her lap, curled head to tail, her black chest rising and falling rhythmically. Rachel pulled a small framed photo from her pocket. A little blonde girl in a blue-flowered sundress, holding a Raggedy Ann doll grinned at the camera, her features indistinct in the darkness.

"I shall always love you, baby," Rachel whispered. "Do you mind if Abigail keeps me company for a while? It can get lonely here, sometimes." A gentle breeze rustled the hibiscus and wrapped itself like a silk shawl around Rachel's shoulders. It carried the smell of lavender and Rachel knew she was there. It was their connection. The breeze tenderly caressed Rachel's scarred cheek. "An owie kiss, sweet little one, thank you."

Rachel sighed and breathed the scented air, until the smell faded. Then she went to bed.

Screams in the night. Nightmare shrieks, but not her own. Rachel no longer had screaming-awake dreams. Something else!

She sat up in bed, still enveloped in a sleep-drugged daze. Abigail! Rachel leaped out of bed and ran into the other room. Abigail sat on the bed screaming. "Mommeeee, help me. Momeeee!"

"It's all right, Abby. I'm here. You're safe." Rachel held the terrified child, who stared into the dark beyond Rachel's shoulder. She fought the temptation to turn around and see what apparition hovered in the darkness.

"Nooooo! Noise! Woodpeckers. Ann, Ann, help me." Abigail waved her arms trying to push something away. "Wind, go away rain. Noise! Boom, boom!"

"Abby, wake up. It's mommy. You're safe. Wake up, darling'." Rachel held her tightly and rocked back and forth.

Abigail stopped screaming and looked into Rachel's eyes. Finally, she breathed raggedly and hiccupped. "Big wind! Loud boom booms! Abby scared." The little girl had reverted to baby talk again.

"You're safe, now, Abby. You were dreaming about a storm. Listen, no wind or rain. No booming thunder. You're safe in your own bed and Mommy is here." Rachel rubbed Abby's back.

"I'm so scared," Abigail shivered again.

"Would you like to keep me company for the rest of the night?"

Abigail nodded.

Rachel carried her into her bedroom and tucked her under the quilt. Then she climbed in and pulled the child close. Soon, she heard the quiet, gentle breathing of sleep. This wasn't the first nightmare nor, Rachel expected, the last. The worst had come after a violent thunder storm last month. Rachel was awakened from a bad dream that might have segued into a full-blown nightmare, if Abigail hadn't chosen that moment to scream in terror from the storm.

They made quite a pair, both running from storms lurking in their memories, sharing terror, the one understanding, the other, innocent of reality.

The sun wasn't fully above the horizon, when Rachel opened one eye.

"Who is this?" Abigail asked, pointing at the photo on the table next to Rachel's bed.

Rachel sat up. "What?"

"This little girl. She's wearing my dress and she has my Raggedy Ann doll and she looks like me, but not like me."

Rachel rubbed her eyes. "Shit," she said.

"Ooh, Mommy said a nasty word. Naughty Mommy," Abigail said, wagging a finger at Rachel.

"I'm sorry. You are right, Abby, it was a nasty word. Mommy will wash her mouth out with soap."

"Yucky icky poopy," Abigail said. "Don't say it again, okay?"

Rachel fell back on the bed laughing.

"Not funny, Mommy. Nasty word." Abigail pulled herself onto the bed and sat beside Rachel.

Rachel took a deep breath. "I'm sorry, Abby. You are a funny little girl, do you know that?"

Abigail cocked her head. "No more nasty words."

"Absolutely not," Rachel said, trying not to laugh.

"So who is this?" Abigail again pointed at the picture.

The laughter died in Rachel's throat. She remembered the stubborn persistence of children until they got some sort of answer. Her mind raced to unearth another lie. "Uh, why that's me when I was a little girl," she said.

"Oh, okay. Can we eat? I'm hungry," Abigail said, jumping off the bed.

Rachel stared in wonder at this little child who took everything at face value, yet could decide if a fish would live or die and named her dog Sandy because he came from the sand.

GAIA'S GIFT

Abigail reached out for Rachel's hand. "Come on, Mommy."

FRAN ORENSTEIN

CHAPTER TWENTY-ONE

Sandy lifted his head from Rachel's thigh and pushed at her hand with his wet nose. She idly scratched between his ears and he lay his head down again and sighed. "You are such a fine, brave dog, Sandy," Rachel said. The yellow lab raised his head again and looked at her with limpid eyes. He softly woofed and dropped his head back on her leg.

Sandy brought her back to that day 4 years ago, the day of the second storm, the day Gaia reached out to replace what she had taken and had brought Rachel back to life. She had awakened from a five-year slumber, like Sleeping Beauty, only it had taken the magical 'owie' kiss of a three-year old to break the spell. There was no Prince Charming in this fairytale. He, too, was gone with the wind, never to return. Instead, a dirty yellow puppy, eventually named Sandy, became Abigail's shadow and protector, a Labrador whose best friend was a black cat, named Charm. The dog was pure bred and beautiful; someone's sad loss, but their joyous gain. Sandy was a magical dog, who never harmed a chicken, who played with the goat and received her love in return, for the goat was lonely. This information came directly from Sandy to Abigail.

They named the goat, Clover, because the goat liked the way clover tasted. Clover had told Sandy, who told Abigail, who told Rachel that the goat claimed clover was sweet and tickled her throat. Charm ruled this mystical configuration in regal splendor as was befitting a royal feline queen. Rachel wasn't sure where she fit into the picture, except as provider and primary caregiver. It didn't really matter because she loved them all and they loved her, even the chickens that guarded the secret hidden in the coop floor.

They sat under a palm tree at the wooden table Rachel had made from left-over lumber. Rachel spread out the set of drawing pencils and paper she had brought to her retreat all those years ago. She had hoped to draw, but had been too busy trying to survive those first years to indulge in what she considered frivolous activity. She had made multiple trips back and forth in the Whaler, hauling supplies. She had hired a contractor to build the cabin and outbuildings and someone else to set up the wind power for electricity, solar panels on the roof, and the emergency generator.

She planted herb and vegetable gardens, and decorated the cabin, not that it was important because no one would ever visit. Rachel worked all day until she was so tired her body dropped onto the bed and her mind fell immediately into a deep sleep. The pain of her overworked muscles drowned out the mind-invading memories of the tiny-voiced screams barely discernable above the pounding thunder and crackling lightning.

That last trip, Rachel filled the boat with seeds, food staples, cloth, some cages of chickens, the rooster, and the goat. When she was done, she decided that she had enough to survive on until the time came to leave this world. Now, all that had changed.

Leaning forward, Rachel sewed a new tee shirt she had cut from one of her own. The child grew so fast, Rachel was afraid she would run out of fabric, so she recycled. She herself could go with less and wash more often. She paid only scant attention to Abigail's drawing. This was the child's time to be creative without grown-up interference.

Abigail held up the drawing. "See, it's Raggedy Ann and Emma and me having a party."

Rachel pricked herself with the needle. "Damn," she said, sucking on her finger.

"Oops, you did it again, Mommy. Nasty word."

Rachel didn't answer. She looked at the drawing Abigail was holding up. My God, there she was. The round pudgy face, the yellow curls, the big blue eyes, that perfect smile of pink lips outlining tiny white baby teeth. Emma's teeth would never fall out. Ever! Emma's teeth that would never taste her wedding cake, or...stop! Rachel bit her lip and willed her heart to beat and the breath to pass in and out of her nostrils. She looked up at Abigail's mischievous grin...her missing front tooth, the small dimples in her cheeks and sighed. Would Emma have looked like this at seven?

Rachel breathed deeply. "Abby, you mentioned Emma before. Who is she? How do you know what Emma looks like?"

"She's my cousin," Abigail said, shrugging.

Rachel froze. "Did you say cousin?"

"Uh, huh. She says my mommy was her mommy's baby sister. It's confusing 'cause you're my mommy, right?"

Rachel closed her eyes and breathed deeply. When she could speak, Rachel said, "That is confusing, Abby. Are you sure you're not making up the story?"

Abigail shook her head. "Nope. That's what Emma told me."

For a moment, Rachel flashed back to the resemblance between Abigail's dead mother and herself and the stirrings in her brain when she had seen Ann's name. Firmly, she dismissed them. It was easier to think of this as a figment of a seven-year-old imagination and not explore it any further. That would be treading on dangerous ground and she didn't want to go there and be mired in quicksand from which she couldn't escape.

Instead Rachel said, "That's fine, Abby, she can be your cousin if she wants."

"That's good. She plays with Raggedy Ann and me and we're a family."

"Um, is she here now?" Rachel's eyes roved. "Do you see her?"

"Well, sort of. It's like the light is different. She's right over there." Abigail pointed to the swing that Rachel had hung from one of the live oak trees. It moved back and forth in the breeze.

Eyes blurred, Rachel stared at the swing, willing a vision to appear. No image filled the void, but the swing kept moving. Saddened by the realization that she did not have the power

Abigail possessed to see and communicate with spirits, Rachel blinked back tears. To see her baby once more…. A lump blocked her throat and Rachel hugged herself. Then she felt Abigail's small arms around her and rested her head on the child's shoulder, inhaling the mixture of Abigail's lilac scent and Emma's lavender.

"It's okay, Mommy. She knows you love her. She said to tell you that she loves you, too," Abigail whispered.

Rachel sighed. Abigail had never asked about Emma, and Rachel wondered what she knew or thought. More secrets….

Rachel got used to Emma being around and she found it a comfort rather than an emotional burden. She never actually saw her, but Abigail talked about their adventures and Sandy seemed to sense her presence. Charm watched and maintained her distance, as if more sensitive to otherworldly experiences and less eager to embrace them. The cat spent most of her days stalking the moles and chipmunks that made up her diet.

Sometimes, after a storm, Charm procured a still-flopping fish from the shore, a rare treat fit for the palate of the Queen of the Cabin. She even proudly shared some of her catches with Sandy, who mostly preferred the rabbits or squirrels he hunted in the woods. Rachel supplemented their diets with eggs, grains and vegetables and Kibbles for Sandy. Abigail, the vegetarian, ignored the animals' partiality for raw meat, as long as they didn't eat her chicken friends or baby rabbits.

CHAPTER TWENTY-TWO

Life surged by, urged on by the ebb and flow of the tide. Ordinary days became weeks and then months, enlivened by the miracle child and her animal friends pouring joy into the empty vessel that once served as Rachel's heart and filling it to overflowing. Rachel, mesmerized, sat on the porch steps and watched the tiny white-edged waves surge onto the beach and then retreat, only to return minutes later, the life force of the never-ending, eternal sea, harbinger of life and death.

"Mommy, I finished my homework." Abigail danced onto the porch. Rachel started and then smiled. The child was never still. She was like the wind, always flitting this way and that, blowing in and out of rooms, jiggling her feet and fluttering her hands even when she sat.

"Excellent! May I read your story?"

Abigail handed Rachel the notebook. "It's about a chicken named Charlie."

Rachel nodded, and kept her face serious.

Abigail looked around. Then she leaned close to Rachel and whispered in her ear. "It's a true story about our Charlie Chicken."

Rachel smothered a smile. "I didn't know we also had a chicken named Charlie?"

Abigail shook her head. "Oh silly Mommy, it's really Charlie Rooster, but Charlie Chicken sounded better."

"I'm sure it's a fine story," Rachel said.

"Oh, yes. And each of his chicken family has a name. There's Sara, Dara, Lara, Dora, Cora, and Lora, and of course Charlie. We wouldn't have chicks without Charlie. They haven't named the chicks because they haven't developed personalities yet."

"I see. Thank you for telling me. Why don't you take Sandy for a walk to visit Clover, while I read your story," Rachel suggested.

Abigail turned to the dog. "Sandy, do you want to play with Clover?"

The dog woofed once and leaped off the porch, following Abigail down the path toward the goat pen. She stopped and turned around. "Uh, Mommy, I hope it's all right that I wrote a true story. I mean, Charlie said it was okay."

Rachel nodded. "It's called a biography when you write about someone else's life."

"Oh, good! I was worried about that. See you later."

Rachel smiled. Even if it was about a rooster with a bad attitude, Abigail's imagination was amazing. Of course the chickens had names, why not? She was glad they had stopped eating meat years ago. How could she possibly eat a chicken named Sara? Then she immersed herself in the story of *Charlie Chicken, King of the Roost*.

Cholly Chikin, King of the Roost, lives in a cooop with his 6 wifes, Sara, Dara, Lara, Dora, Cora, and Lora. His wifes make egs. Cholly makes chiks. Lots of chiks. Well, the chiks come from the egs, but Cholly Chikin helps. Cholly likes to make noyse in the mawning. He wakes us all up with his cocadools. Cholly Chikin is King of the Roost. Sara, Dara, Lara, Dora, Cora, and Lora are his queens. Sometimes, Cholly Chikin is not nice. He chases Sandy and me. He makes a lot of noyse; Cocadoodl, Cocadoodl. His 6 wifes love him. He makes good chiks.

Abigail Wells, age 7

Rachel sat back and laughed until tears rolled down her cheeks. *Cholly Chikin*! Okay! When she could write without her hand shaking, she picked up a pad and wrote a list of words misspelled in the story, Abigail's spelling list for the week. It seemed almost a shame to spoil her originality, but one day she would have to spell correctly. Rachel pushed the thought of the future out of her mind. There were many years to go before she had to worry about Abigail's higher education. Rachel could teach her. After all a lot of kids were home-schooled now. Her only concern was isolation. There were no other children for Abigail to play with and although the animals were wonderful fodder for her imagination, they were not playmates. On the other hand, Abigail was protected from the teasing, bullying, and nastiness that went with along with groups of kids and friendships happily formed and cruelly unformed or deformed.

Her own life was littered with forgotten friends, discarded like the debris brought in by the tide. Friends, who deserted her after Gaia beat her breasts and sent her sons from the sky and sea on a mission of vengeance and destruction, leaving Rachel bereft and in the throws of insanity. Friends disappeared, because they could not understand or accept the madness that overwhelmed her mind and threatened to destroy her soul.

Everyone, that is, but Mary, who hung in there, the steadfast friend, never giving up on her. She missed Mary, but called her as promised whenever she and Abigail sailed to the mainland. Rachel guarded the satellite phone's number, even from Mary. The computer's internet hadn't worked on the island and they used it for Abigail's school work. Rachel had an email account that she could access at the library and in their first exchange three years ago, Mary said it was mutual love at first sight, between her and Dr. Peter Grimes, the vet who bought Jack's practice. Married two years, they had infant twin boys. Mary was ecstatic with married life and motherhood. Rachel was thrilled for her and happy, too that the practice Jack had worked so hard to develop was in the capable hands of Peter and Mary. Rachel kept their family photo on the table in the parlor.

Her only regret was not telling Mary about Abigail, but this was forbidden territory, which Rachel refused to enter. She stood to lose everything, even her freedom. Rachel clearly understood what she had done and the consequences that would come if anyone found out about the child, especially the consequences for Abigail.

Rachel's life was like latticed webs woven in intricate patterns…lie upon lie upon lie and the liar impaled upon the sticky surface like a fly watching from the corner of its eye as the spider approaches, helpless to escape its destiny.

CHAPTER TWENTY-THREE

Sometimes Rachel felt a prick of guilt. Was there a family out there wondering about a woman called Ann, an unknown man, Paul, probably her husband and a baby named Abigail? Was she wrong to keep this gift from the Goddess? Didn't she, Rachel, deserve some redemption and happiness for all those years of anguish?

Then Rachel felt a stab of fear. What if something happened to her in this isolated place? How would Abigail survive? She had played a game all these years, testing fate, testing the patience of the Goddess, betting her strength and health against the safety of this precious child.

She thought of the cell phone in her room, never turned on, although she charged it regularly. Mary's number was programmed in, as well as Gary's. She also programmed the Coast Guard number. She had taught Abigail how to call out and made her practice every month. That and the boat were their only escape from this haven that had been her salvation for so many years. The thought of Abigail sailing alone out to sea terrified her. There were sleepless nights when she agonized over what she had done; hours spent fighting the pragmatic voice in her head, arguing right and wrong, justifying, rationalizing, and always coming back to the honorable thing to do. But emotions, loneliness, grief and the terrible, terrible need to fill the black hole that lingered, waiting to suck her down into oblivion, vanquished the pragmatist.

She still recalled the 'other' almost every day, and if she forgot, the sudden scent of lavender on the breeze reminded her. A little nudge, not to forget the past; an impossibility, since the past always lingered just out of reach, altered in tiny ways, but insisting on this subtle reminder, I am waiting….

Me too, Rachel thought…some day. "Be patient baby girl, I still have much to do in this realm." Rachel was astonished at the realization of what she had just whispered. Twelve years ago, she was hiding from the world that rejected her, a world that had pushed her into isolation on this remote beach, a world that had looked on her as eccentric, bizarre, dangerous, seeing only a mad woman, deranged by grief, who retreated from their reality; a lunatic who healed with herbs and hands, an animal whisperer, a seer, a witch. Hide your children when she appears, they would say. She's the crazy witch and who knows what evil she can do. Ignorance and fear! Rachel leaned back and closed her eyes. A single tear squeezed out between her eyelids and etched a wet path down her cheek. She sank into the morass of black memory.

The child stood on the porch watching Rachel. The faint smell of lavender wafted the air surrounding them. "Do you think she's okay, Emma?"

A whisper on the breeze touched Abigail's ear.

Abigail nodded. "She's sad. I don't know why she's sad. I wish she was happy."

The breeze floated by in a lavender mist.

"She misses you," Abigail said. "But she has me."

The breeze grew stronger lifting the palm fronds, swirling the air around Abigail's head.

"Okay, okay. You were there first. I know. Don't get mad."

The air settled down and the lavender scent drifted away in the gentle breeze. Abigail thought she heard the faint sounds of a tiny voice singing.

Abigail didn't know why only she could see and hear Emma, and she didn't mind, except when Emma grew angry. Then it was like a little girl's tantrum. Last week, a cup from her tea set flew across the porch, missing her head by inches. Emma had a temper.

Abigail walked toward her mother. "Mommy, are you okay?" She clasped Rachel's hand in her small fingers. Rachel opened her eyes and blinked.

She pulled Abigail close in a hug and smiled. "I am just handy dandy, Abby Dabby."

Abigail giggled and climbed up beside Rachel. "Did you like my story? I read it to Sandy and he told it to Clover, who told Charlie, who just loved it. All his chicken wives loved it, too."

Rachel peered at Abigail. "And you know this because…?"

"Dora Chicken told me."

"Of course, Dora." Rachel nodded.

"Yes, she's Charlie's favorite wife. He tells her everything."

Quelling the laughter that threatened to erupt from her lips, Rachel squeezed Abigail. "I love you."

"Mommy, I can't breathe. I love you, too."

"Sorry! I really like your story and I made a list of some new spelling words for this week. Let's see if you can read them, then you can practice writing the words and putting them into sentences."

Abigail made a face. "I don't want to do any more school work today."

"Hmm. Let's see, look at the sun and tell me what time it is."

Abigail looked up at the sky. The sun was nearly overhead. "It's almost lunch time and my tummy is growling."

Rachel laughed. "So lunch, math for an hour…."

Abigail frowned.

"Very well, half an hour," Rachel relented. "Then we'll walk the beach and have a science lesson about bi-valves."

Abigail danced away toward house, waving the story and the list of words. "Bi-valves, bi-valves," she chanted. Her ever present shadow, Sandy pranced at her heels.

CHAPTER TWENTY-FOUR

The afternoon was warm, with a gentle breeze blowing from the ocean. "This way, Abby," Rachel said, leading her to the left, away from the house.

"But I want to go this way." Abby pointed in the opposite direction, the path to the past.

"We'll go that way another day. I bet you can't beat me to that tree hanging over the water." Rachel took off, running.

The warm sea air cleared Rachel's head and blew the last remnants of black memory into the breeze. She pounded along the surf looking over her shoulder at the golden-haired girl and the golden dog chasing after her. Imperceptibly, she slowed her pace.

"No fair, you started ahead of me," Abigail yelled running behind Rachel, the dog running beside her. Her little feet pumped faster. Rachel slowed some more, allowing Abigail to catch up and then pass her.

"I won, I won," Abigail shouted, hugging the trunk of the tree. Sandy barked and jumped up against the tree.

Rachel bent over, gasping. "You are a fast runner, Abby."

Abigail tilted her head and looked suspiciously at Rachel. "Are you sure you didn't slow down, Mommy, and let me win?"

"Now why would I do that? It would be unfair," Rachel panted.

Abigail nodded. "Well, okay." Then she pointed to the water. "There's a boat. Do you think it will come here?"

Rachel looked at the boat far out on the water. She glanced at the sky, a clear blue, no clouds. Gaia was sleeping. *I hope not*, she thought and said, "I don't think so, honey. It seems to be sailing away from us toward open sea."

"Pooey, I was hoping they would come to visit us."

"Are you lonely, Abby?" Rachel asked, kneeling in front of the child.

Abby shrugged. "Sometimes, I wish there was other kids to play with. Raggedy Ann gets lonely, too. She's glad I'm here to play with her. She used to play with Emma, and sometimes Emma comes to play with us. But she's younger than me. She spills her tea. Sandy likes Emma. She says I look like her. You know, Mommy, Emma says she was here first. Sometimes she gets really mad about it. I'm not sure I know what she means."

Rachel blanched. Abigail's voice receded into the far distance. Rachel's heart skipped and she couldn't catch her breath. She sat down on the ground and hugged herself to ward off the sudden chill that suddenly wrapped her body in a frozen blanket. Rachel put her head on her knees against the wave of dizziness that threatened her balance.

Abigail wasn't watching; she was looking at the boat that grew smaller with every second that passed. "I wish you could see Emma, too, then, we could all be friends. We could have tea parties together." Abigail turned around. Rachel was sitting on the ground, rocking back and forth, whimpering.

"Mommy? Mommy, look at me. Mommeeee!"

At that final scream, Rachel tore her ravaged mind back to the present and looked up. "It's...it's okay, um, Abby. L...let's go back home, Mommy doesn't f...feel very well."

"Okay Mommy, don't cry, I'll take care of you." Abigail pulled Rachel's arm trying to raise her up off the ground. Rachel stumbled and almost fell back again, but she locked her knees and willed her body to stand and walk back towards the cabin. Sandy, sensing something amiss, stayed close by her side. Rachel moved like an ancient, arthritic old woman, as she shuffled slowly, barely able to raise her feet above the sand. Abigail put her arms around Rachel's waist and tried to keep her from falling.

Abigail's fear drowned her like a sudden summer rainstorm. She had never seen her mother like this. Mommy was always so strong. Was it her fault, she wondered? Maybe it was something she said, something she did that was bad. Would Mommy die? What would she do, all alone out here?

Mommy said if anything ever happened to use the cell phone and call for help. Abigail wasn't sure she could remember how to turn it on, 'cause there were so many buttons. Wait, mommy wrote down the instructions, but where did she put them. Abigail's brain threatened to burst. She couldn't remember. Where were the instructions? What would happen to her? Panic welled in her chest and bile rose like sour milk in her throat. Abigail stomach roiled. She wanted to run screaming, but there was nowhere to run to. Sandy pushed his damp nose against her leg. Absently, she reached out and placed her hand on his head. Instantly, a calming heat filled her hand, releasing a peaceful pulse of energy into her palm.

The panic retreated as though a giant plunger had pressed it back into place. Her brain cleared and she saw the paper with the instructions taped to the side of the refrigerator. Abigail breathed.

Don't die, Mommy, please, she silently pleaded. She knew about death because two of the baby chicks had died last year and just weren't anymore. They were Lora's chicks and she was very sad. So was Charlie. They buried them behind the coop and all the animals came to watch. Would she have to bury Mommy, too? Then how would she take care of the animals and the garden? She wasn't big enough yet. "Please don't die, Mommy," she whispered.

Rachel's mind clouded with a despair she hadn't felt in eight years. Oh, my God, Emma...! The subtle scent of lavender drifted in on the breeze, surrounding Rachel in a gentle touch. It soothed her bare skin and calmed her whirling brain. Then she heard the tiny whisper from the child at her side, "Please don't die, Mommy." Reality rushed in.

Rachel collapsed to her knees and clasped Abigail to her. "Oh, Abby, I'm so sorry. I'm not dying. I must have eaten something bad at lunch. Don't you worry, I'll always be here to take care of you."

Sandy sat down and licked Rachel's hand.

Abigail pressed against Rachel and sighed. Her child breaths cooled Rachel's hot skin. "Promise, Mommy?"

Rachel held her back and looked into her eyes. "I promise, Abby. I won't leave you, ever."

But, you will leave me. Suddenly, in her anguished mind, she saw a boat pulling away from the shore, a blonde girl, hair streaming in the wind, alone at the helm. There it was, the vision she had dreaded. Abigail would leave her. She would find out the truth and leave.

Abigail smiled. "Are you better, now?"

Rachel shook off the image of the future. "Yes, Abby Dabby, I'm feeling better. Let's go home. Maybe we can bake cookies." Then she turned to the dog, "Good boy, Sandy. You take care of us both. You're a good friend and protector."

Sandy grinned, his tongue lolling from the side of his mouth.

The three walked back along the beach, bathed in a lavender scented breeze.

CHAPTER TWENTY-FIVE

The millennium had come and gone, the world was still in orbit, spinning on its axis, and nothing had changed on their end of the Island of Nowhere. The fateful day, 9/11/2001 the day that would change the world had happened but they knew nothing about it and would not know until they sailed to the mainland, whenever that occurred.

Abigail, tall and leggy, had grown out of babyhood, displaying the stubborn, independent personality Rachel had detected years ago. She had a sharp wit and a quick tongue, but still retained a loving kindness, especially toward the animals.

Rachel wanted something special for Abigail's twelfth birthday, which Rachel celebrated every year on the day she had found her, although Abigail knew nothing about this.

"Happy Birthday, Abigail," Rachel sang, taking her hand. "I have a surprise for you."

"I love surprises, Mom. What is it?"

"Silly girl, it wouldn't be a surprise if I told you, would it?"

Abigail nodded and danced alongside Rachel. "I hate surprises. I mean, I love surprises, but…oh you know what I mean."

"Just another minute, be patient, beautiful Abigail." Rachel led her down a path in the woods to a small shed. She took a key out of her pocket and opened the lock hanging on a hasp high up on the door. "Wait here!"

Rachel went into the shed and came out pushing a black dirt bike with a bright red ribbon tied on the handlebars.

Abigail's mouth fell open. "I know what that is, I know, I know. It's a...a...um...." Tears welled up in her eyes. "I can't remember the word. I'm so stupid. I can't remember."

Rachel put her arm around the child. "It's a bicycle and you're not stupid. You just haven't seen one, so how could you know what it is?"

"But I have seen one, I remember. She called it a bike and I rode on a seat in the back." Abigail put her hand over her mouth. "What did I just say? Who am I talking about? Who is she? Why would I ride on a seat? Mom?"

Rachel saw the panic in Abigail's eyes. "It's okay, honey. When you were a very little girl, you used to ride on the back of this bicycle. That's what you're remembering." Rachel crossed her fingers at the fabrication. Forgive me, Ann, wherever you are. Forgive me, Emma.

Abigail relaxed. "So this is your bike?"

Rachel nodded. "And now it's yours. Come on let's try it out."

Abigail swung her long legs over the seat. Rachel steadied the bike while she put her foot on the pedal. "Now, you push forward and then put your left foot on the other pedal as it rises and push forward on that. You have to keep the pedals moving and always look directly ahead of you. The bike will go where you look, always remember that. Oh, and sit up straight. To stop, just push down on these clips on the handle bar, easy, so you don't stop short. Then put one foot on the ground, and you're fine.

"Don't let go, Mom."

"I won't." Rachel held onto the back of the bike and Abigail pedaled forward. After a few yards, Rachel let go. "Keep pedaling and look straight ahead, you're doing great."

"I can't stop, Mommy, help!"

Rachel ran forward, shouting, "You can stop. Press down on the clips and put your foot down on the ground."

Abigail stopped short and the bike fell over. Rachel ran up. "Are you all right?"

Abigail stood up, rubbed her skinned knee and righted the bike. "That was great! Can I do it again?"

Rachel spread her hands, "Go for it, girl."

Abigail got back on and after a wobbly start, took off down the path toward the cabin. Sandy chased her, barking. When Rachel reached the cabin, Abigail was dancing around the yard, the dog prancing and barking in her wake. She ran up to Rachel and threw her arms around her neck. "I love it. It's the best birthday I've ever had. Thank you, thank you, Mom. You're super-great-terrific."

Rachel smiled and watched her miracle child ride around the yard, the dog at her side. The bike could be Abigail's escape, should something happen to her. There was a sealed white envelope addressed to Abigail, in the drawer of Rachel's dresser with instructions directing her to the waterproof bag hidden in the chicken coop. The enclosed letter explained what Rachel had done and contained a map and instructions along the shoreline to civilization at the far end of the island. It would be a difficult ride, but doable.

She had also written down information on her attorney, Gary and her friend, Mary. Several years ago, Rachel had shown it to her and told her it held important papers. Abigail had probably forgotten about it because it had never been unsealed. Rachel made a mental note to show it to the child again.

She hoped Abigail would forgive her some day, for what she had done in the aftermath of the storm that fateful July, forgiveness in light of the circumstances that had befallen them. Abigail had been Rachel's survival and Rachel was hers, at the time they each needed the other. What followed was unforgivable deceit, but Rachel's sanity was at stake. She could not bear to lose this child, certainly not one that had been a gift from Gaia. Would she be punished for this deception one day? Probably, but at this moment, watching her daughter pedal around the yard, Rachel didn't care. She turned to the swaying swing and whispered. "You understand, baby girl, don't you?" The breeze picked up and the swing moved higher. A fragrant waft of lavender permeated the air.

FRAN ORENSTEIN

CHAPTER TWENTY-SIX

They celebrated Abigail's twelfth birthday with a trip to the mainland. Abigail was no longer fearful of the boat, but it had taken many years to convince her that it was safe to sail out to sea, as long as the weather was clear and the sun shone.

She remembered when they had brought back a young Billy goat for Clover. He was not a happy sailor and nearly ate his cage on the voyage back to the island. Now Billy and Clover were a family of four. Clover and Billy named the babies Buttercup and Daisy, or so Charlie told Sandy, who told Abigail, who of course, passed the news on to Rachel. Abigail insisted they had to have a party to celebrate. Everyone came…even Queen Charm deigned to make an appearance.

Abigail whispered in Rachel's ear that Emma was there, too. Rachel no longer reacted to the news about Emma, she accepted it and was at peace. The family was together on that special day and Abigail was content. There was no longer a rivalry between her and Emma. She understood that Emma had been Rachel's child before she had been born, and that was okay. Abigail was happy to be in Rachel's life now and to help lift the sadness her mother had felt about losing Emma.

On occasion, Abigail wondered about the memories she and Emma shared about a storm that sent woodpeckers beating tattoos on a boat and roaring winds that seemed to turn and whip the boat around on the water. They both remembered…but what they recalled neither could express.

On Abigail's birthday, or on the day Rachel designated as Abigail's birthday, they set out early. It was a special journey, because Abigail would be handling the boat herself.

"Are you okay doing this?" Rachel asked as they climbed on board.

"Of course, Mom. You've showed me enough times. I can do it in my sleep, or at least with my eyes closed."

"Not a good idea, Abby, you might hit a reef."

Abigail laughed. "Oh, Mom, you're so funny." She pulled on her life jacket and tied the strings. For a moment she paused, seeing the image of another tiny life jacket and the word "no".

"Mom, did I ever fight you about wearing the life jacket, I mean when I was a baby...in a storm?"

Rachel bit her lip. "Um, sometimes." She busied herself fussing with lines.

Rachel hated those pinpricks of memory that crept out of Abigail's mind at odd times. It was unnerving, but she had become adept at little lies, especially when she really didn't know the answer. Perhaps there had been a brief battle over the tiny orange life vest Abigail had been wearing that fateful day seven years ago. A battle won by the woman named Ann, a victory that had probably saved this child's life, but not Emma's.

Rachel watched Abigail check the boat as she had taught her. The girl started the engine, which caught after a few tries, then slowly backed it out of the inlet. She put it in forward and waving to the yellow lab sitting on the shore, sadly watching their departure, Abigail powered the boat out to open sea.

"How did I do, Mom?" Abigail asked, excitedly.

"You did very, very well. I'm very proud of you," Rachel said, patting her shoulder.

The trip across to the mainland was uneventful, and Rachel talked her through her first docking. "Fantastic job, Abby. You're a true sailor."

Abigail beamed. They tied the boat and walked up the dock together. A group of kids her age were gathered around a table at the restaurant drinking shakes. One of the girls waved and Abigail smiled and waved back. She turned and looked back at them as they passed by, a wistful expression on her face. Rachel felt a tremor of fear. One day, Abigail would have to leave, at least to go to college, or maybe even high school, and once she learned the truth, perhaps she would never return.

Rachel made a quick decision. She put her hand on Abigail's arm and stopped her. "Honey, would you like to join them for a bit while I go to the post office across the street?"

Abigail looked back at the kids and the girl waved again. One of the other kids, a boy, gestured for her to join them. Abigail turned back to Rachel. "I don't know, Mom. I'd like that, but I'm scared. What do I say? I've never talked to kids before."

"Now look what you've done," the pragmatist admonished.

"Oh, please," the idealist scolded. *"Stop pushing the guilt button all the time."*

"Don't tell me...."

Rachel cringed at the words, but lifted her shoulders and said, "Supposing I walk back with you and we can both talk to them, then if you want, you can stay and I'll go to the post office and meet you over there. It will be your choice."

Abigail hesitated. Rachel leaned over and whispered, "Smile, Abby and just be yourself."

"I can do this myself. I'll be fine." She hesitated, then took a deep breath and thought, *"I can do this."*

"Sure you can. Here's some money." Rachel pulled out her wallet and handed Abigail ten dollars.

"Thanks, Mom." The girl tucked the money in her shorts and strode with determination toward the table.

Rachel walked down the street, glancing back every so often, then watched for a few moments from the entrance to the post office. Abigail stood by the table. Rachel could almost taste the chocolate shake and smiled. Rachel knew that some of today's purchases would be an ice cream machine, a blender and plenty of chocolate syrup. She just hoped this meeting with her peers didn't spark a need in Abigail, Rachel wasn't prepared to fulfill. She knew it was inevitable, but kept pushing it off into the distance and would deal with Abigail's emergence into teen years when it happened, although it was too fast approaching.

CHAPTER TWENTY-SEVEN

Abigail walked to the counter and ordered a chocolate shake. The girl behind the counter smiled at her. "You sitting with those kids? I'll bring it over."

"Hey, we haven't seen you here before," the girl who had waved said. "I'm Becka and this jerk is my little brother Jacob." He looked up at her and snarled. Then she pointed to the other two. "That's Missy and her sister, Mandy. They're twins.

"Hi! It's really Amanda and Melissa, but Mandy and Missy are fine," Mandy said. "And, we're not identical twins and I'm older."

Missy frowned. "You always have to add that don't you?"

Mandy smirked.

"Well you're not as old as Tara," Missy sniped.

"You always bring that up…of course I'm not…she's 6 years older than us," Mandy shot back.

"Uh, who's Tara?" Becka ventured.

"Oh sorry, she's our older…" Missy answered

"…bossy sister…," Mandy interrupted.

Abigail didn't quite know what to make of them. They certainly looked alike, straight brown hair, green eyes, and long, lean bodies. "Um, hi," she ventured, "I'm Abby Wells."

"Hello, Abby. Did you just come in on that Boston Whaler? Neat boat. We have one of those; it's bigger, though, 21 feet. It's docked down there," Becka said, pointing in the general direction of the pier.

Missy spoke up. "Hey, why don't you sit with us? Where do you live? Did you order a shake? They only have chocolate and vanilla – boring."

Overwhelmed, Abigail accepted the empty chair.

"We're up from Miami for the week with our parents, kind of a vacation before school starts," Mandy interrupted.

"Where do you go to school, Becka?" Missy asked.

The waitress brought Abigail's drink and placed it on the table. Abigail thanked her and took a sip. Wow! She took another and another. This was super delicious; nector from the Goddess, her mom would have said.

Jacob seemed to be in a world of his own, loudly slurping his drink, staring at a small box in his hand, pushing buttons with this thumbs.

Abigail watched Rachel disappear into the post office building. She looked down at her hands, afraid to look at the other kids. *Maybe they'll ask me questions I can't answer,* she thought.

"So, where do you go to school?" Missy asked Becka again.

"Oh, sorry. Jacob and I go to a private school in Baton Rouge. I'm in sixth grade and Jacob is in fourth. What about you?"

Missy answered, "We're in sixth grade, too."

"Right, we live in Miami," Mandy added.

Miami, the name nudged at the edges of Abigail's brain. Where had she heard that before?

But, before she could respond, Becka asked, "So where do you live, Abigail?"

"Oh, um, we live on an island," Abigail said tentatively.

Jacob finally looked up. "Hey, that's neat. Boy, I'd love to live on an island, like is there buried treasure and pirates?"

Abigail giggled. "No pirates, but there might be buried treasure. I haven't explored a lot of the island."

"Oh boy, hey, maybe we can sail over to your island? Becka, you think dad would stop there?"

Becka shrugged. "Maybe when he comes back from the store we can ask him."

"So where is this island?" Mandy asked.

Abigail pointed in the general direction of the water. "Out there!"

"Out there, huh? I bet there's no island. I bet you made it all up," Jacob said.

Abigail shook her head. "No, I didn't, really. My mom would know the coordinates, she's the navigator."

"Who's the captain?" Missy asked.

"Me!" Abigail responded.

Jacob snorted. "Right...you captained the boat."

"Well, I did this trip. My mom wanted me to practice," Abigail replied.

"Wow, I wish my dad would let me do that. He won't even let us steer," Mandy said, pointing to Missy and herself.

"Our dad won't even let our mom steer the boat unless he's right next to her. He's a control freak," Becka said.

Jacob stood up and squared his shoulders. "This is my boat and I'm the captain," he shouted, imitating a deeper voice.

Everyone laughed. Abigail felt comfortable. They were nice kids and she listened carefully as they talked about school and their friends. There was a void inside her. It wasn't something she could name, but it lingered there, a thirsting soul finally arriving at an oasis in the burning desert, filling the emptiness, but the thirst never got quenched. She watched Jacob out of the corner of her eye and finally got up the nerve to ask, "Uh, Jacob, what's that you're playing with?"

Jacob looked up, startled. "Huh? It's a game box...you know it has games and you can play them."

Abigail realized the others were looking at her strangely. "I'm sorry, I didn't mean to sound weird, but we don't have anything like that on the island."

There was a collective expelling of breath.

"It's okay. Here, I'll show you," Jacob leaned over and gave Abigail a lesson on Tetrus.

"Wow, that's fun," Abigail said, grinning. "Thanks, Jacob. Maybe I'll ask my mom to get me one of those."

Jacob shrugged. "No problem. There're big ones you can play on the internet or the television."

Abigail had no intention of telling them they had no working internet or television and had never seen any, other than the floor models in the store. She figured they thought she was strange enough. Jacob went back to his game box and the girls talked about boys. Abigail had never known boys and eagerly absorbed everything she heard like a dry sponge. According to her new friends, boys were nasty, terrific, dorks, nerds, jocks, brains, gorgeous and a variety of other descriptions. Abigail wished she knew some boys so she could chime into the conversation. She would have to check out these words in the dictionary and discuss all this with Rachel.

"So do you have a boyfriend?" Missy asked.

Abigail swallowed and thought fast. "Um, not right now. There's this boy I like, um, Sandy, but um, I wouldn't call him a boyfriend, more like a good friend."

"So what does he look like?" Mandy asked.

"Oh, he's strong and handsome. Oh, and he has blonde hair and big brown eyes."

"Awesome, he sounds like a god," Becka said.

Abigail shrugged. Out of the corner of her eye she saw her mom appear in the street and wave. Abigail almost ignored her. She wanted to stay here, with these kids, strangers, yet companions. They understood her and she understood them. It was like nothing she shared with her mom or with the animals.

Abigail felt the rising force of anger. It was a feeling she had never experienced before. She wanted to scream at her mother and vent her rage at their isolation. This was a new thought that had never occurred to her before today.

Then guilt and love overpowered the other emotion. She remembered the loving animals, the peaceful beach and forest, her mother's love.

"Sorry, I have to go. We need to get some shopping done and leave before it gets dark."

"Nice meeting you," Missy slurped some more of her shake.

Becka raised her hand. "Maybe we'll meet here again."

Jacob never looked up from his game box but said, "Uh huh, we stop here all the time when we sail down the coast."

"See y'all," Mandy said waving.

"Bye, safe sailing." Abby reluctantly crossed the street to meet her mother.

FRAN ORENSTEIN

CHAPTER TWENTY-EIGHT

Turmoil boiled in Rachel's gut. She smoothed the girl's hair to delay the inevitable question. Finally, she asked, "Did you have a good time?" Rachel held her breath, fearful of the answer.

Abigail nodded. "I had a great time. They were really nice. I wish...." She turned but the table was empty. It was like a dream. "Where'd they go?"

"I guess, back to their boats," Rachel said, relieved yet wary.

"Where are they from?"

"Oh Mandy and Missy are from Miami, Florida and Jacob and Becka are from some place called Baton Rouge in Louisiana. Mom, did we ever go to Miami?"

Rachel looked closely at Abigail. "Why do you ask?"

"It just sounded so familiar, like someplace I'd been in a dream. It's a nice word, Mi-a-mi. It makes me think of pretty colored houses, pink like the inside of some shells, blue like the sky, and turquoise, like the sea around the beach. I don't know why that name is like a picture. Are you sure I've never been there?"

Rachel's heart flipped. Memories again, like forbidding shadows intruding on the sun. More lies, yet not lies. "We did sail down there when you were a very tiny girl. I can't imagine you would remember it."

Abigail shrugged. "I don't know. I just remember the colored houses. Silly. Anyway, the kids couldn't believe we live on an island. Jacob wanted to know if there were pirates and buried treasure. And they were so jealous that I had piloted the boat over here...."

Rachel listened to Abigail chatter away about her experience. Guilt pricked her heart, which she flicked away after brief consideration of the ramifications of moving back to civilization. Perhaps one day in the future, she would send Abigail to school. What would she do about a birth certificate and inoculations, all the encumbrances of civilized society? Rachel couldn't deal with that now.

"So could we, Mom?" Abigail tugged at Rachel's arm.

"Could we what, honey?"

"Were you even listening to me?" Abigail asked, annoyed.

"Of course, I missed what you just said because of the noise of that motor." Rachel had become adept at lying at a moment's notice.

"I asked if we could have a television and can I get a game box."

"Oh!" Rachel had visions of a bigger generator and quickly probed for an answer. "I don't think it will work on the island, Abby. Besides, it's much more fun to read and ride your bike and play with the animals. Television is boring and a lot of the programs are bad, really bad."

"Could we just buy a small one and try it out?"

"I'll tell you what, what if I buy you an ice cream maker and a blender so you can make shakes."

Abigail grinned. "Well, I was going to ask for that anyway. The kids said television is so great and you can learn so much. Jacob said they have this satellite dish that can pick up stuff from all over the world."

Rachel looked down at the miracle child. Abigail existed in this world and her successful negotiation of its treacherous shoals was tantamount to her survival beyond the island. She needed to experience and explore the ugliness and the beauty. The girl was growing up and one day would leave their island sanctuary. Why was it always a mother's cruel job to push her child from the womb and then the nest? Rachel brushed her hand across her scar and sighed, "Okay, we'll go and check it out."

Abigail threw her arms around her mother. "You're fantabulous, Mom. I love you. Uh, can we check out a game box, too?"

Rachel sighed. "I haven't said yes. We still have to see if it's possible."

"Oh, I have a feeling it will work perfectly." Abigail nodded sagely.

She took her mother's hand and squeezed. "So when we get back will you tell me about boys?"

Rachel swallowed hard. *Couldn't she have held off a few years?*

Rachel, consumed with guilt, bought everything Abigail asked for; even the game box. There was barely room for them on the boat as they sailed across the Gulf to their island, hauling Abigail's booty. "Yo, ho, ho, I'm a pirate," she sang, steering the boat deftly through the water. Rachel grinned and stilled the voices in her head.

The television proved to be an education for Abigail, especially 'tween shows and sitcoms that dealt with families and relationships. They had brought back DVD's of movies and continued to add to the collection on every trip, which became more and more frequent. Abigail did get a game box with the requisite games, but now it languished on a shelf in her room, forgotten in the process of growing up.

"Boo!"

Rachel jumped and dropped the pail of fertilizer. "Oh! Don't do that…you scared me."

"That's what was supposed to happen, Mom."

Rachel cringed at the 'Mom', it sounded so disconnected, almost like a name. "So why are you trying to scare me?"

"I have a surprise for you," Abigail said.

Rachel rose and turned. Abigail was almost as tall as she was. Lean and strong, her hair, now a dark blonde, gleamed in the sunlight. Her figure was filling out, small breasts and the indication of hips and waistline belied the still exuberant, ever moving girl inside the burgeoning woman's body. Rachel grinned. "What's the surprise?"

"I got my period!"

For a moment, Rachel didn't understand. Then she did. Her heart pounded and she was sure Abigail could hear it thumping inside her chest wall. Rachel breathed and hugged her daughter. "Congratulations, Abby. Any discomfort, trouble with the tampon?"

Abigail shrugged. "I had a little cramping, but nothing terrible. I took those herbs you showed me and it's already better. The tampon was a struggle and it hurt, but I won."

"Well, all right, woman. This calls for a celebration." Abigail giggled. Rachel took her hand and they walked up the path toward the house. "Chocolate cake a la mode…chocolate ice cream, of course."

"Of course," Abigail laughed. "Is there anything other flavor?"

"Well, vanilla, coffee, butter pecan, strawberry…."

"Oh, Mom, you're so funny."

"Pistachio, cherry vanilla, raspberry…."

Okay, okay, I get it." Abigail said, laughing.

CHAPTER TWENTY-NINE

Sandy picked his head up off his cushion on the porch as they approached and rose stiffly, his arthritic hind legs struggling to straighten. The dog's muzzle was speckled white and his eyes rheumy and heavy-lidded, but he still did his best to follow Abigail, slowly of course. Rachel knew he was getting old for a dog his size. Charm, too, now 17, lazed around in the sun. She could no longer leap to the roof and climb trees. Maybe another year or two left with them on this plane. *Cycles of life*, Rachel thought, her thoughts drifting. She pulled herself back from the cliff along the chasm of despair. *Don't go near the edge, the ground will crumble and you'll fall in and one day you won't be able to climb out.*

Abigail placed her hand on Sandy's bent head. "Not yet, sweet puppy, not yet."

Rachel watched the interaction, a lump rising in her throat. "Abby, talk to me?"

Abigail turned to Rachel. "He's tired, Mom. He told me he's very tired. He's almost ready, but not quite yet. He's waiting for Charm and they'll go together. Then they'll be able to run again and hunt, and wait for us to join them."

Rachel brushed the tear off her cheek. The child said it so matter of fact, like it was something she experienced every day. Abigail hugged Rachel and the old dog rubbed up against her. "It's all right, Mom. He's not sad. Sandy has had a good life with us. He's been a very happy dog, haven't you boy?" She reached down and smoothed his graying head. "We've had so many good times together running on the beach and he loved chasing my bicycle. He's just tired, now."

Rachel's shoulder's shook and she recalled the first time she saw the dirty, half-starved puppy, so valiantly protecting baby Abigail. All those devoted years following the child, prepared to give his life to keep her safe; such a brave, loyal friend.

"Mom, please don't cry; Sandy doesn't want you to be sad. He loves you so much. See?"

Rachel looked down at the beautiful eyes that peered up at her. She knelt down and put her arms around his neck and he ran a wet tongue over her cheek, wiping away the tears. "I love you Sandy," she said. "You are the bravest, most beautiful puppy in the whole world. Thank you for being our puppy."

Rachel sniffed. "How would you like a biscuit, Sandy?" Sandy smiled his doggy smile and sighed. "I thought so," Rachel said, rising. Out of the corner of her eye she saw the swing moving in the breeze. *"You'll have company soon, Emma, baby."*

"Don't worry, Mom. It's not going to happen, yet. Charm isn't ready. But Sandy says if you would give him more of those herbs to help his legs, he would really be grateful."

"Oh, God, I'm sorry. Of course, Sandy. Right away, with the biscuit, okay? You go ahead, Abby, I'll be right there." Rachel detoured to the small shed where she stored her herbs. *"I've been so selfish; I couldn't see the dog was suffering. Get it together, Rachel pay attention to what's going on around you,"* she thought. *"Around and around, the endless cycle...."*

Suddenly, Rachel understood as surely as she knew the sun would sink into the horizon as the Earth spun in its never-ending, ever-changing cycle. The vision hit her like a blow to the gut, knocking the air from her lungs and sending her to the ground. She doubled over gasping. She saw Abigail, her beautiful, glorious miracle child, her face an ugly grimace of anger and loathing, mouth spewing forth words that hurtled toward her like stoning rocks falling on a Biblical sinner, Abigail waving an orange life preserver like a beacon of light filled with Rachel's sin.

GAIA'S GIFT

Death took many forms and the heart died in too many ways to count. But not yet, in a few years perhaps it would come to pass, but not yet. There was still time to…to what, reverse the Earth on its axis; send time spinning back, to undo the done? Was she a reluctant time traveler, playing poker with Death, holding a pair of deuces against a full-house? Death always wins, as the duped gambler learns in the end. "Lay your bets," Death cackles madly to the unsuspecting fool.

Rachel pushed herself up and drew in a long breath of the sweet sea-scented air. "Time, a little more time, Gaia…just until she's old enough to live her life, then you can have me". As Rachel walked slowly toward the spice shed, a lavender-scented breeze wafted up from the ground to engulf her body. "I know, I know, my baby," she whispered. "I'm coming."

FRAN ORENSTEIN

CHAPTER THIRTY

The twins were back at the marina's ice cream shop when Rachel and Abigail made the next trip across the Gulf. Abigail's face lit up at the sight of the two sisters arguing over which current rock star was better. They seemed older somehow, matured. Abigail waved as she and Rachel went down the pier. "Hey, come on over, Abby," Mandy called.

"Can I, Mom?" Abigail's implored a 'yes' from Rachel.

"Sure, I'll meet you at the market in one hour," Rachel said, handing her some money. "Hi, girls," she called, waving.

"Hi, Abby's Mom," Missy called.

Abigail ran across the street and slid into a chair. "It's so nice we could meet again. I'm glad you're here."

"It's spring break and dad decided it would be fun to sail north for a week," Missy explained.

"It's cooler up here, anyway," Mandy said.

"Our dad's a lawyer," Missy said.

"He used to be a prosecutor," Mandy offered.

Missy frowned at her sister. "He put people in jail, but…"

"…Now he just does family law stuff…," Mandy finished.

"…And some defense work…." Missy added.

Abigail nodded as though she knew just what they were talking about. *If this continues, I'll have to carry a pocket dictionary. File that away in the 'I'll-ask-mom-drawer',* she thought.

"What does your dad do?" Mandy asked.

Abigail hesitated. "Uh…my dad went to sea and didn't come back," Abigail gave the only information she had. She filed it away as another future topic for discussion with her mother.

"Oh, I'm sorry…was he in the Navy?" Mandy asked.

"Yes, I guess. My mom doesn't like to talk about it," Abigail said.

"Our mom couldn't get off work…," Missy started.

"…she's a doctor," Mandy finished.

"Oh, that's exciting. What kind of doctor?" Abigail asked, happy to change the subject.

Mandy opened her mouth, but Missy jumped in, "She's a dermatologist."

"Right. She says that way nobody's calling her at 2 a.m. to deliver a baby or perform emergency surgery in the middle of the night," Mandy said.

"I mean, a zit's not exactly an emergency, right?" Missy's giggles setting them all off until the waitress came to take Abigail's order.

Mandy managed to snort some shake through her nose. When she had her breathing under control, she said, "It sure is an emergency when it pops out the morning of the spring dance."

Missy nodded. "Okay, I'll give you that, but even a mom who's a dermatologist can't do an emergency zitectomy."

They were off and laughing again.

Abigail wondered what a spring dance was like. The waitress put Abigail's shake on the table and looked at them strangely. More giggles and snorts.

"Oh, yuck, that was disgusting," Missy said screwing her face into a wrinkled scrunch.

"It was an accident," Missy said blowing her nose into a napkin.

Abigail rubbed her mouth to keep from laughing. These two were the bomb. She learned that word from the latest sitcom on T.V.

Abigail sipped the shake and the discussion reverted to the latest rock star heart throb. Abigail was comfortable because now she could join the discussion and not feel like she'd been living in a cave somewhere.

The hour passed too quickly. Abigail wished she had friends like this she could talk to every day. Meeting the twins brought home the lonely existence she lived on the island. Guilt tweaked her conscience as she thought of her animal friends and Rachel, who loved her so much. It wasn't this, though. It wasn't girl talk and laughing at stupid stuff. It just wasn't...the same.

"Hey, I have to go. I wish I could stay longer, but my mom worries about me and she said an hour. So...hey, maybe we'll see each other this summer," Abigail said.

Mandy scribbled something on the napkin and thrust it at Abigail. "Here's our email address, send us a message and then we can talk on-line."

Missy's hand shot out and she intercepted the napkin. "Wait, here's our cell phone number...you can call anytime up to 9 p.m. My mom gets really mad if we stay up talking on the phone too late."

"Uh, okay, sure" Abigail said carefully folding the napkin and tucking it in her pocket. She knew there was no way she could get in touch with the girls through a computer, but maybe a cell phone....

Mandy looked at Missy. "I bet Danny would love to meet Abby."

Abby raised her eyebrows. "Uh, who's Danny?"

"He's our friend," Missy said.

"He lives down the street," Mandy added.

"He's okay, but we like know him since kindergarten," Missy said.

Mandy nodded. "We keep trying to get him to meet girls..."

"...he's shy," Missy finished.

"He is not," Mandy argued.

"Yes he is," Missy insisted.

"He spends his life on the short-wave radio," Mandy said.

"Girls...uh, hey, girls?" Abigail interrupted the burgeoning argument. "We have a short-wave radio. Let me write down the call numbers and maybe you and Danny can call me." Abigail hastily scribbled the information on a napkin.

"Great idea." Missy raised her glass and toasted in a smooth silky voice, "Here's to our yearly rendezvous."

"Ooh, sounds delicious." Mandy giggled.

Abigail touched her mostly empty glass to theirs. "Next year, same time."

"Same place, salud." Mandy saluted with her glass.

"Bye." Laughing, Abigail ran down the street toward the market. Rachel stood outside waving.

CHAPTER THIRTY-ONE

Rachel watched Abigail cross the street. She thought her heart would burst with love and pride. Rarely thinking of her as other than her own child, Rachel marveled at the vibrant beauty Abigail was becoming. Slim long legs, dark blonde pony tail bouncing with every step, and a mischievous gleam in her eyes that sometimes turned flirty, Abigail radiated wholesome health and youth.

"I had such a good time, Mom. Missy and Mandy are so funny, they are always arguing, but they love each other. I can tell. I wish…."

Rachel cringed waiting for the next words but Abigail shook her head and smiled instead. "They have a friend, his name is Danny and he has a short-wave radio. Anyway, he goes to school with them and they've known him forever. They gave me their cell phone number and I gave them our call numbers on the radio. Maybe in a week or so I can call them? Please? Okay? Wouldn't that be neat?"

Rachel listened to Abigail's enthusiastic description of her visit with the twins and their friend Danny. In the next year, Rachel would have to make a decision, either move to the mainland or send Abigail to boarding school. She couldn't keep her isolated from the world any longer. Perhaps it would be time to tell her the truth. The lump of fear grew to such proportions, that Rachel could barely inhale enough air to sustain her. Could she survive if she lost this miracle child gifted by Gaia? There would be no purpose to live…and Emma was waiting, Emma who would have been almost 20 by now, wandering in another world, forever three years old…and Jack, her beloved Jack. Would he recognize her after all this time?

"I won't think about it, now," Rachel thought. She searched for a distraction to tamp down the fear. "Let's do something special, Abby,"

Abigail looked up expectantly.

"How would you like to go to a beauty salon and we'll get our hair and nails done?"

"Toes, too? I want bright red polish," Abigail announced, twirling in the street, pony tail flying.

"Absolutely, manicure and pedicure, bright red polish. We'll buy a bottle and take it back with us, then you can wear red polish every day."

"Can we buy different colors, you know orange and pink, oh and black, so I can look like a vampire, like on Buffy," Abby asked.

"I knew I should never have agreed to the satellite dish. I raised a vampire child. I guess I should be happy, at least you haven't asked for a tattoo or piercing."

Abigail grinned. "I don't know about a nose ring, but a tattoo, now that's cool. Just a little one? Uh? Uh Mom? Maybe a butterfly?"

Rachel laughed. "Absolutely not, no tattoos, no nose rings, at those I draw the line."

Abigail pouted. "Well, okay, for now. But next year, we'll see."

"I think I'm taking down the satellite dish tomorrow," Rachel said.

"Mo-ohm." Abigail turned the word into two syllables.

Rachel put her arm around the girl's shoulders and squeezed. "Just kidding, Abby Dabby, just kidding. You're growing up so fast."

"Too fast," she thought.

"Kids do that, Mom."

Rachel swallowed. Some kids.

CHAPTER THIRTY-TWO

This will be the year of reckoning. The thought flew into Rachel's mind unbidden on the wings of an orange butterfly. She watched the gorgeous creature settle its delicate body on a yellow flower and fold its wings together. It looked at her, and that's when Rachel knew that events were about to unfold that would alter their lives and she was helpless to stop them.

Most of the animals were gone, now. Buttercup and Daisy were growing old and their parents, Clover and Billy had passed on several years ago. Charlie Chicken and his wives, too, had left this world and only a few of their offspring hens remained with no rooster to continue the line. Rachel missed the feisty rooster and his hens, and the two goats…the world was a lesser place without them in it. Sandy now moved slowly with painful steps despite the herbs she gave him and Charm spent most of her days sleeping in the warm sun. Life…and death…moved inexorably onward.

Tears welled and Rachel sniffed. This had been her family and soon they too would pass into the next world and wait for her with Emma, sweet baby Emma. The scent of lavender permeated the air and Rachel breathed deeply.

"Mom?" Abigail called from across the yard.

Rachel stood up and walked to the girl. Tears streaked Abigail's cheeks. Rachel put her arms around her and smoothed her hair. "What is it honey?"

Abigail sniffed. "It's time, Mom. Sandy says it's time."

Rachel wilted. *"No, I'm not ready for this, not Sandy,"* she thought. Not this brave, wonderful puppy. Then she closed her eyes and willed herself to be strong for Abigail and for Sandy and Charm. Oh my God, Charm. Was it time for her, also? Sandy said he was waiting for Charm. Charm was from before. Charm shared her memories of Jack and Emma. There would be nothing left of reality in her memories once Charm left.

"Where's Charm, Abby?"

"She's with him, Mom. Come on. They're down at the beach."

Rachel followed Abigail down the path to the beach. The beautiful yellow lab lay on the sand, his head on his front paws. He slowly raised it as they approached and gazed at them with his beautiful brown eyes, now milky. Charm lay beside him, her head on his shoulder. She looked up at Rachel and softly mewed. They knelt down and Abigail placed Sandy's head on her lap. Rachel put her arms around Charm and they watched the sun drop behind the horizon and turn the sky blazing red and orange. Sandy thumped his tail once and expired with a great sigh. Charm licked Rachel's hand and lay her head back down, as her life force left her body.

Only the lapping waves against the shore disturbed the silence. Finally, Abigail looked down the beach. "They're free now, Mom. I see them running together in the sand. Sandy doesn't hurt any more and Charm is climbing a tree. Emma's there too with a man and they're waving at us. Is he my daddy?"

Rachel's heart stopped and she couldn't breathe. *Oh my God, Jack...?* "Mom, answer me, are you okay?" Abigail shook Rachel's arm. "Mom?"

Rachel gasped and nodded.

"It's okay, Mom. I didn't mean to scare you it's just that I see these things."

Forcing herself to breathe, Rachel whispered, "I know and it's fine, darlin'. You just took me by surprise."

"Are you sure you're okay?"

"I'm fine, Abby. So you saw them all together…"

"Oh yeah! They're really happy, but sad, too because we aren't with them. But they'll wait for us, I know they will."

Rachel forced a smile at the vision Abigail painted. "Thank you for that Abby. It's easier if I know they are happy." She bent down and lifted the cat and cradled her in her arms. Then she carried her to the small cemetery where they had buried all the animals. She laid her gently on the ground and returned for the dog. She and Abigail lifted him gently and brought him to his place beside his lifelong companion. They wrapped them carefully and buried them together next to the other animals, placing a wooden marker on their grave that they painstakingly carved with a chisel and hammer.

OUR BEST FRIENDS
SANDY, A BRAVE DOG AND
CHARM, A LOVING CAT,
TOGETHER IN LIFE, TOGETHER IN DEATH
JULY 2006

Rachel spoke first. "Our Charm…in regal beauty she graced our lives with her gentle presence, finding pleasure in a forest of trees to climb, chasing a butterfly, stalking a bird, unearthing a mole. She liked to be scratched between her ears and in front of her tail, purring and kneading, never unsheathing her claws. She adopted a golden puppy as her own, caring for him as she would a kitten, had she born any. Charm lived a long and happy life and we shall miss her every minute of every day."

Abigail wiped her eyes and took a deep breath, shuddering. "Goodbye Sandy…strong and loyal, my best friend and protector who will always live in my heart. I know you are running free along a sandy beach, splashing in the surf, chasing wavelets and red rubber balls. I'll always remember you and miss your grin and waving…" Abigail's voice broke and she slumped against Rachel, sobbing.

Rachel eased her onto a log and they held each other and cried for a long time.

***

Abigail wandered the shoreline for days, bereft and lonely. Tears came at odd times, unbidden, with memories that surfaced briefly like flashes of lightning in the night sky. Glimpses of a sleek yellow-hued flicker of shadow out of the corner of her eye pierced her heart and rendered her inconsolable. He had been her best friend and protector for as long as she could remember. Mom had explained the life-span of a dog, particularly a big dog, and in her head, Abigail understood, but the reality was a dose of Chinese mustard on the tongue.

Abigail curled up in bed at night, reaching automatically for the warm pulsing body of her constant companion. Her shoulders shook and the pillow dampened with the salty waters of grief. Her bed, once a sanctuary, was no longer a friendly place to feel secure; instead it became the cold slab of a sepulcher. She turned to Jon Bear, abandoned after childhood, his tired body worn and bald in patches from loving caresses over many years. When she slept at all, she would awaken suddenly, listening for the soft snuffle of a wet black nose, a sound that existed only in her mind, now.

Sometimes outside, Abigail would glance at the sun-drenched porch railing, expecting to see Charm curled up in kitty bliss, ears twitching in dream-world pursuit of wild-bird delicacies. She sat on the top step of the porch where Charm would crouch, and spring at an unsuspecting Sandy, sunning himself on the bottom step. Wherever she went, Abigail besieged by memories, saw remnants of her childhood friends: Sandy's red ball, abandoned under a Bougainvillea or Charm's furry catnip mouse peeking out from behind the flower pot. She collected them all in a covered plastic container and placed it on the grave, an offering of love. The girl added to the box whenever something else revealed itself from a kitty or puppy hiding place.

On the table next to her bed, she placed a framed picture of Sandy and Charm so she could say goodnight to them when she went to bed and good morning when she awoke. Their gentle eyes looked out at her from the photograph and she felt safe knowing they still watched over her.

GAIA'S GIFT

CHAPTER THIRTY-TWO

Gradually, as the months passed, the pain of loss eased, and although it never left completely, it receded to occasional tear-stained nights and moody daytime meltdowns when she unearthed another memory. The short-wave radio proved to be a distraction for Abigail. She and Danny developed a friendship and spoke at least twice a week. His full name was Danny Winters. They mailed each other pictures and as soon as Abigail saw his, she was convinced she was in love. His hair was dark and curly and his smoldering brown eyes seemed to penetrate deeply into hers from the photo. Danny's grin was boyish and a deep dimpled chin gave him an impish look. She thought he would look great in a pirate's hat, swinging a sword; Dan the Pirate, terror of the Florida coast.

Abigail thought about her dilemma a long time before approaching Rachel. "Mom, can you fall in love with somebody even though you've never really met them?"

Rachel, kneeling in the herb garden, weeding, looked up startled by the question. *Uh, oh*, she thought, *how do I answer that one?* "I guess if you see someone who appeals to you and then you like what they say and you have things in common that you both like and enjoy, you can fall in love."

"I thought so...I mean people fall in love on email, don't they?"

"Oh, you mean like in the movies?"

"Well, yes," Abby answered.

"Real life isn't the movies, Abby. We talked about that."

"Well, it could be. I mean what's so hard about it, if like you said you get along and like the same things, and you like the way he looks."

Rachel racked her brain to answer that one. "There's more to loving someone than a picture and a conversation."

"Well, what more?"

"I'll have to think about that, Abby, okay?"

"Sure, Mom. While you're thinking, I think I'm in love with Danny."

Rachel sighed. *"Already,"* she thought. *"She's only 14."*

"Ah, young love, so delicious," the idealist purred.

"But, she's so young," Rachel thought.

"And how old were you when you 'fell in love' with that Mike Barnes on the football team?" the pragmatist asked.

Rachel cringed. He had dumped her in six months for Lori with the big boobs.

The idealist stepped in. *"That was unfortunate. He was a creep. Isn't this all part of growing up?"*

Once more the pragmatist butted in. *"You see everything through rosy glasses. She could get hurt."*

"All part of the growing up game," answered the idealist.

"Shut up!" Rachel closed her mind to the voices.

"Anyway, Mom, In April during Spring Vacation, Danny is going to sail up with the twins and they'll dock at the pier where we meet. So, I was thinking, could we go and maybe stay for a few days, instead of sailing right back? Could we?" Abigail was bouncing up and down in excitement. "Please, please, can we do it?"

Rachel wiped her forehead. "You're smashing the herbs. Can I think about it?"

"Sorry, but Mom, what's to think about. It's just a few days…please? I really want to see my friends."

It suddenly dawned on Rachel that Abigail must be very lonely now without Sandy. She also needed her peers. Living alone with her Mom wasn't going to cut it any more. Abigail was growing up and Rachel had to face the fact that life was going to change.

"Aha, finally," said the pragmatist, triumphantly.

"Go away!" Rachel commanded.

"All right, Abby. We'll go for three days. I'll get us a hotel room."

"YES!" she shouted, dancing off.

"Watch the herbs, Abby. You're trampling the garden."

"Sorry, Mom, sorry. Buttercup, Daisy, wait 'til you hear. We're going to stay on the mainland and I'm going to meet Danny."

Abigail's voice faded as she hurtled toward the goat's pen to tell them.

"I'm not ready for this," Rachel said aloud to the breeze. But she wondered if she would ever be ready for it. Was any parent? Children grew up and went away. Sometimes they came back, but mostly they went forward with their lives, leaving parents behind. They had done that when she married Jack and moved to Florida, leaving his parents behind. Then his baby brother, Chip, left and never came back from the war.

Which war? Rachel couldn't even remember there had been so many. Was there ever a gap between wars or did one just merge into the other? Rachel always believed that loneliness and grief murdered his parents, two loving people, before their time, devastated by the loss of their beloved son to something they had reviled since their protest marches in the 1960's. Jack's flower-power, peace-loving parents had been devastated as their dreams of the future exploded with a roadside bomb in a desert hellhole they couldn't even find on a map.

Rachel sighed. She still faced the dilemma of Abigail's education and socialization. It kept her awake nights with anxiety gnawing at her stomach. She knew what her future was once Abigail was grown and moving on with her own life. Rachel fully expected to join Emma and Jack. This time she would not hesitate at the shore, but walk steadfastly into the sea, until Poseidon reached out and took her home. Lately, though she had formulated another plan, sail out to sea and scuttle the boat, then, she could not turn back. If Abigail still cared by then, she would at least think it was an accident and not a suicide.

The child would want for nothing, except a mother, but by then she would know the truth, so it wouldn't matter. Rachel herself had managed to grow up anyway, most kids did.

The trust fund was set in stone and Abigail could not break it. The money would just continue to grow, even if she rejected it in anger. Besides, she would no longer be a child, but an adult and independent.

Sometimes, though, Rachel wondered what it would be like to witness Abigail walking down the aisle in a white wedding gown and living happily ever after, if anyone actually did that in this century. Sometimes she looked in the mirror and saw the few gray hairs that had begun to sprout and the tiny tell-tale lines around her eyes and mouth. She pictured being a grandmother, but this vision eluded her imagination. Besides, was it worth going on for that?

"You're rushing too fast," The pragmatic voice warned.

"Leave me alone," Rachel said. "It's not a crime to dream."

"First steps, first," the voice admonished.

"Idiot," the idealist interrupted, *"Life's too short, live it."*

"Don't call me an idiot," the pragmatist protested.

"Hush, both of you," Rachel said aloud.

But, for once, Rachel admitted the pragmatist had a point. Abigail was only fourteen…well, going on fifteen. Still, she had to figure out the school dilemma and this would require more subterfuge than Rachel had energy to accomplish. Perhaps these three days on the mainland would be helpful. She would go on-line at the Internet Café and check out boarding schools, then explore the very remote possibility of moving to the mainland.

Deep in the pockets of her brain she flashed on a family named Stern from Miami who had perished in a small boat on the isolated and remote end of a long key off the west coast of Florida…and a woman named Ann, cut off from life too early. There were times Rachel wondered about this woman and the eerie resemblance they had to each other. She recalled many years ago when Emma told Abigail they were cousins.

At the next opportunity she went to the chicken coop and removed out Ann's passport, staring at her picture. Could fate create such a bizarre situation? Was there a connection between them? Tamping down the thought, she gathered the herbs and carried them into the house.

FRAN ORENSTEIN

GAIA'S GIFT

CHAPTER THIRTY-FOUR

They sailed to the mainland again and this time packed enough clothes to last a week. Rachel left out plenty of feed and water for the remaining animals. When Abigail had not appeared, she found her kneeling before the grave of Sandy and Charm. Ashamed of herself for eavesdropping, she turned to walk away when she heard, "I'm very lonely, Sandy. I miss you so much. Remember when I told you, I want to meet other kids, especially Danny. I think I'm in love with him, but I've never really met him. He might just think I'm awful and ugly and not want anything to do with me. I don't even know what to say to him. I don't know how to act...I'm such a loser. I hope you can hear me, Sandy, 'cause I just want you to remember that you were my first love and I'll always remember you."

Rachel backed silently out of the tiny animal cemetery, tears coursing down her cheeks. She sat down on a log and put her head in her hands. "What have I done?" she moaned.

"You stole a child," the pragmatist said.

"Nonsense, she saved her life," the idealist argued.

"She lied," the pragmatist stated.

"She gave her love and happiness," the idealist insisted

"You don't know what you're talking about. She built a giant web of deceit and now she can't get out," the pragmatist taunted.

"What do you know about love, anyway...?"

Rachel clutched her head. "Shut up, shut up. I've got to make this right."

"See what you've done?" The idealist shouted.

"Me? I haven't done anything...she did it."

"Leave me alone," Rachel said, running toward the beach.

Abigail shut the gate of the cemetery fence and saw Rachel race across the grass. "Mom, come back. Where are you going?" Abigail shouted.

Rachel stopped at the edge of the water and bent over, hands on her knees, panting. Abigail caught up and clutched her mother's arms. "Hey, are you okay? You've been crying. What's the matter, Mom?"

"Nothing, honey."

"Don't treat me like a baby, Mom. Something's wrong."

"I'm sorry, I didn't mean to listen in on your conversation with Sandy, but I was looking for you and couldn't help hearing you tell Sandy that you were afraid Danny would think you are ugly and...." Rachel sobbed so hard she couldn't finish.

"Oh, come on, Mom. It's just stage fright, that's all. It'll be fine. You remember when you were fourteen; didn't you worry about boys liking you?"

Rachel hiccupped and looked up at her beautiful daughter. "You are so wise for your age, Abby. When did you get to be older than me?"

Abigail laughed so hard she sat down on the grass. Rachel looked at her and started laughing, too, through her tears. Soon they were both lying back on the grass laughing.

"Oh my God, my stomach hurts," Abigail said. "I think I'm going to throw up."

Rachel sat up and hugged the girl. "You are the light of my life, Abby Dabby."

"I know, Mom, and you are mine. So can we leave, now?"

Rachel shook her head. The resiliency of children, she marveled. "Indeed, Miss Abigail, we can leave now."

They sailed across the bay and docked the boat. Missy and Mandy stood on the dock with a tall, good-looking boy. The girls were practically dancing in anticipation. "Abby," Mandy called. The twins waved, and Abigail tossed the line to the boy.

As she stepped off the boat onto the dock, he reached out and grasped her hand to help her off. Abigail's knees felt like mush. "It's great to finally meet you in person," she said, hoping her voice wouldn't shake.

"Whew, you're gorgeous," he said, staring.

"Thank you, Danny," Abigail blushed and let go of his hand. She looked down, busying herself with the rope.

Rachel grinned. *"Yes," she thought, "perfect."*

"Hi, Mrs. Wells," Missy said.

"Hello, girls." She turned to the boy. "You must be Danny Winters. I'm Abby's Mom, Rachel Wells."

Danny dragged his eyes away from Abigail. "Uh, pleased to meet you, ma'am," Danny said, reaching out to help her off the boat.

Rachel handed him the bags and then accepted his assist onto the dock. She reached down to pick up the bags.

"Oh, let me do that, ma'am." Danny hefted the bags.

"Ah, a true son of the South," she thought.

"Thank you, Danny. I surely appreciate that."

"Yes, ma'am."

They trailed up the dock toward the hotel. While Rachel checked in, the kids caught up on their sailing adventures.

Danny carried their bags to the room. His eyes were glued to Abigail. The twins, walking behind, whispered and giggled.

Rachel, trailing the group, heard Mandy whisper, "I think Danny's in love."

Rachel smothered a smile. She would have to keep a close eye on them, a very close eye.

Rachel shooed them away. "I'll unpack. You kids go have a shake on me. I'll see you later, Abby." She handed Abby some money and kissed her cheek.

They turned to leave, when Mandy stopped. "Oh, Mrs. Wells, I almost forgot. My Dad said to tell you he's sorry he wasn't here to meet you at the dock, but he had to go see about a client or something. He's invited you both to dinner tonight at the Fish

Market restaurant. Seven okay? Nobody gets dressed up, so you're fine."

Rachel wondered what her father did for a living. "Well, that will be nice, Mandy. I'll get to meet your parents."

Mandy glanced at Missy. "Uh, Mom's not here."

"Don't be stupid, tell her," Missy said, poking her sister.

"I'm not stupid and you tell her, you're so smart."

Missy made a face at Mandy. "Our parents got divorced. There, that wasn't so hard."

"I'm sorry, girls," Rachel said.

"Yes, well, we're getting used to it," Mandy looked down at her pink toenails poking out from the sandals, as if they were about to fall off and walk away by themselves.

"Anyway, Dad wants to meet you and Abby. So is tonight okay?" Missy asked.

Rachel smiled. "Of course! I look forward to meeting him."

"Great, we'll meet you in the lobby of your hotel at six," Mandy said.

"Have fun, and Abby, I'll meet you back at the hotel around five," Rachel said.

"Sure, Mom. Thanks for the treat."

"Oh, right, thank you, ma'am, for the shakes," Gentleman Danny said.

"My pleasure, Danny."

"Me, too. I mean thanks, Mrs. Wells," Mandy said, poking her sister.

"Right, what she said," Missy said, making a face at Mandy.

Rachel smiled. The door shut behind them and she heard their feet pounding down the hall. Rachel sat down on the bed. She was suddenly as nervous as Abigail had been on the trip over. She hadn't spoken to a man in years, well other than the checkers at the market and the postal worker. Oh, and there was the nice salesman at the electronics store.

"Stop this, idiot. You're acting like a teenager on a first date," she mumbled.

Then she opened her suitcase throwing the clothes all over the bed. "Oh dear, didn't I bring anything along that's nicer than shorts and a tank top?"

Suddenly, she started to laugh hysterically. The reaction was so foreign that she couldn't control it. Tears rolled down her cheeks. Finally, she gasped. "Here I am worrying about what to wear to dinner with a strange man and I'm in hysterics."

FRAN ORENSTEIN

CHAPTER THIRTY-FIVE

Danny was gorgeous, better than his picture, and a gentleman, too. He pulled out her seat and waited until she was comfortable before he sat down next to her. Somehow, his chair had moved closer to hers. The twins smirked across the table. Abigail didn't care, she was happier than she had been in a very long time.

"So what's it like to live on an island?" Danny asked.

Abigail shrugged. "I have nothing to compare it to. It's simple, I guess. There's just Mom and me and Sandy and…." She stopped bit her lip to keep from crying.

"Who's Sandy?" Mandy asked.

She wondered if they remembered her long-ago lie about a boyfriend named Sandy.

Breathing deeply, she answered, "He was my golden retriever. He died last month along with our cat, Charm."

Before the twins could say anything, Danny said, "I'm sorry, Abby. I had a dog once, too. A shepherd named Buster. I remember being sad for a long time because he wasn't there any more."

Abby looked up into his beautiful eyes. "Thank you, Danny."

The twins looked at each other. "We had a cat named Snuggles," Missy said.

"She got hit by a car last year," Mandy added.

Abby tore her eyes away from Danny's face. "I'm sorry. That must have been awful."

They both nodded. Mandy opened her mouth but closed it again when Abby turned to lock eyes with Danny.

Missy looked at her sister and rolled her eyes.

Mandy giggled and pushed back her chair, "We're gonna check out the uh…

"…shoe store," Missy finished.

"Okay," Abby and Danny said at the same time.

"See you later," Mandy said, grabbing her sister's arm and pulling her to her feet. They giggled all the way down the street.

Abby sighed. "So tell me about your school. Do you play sports?"

Danny nodded. "I go to high school and I play saxophone in the band, but I also play soccer."

"That's great. Mom says maybe we'll move to the mainland soon so I can go to school and be with other kids."

"It must get lonely on an island with just your mother." Danny said.

"Yes, it does get lonely sometimes. I mean she's a great mom, but I miss having other kids to talk to."

"You have me and the twins." Danny took her hand.

Abby felt a strange tingling sensation in her body. She cleared her throat. "I know, and that's great, but it's not like every day. I can't just pick up a phone and call or go over after school."

"Wouldn't it be great if you could live near us? Then we would go to the same school and everything. You could meet all my friends and the twins' friends."

"Maybe their dad can convince my mother to move to the mainland."

Danny grinned. "You could come down to Miami to live."

Abby wrinkled her forehead. "Danny, are the houses bright colors in Miami, like pink and blue and turquoise?"

"Well, maybe in Miami Beach and some other places. Mostly they're high-rise condos and regular houses," he answered. "Why?"

She shrugged. "I don't know. I just have this memory of lots of colors and the word Miami."

"Did you ask your Mom?"

GAIA'S GIFT

"She says we sailed down there once, but I was a baby. It's really weird, I get these snatches of pictures and sounds, like I'm watching a film flickering in and out, but I can't keep them for long enough to figure out what they are."

Danny squeezed her hand. "Sounds like things you want to remember but can't."

"I'm just being silly. Let's talk about you. What's your favorite food?"

"Pepperoni Pizza, hands-down." Danny licked his lips.

Abby pulled her eyes away from those wet lips. "Mine's chocolate ice cream with blueberries and chocolate syrup."

They sat there for a long while, learning about each other. Abby devoured the information on life beyond her island and the more she heard, the more she craved. She became obsessed with moving to the mainland and vowed to talk to her mom in earnest now.

FRAN ORENSTEIN

CHAPTER THIRTY-SIX

Rachel was obsessed with what to wear to dinner that night. She knew nobody got dressed up in Florida, but her shorts and tee were just not going out tonight. Finally, she went shopping and found a flowered sundress that was perfect for casual dining. She picked up a few other items before returning to the hotel. A leisurely shower and shiny clean hair rejuvenated her spirit. She pulled the sundress over her head and smoothed it down along her hips.

"This is ridiculous," she said to herself. "I'm acting like, like...like a teenager."

"*So???*" *oozed the idealist.*

"*It's stupid...she's not a teenager,*" *muttered the pragmatist.*

"*You don't have to be a teenager to be excited about a date,*" *the idealist countered.*

"*It's not a date, it's a meeting,*" *the pragmatist argued.*

"*Meeting, schmeeting, it's a date....*"

"Be quiet, both of you," Rachel demanded. She twirled in front of the mirror just as she heard the key card in the door and Abby came in.

"Ooh, Mom, you look gorgeous. Did you go shopping?"

Rachel blushed. "Well, I wanted something a little nicer than shorts and a tee shirt."

"I love it."

"Thank you, darling. So did you have a nice time with the kids?"

Abby flopped onto the bed and spread her arms. "I had a fantastic time. Danny is so nice. He plays saxophone in the school band and plays soccer. He has two younger brothers and his father is an engineer and his mother is a math teacher."

Rachel sat down and listened to Abigail rattle on about Danny and marveled at her excitement. On the one hand she was thrilled, on the other she was terrified that the end of their world was rapidly approaching. Gone was the little girl, enter the young woman.

"...so what am I going to wear tonight? I didn't think to bring anything nice," Abigail wailed.

Rachel rose and picked up a shopping bag from the dresser. "For you," she said handing the bag to Abigail.

"What, what?" Abigail shrieked.

"Well, look inside, silly girl."

Abigail reached in and pulled out a light blue sundress. She held it up against her body and looked in the mirror. "Oh, Mom, it's gorgeous. It matches my eyes. Gotta shower, gotta wash my hair, and look at these nails, I'm a mess."

She laid the dress on the bed, stripped off her clothes and disappeared into the bathroom. Rachel smoothed the dress and added clean underwear. Then she sat down and waited.

Finally, Abigail reappeared, wrapped in a towel. She dropped the towel and slipped into her underwear. Pulling the dress down over her head, she stood before the full-length mirror and twirled. "I feel like a princess again," she whispered.

Rachel moved behind her and put her hands on Abigail's shoulders. "A grown-up princess."

"Well, I'm almost 15," Abigail said tossing back her curls.

Rachel smiled. "You most certainly are."

Her stomach roiled and she wanted to scream, *"Not yet, not yet, I'm not ready to lose you. I'm not ready to lose me."*

In her head the pragmatist sang, *"Let the punishment fit the crime, the punishment fit the crime...."*

"Shut up, shut up, shut up," Rachel's mind screamed silently. *"You won't spoil tonight."*

CHAPTER THIRTY-SEVEN

The elevator doors opened and Rachel stared at the man seated on the sofa beside Missy, Mandy and Danny. He was dark...the opposite of her fair-haired Jack; sleek dark brown hair, cut long around his ears, tanned skin, aquiline nose and lush full lips. *"Oh my, those lips,"* she thought...kissable lips. Rachel shook herself. Grow up woman, you're almost forty. Stop behaving like a teenager, like your daughter. She smiled at the thought and watched him rise, unfolding his lean, tall body. He smiled back, cheeks dimpling.

"Of course, he has dimples and let's see...green eyes. Perfect!" the idealist groaned.

"Probably a con-man. You're always taken in by good looks," the pragmatist countered.

"Please, can't you ever be positive?" said the idealist.

"Kindly shut up!" Rachel thought.

He held out his hand and engulfed hers in his firm, but gentle grasp. "You must be Rachel Wells, I'm Bennett Ross, father of these two conniving young ladies. Everyone calls me Ben." Then he turned to Abigail and dipped his head. "You must be Abigail. Danny has been talking about you all evening. Girls, you forgot to tell me how beautiful your new friend is, just like her mother."

Rachel felt the heat rise in her face. Cool it! He's a flatterer, that's all.

Abigail blushed furiously as Missy and Mandy giggled.

Danny grinned and took Abigail's hand. He leaned over and whispered, "He's right, you know."

If it were possible, Abigail reddened even more. In fact, her entire body was on fire. The twins covered their mouths to smother their laughter.

Rachel smiled. "Now, Mr. Ross, you're embarrassing my daughter." There was a lilt to her voice that Abigail hadn't heard before. *Was her mother flirting?*

Ben feigned horror as he looked at Abigail. "I am so sorry, Miss Abigail, can you ever forgive me?"

"I'll try, Mr. Bennett, uh sorry, I mean Mr. Ross," she said in a squeaky voice.

Ben turned back to Rachel. "And please call me Ben and if I may, I'll call you Rachel."

"I'd be delighted, Ben." Rachel took his proffered arm and the teens trailed behind, following them out of the hotel.

Dinner was a blur of conversation that Rachel participated in but remembered little about the subjects, her responses on automatic. She was too aware of the man seated next to her to concentrate on anything but the heat generated from his body. Once his arm touched hers when he reached for something and it felt like a third-degree burn. It had been a long time since she had been so aware of a man, too long.

The idealist reared his head. "That's the answer, it's been too long".

"He's too handsome and charming? There has to be a flaw somewhere." The pragmatist ventured.

"Nonsense," the idealist retorted. "His ex-wife must have been insane. There are insane doctors, aren't there?"

"Maybe he's a workaholic or an alcoholic. Maybe he ran around with other women." The pragmatist snorted.

"Stop it! The only thing lacking is love." The idealist sighed.

"Take a cold shower," stated the pragmatist.

"Nonsense, go to bed with him," the idealist suggested.

"He could have all kinds of diseases," the pragmatist yelled.

"So she uses protection...don't be a pragmatic idiot," retorted the Idealist.

"Who's an idiot...?"

GAIA'S GIFT

Rachel turned off the bewildering argument in her head, but possibilities lurked in the background.

The kids went in different directions after dinner; Missy and Mandy to explore more shops and Abigail and Danny to check out the marina.

"Would you care to join me for a walk on the beach?" Ben asked.

"I'd be delighted, Ben," Rachel said.

Rachel hadn't felt this happy in years. Being happy with Abigail was different from happiness with a handsome charming man at her side. She never realized how much she had missed the company and admiration of men. She didn't need it to survive, but life was surely better if it came along. As they walked and talked, she felt a twinge of betrayal to the memory of Jack, but pushed it back under the surface. Jack was gone, her first love, a lost love. Rachel would remember him forever, but she needed something now.

Ben's voice penetrated Rachel's brain. "So when I realized that I wasn't cut out for the politics of government and the stress of the attorney general's office and that I would never reach the top or actually want to go there, I switched careers."

Rachel's stomach lurched. *What had he just said?*

"Switched to what?" she asked, her voice barely audible.

"Well I resigned from the prosecutor's office and opened my own law firm. I do some defense, but mostly family law."

FRAN ORENSTEIN

GAIA'S GIFT

CHAPTER THIRTY-EIGHT

It suddenly hit like a flaming meteor falling from space and blew up her world. This man walking beside her, someone she might possibly come to uh, never mind, had been a prosecuting attorney. He put people like her in jail. She was a kidnapper, nothing more. Extenuating circumstances didn't count when you stole someone else's child, even if they were dead and buried. No one would care about her own loss, her lost mind, the love and care she had given this child; that she had saved Abigail's life. They would look at her and see a crazy woman who found and kept another family's baby. They would put her away forever...he would put her away forever. What was she thinking? She had to sever this now before it developed into a full-blown relationship.

Unaware of her distress, Ben continued, "Now I put families back together with adoptions or take them apart with divorces."

Rachel barely heard him. Two more days and then she wouldn't see him ever again. The friendship Abigail had developed with the twins and Danny would have to be severed. That would hurt the child, but it was necessary. She would move Abigail to the mainland far north of Miami, perhaps on the east coast of Florida, or better yet, to another state; maybe the Pacific coast. Abigail would adjust and make new friends. Kids were adaptable, weren't they?

"You can make a nice life for yourself and the child," said the idealist.

"They'll still find you," the pragmatist countered.

"*People change identities all the time and disappear,*" the idealist argued.

"*Too many variables with a child,*" the pragmatist shot back.

"*Do you ever see the positive side of anything?*" shouted the idealist.

"*Quiet! I can't think with your voices pounding in my head all the time,*" Rachel thought.

Panic welled up in her chest, constricting her throat. Her body tensed, prepared to run and find Abigail and rush to the boat. Then she would head to the island and pack up what would fit in the boat and leave. Leave everything behind. Everything they had built and loved for the past 11 years. All the memories she had created there with Abigail. Leave behind the memories of Sandy and Charm, Charlie the Rooster and his harem of hens, and Clover and Billy. They would have to abandon the chickens and the two goats to the wilderness and hope for their survival.

Stop! She closed her eyes and breathed deeply. Panic caused mistakes. Take it one step at a time. Just get through tonight and the next two days. Maybe she could feign illness and leave in the morning. No, Abigail would be too disappointed. Be strong!

"Hey, are you all right?" Ben had stopped and was peering down at her.

"I'm sorry, I was lost in thought," Rachel said quickly. *Get control, now, before you do something stupid.* "I lost track of the conversation."

"It wasn't important, anyway. Just a story about a case I once prosecuted."

Rachel forced a smile. "No, I'm interested, please continue."

Ben told his story about blackmail, revenge and murder.

"Sounds like something you would see on television," Rachel commented.

"Lots of times they take their stories from the headlines, so that's not farfetched at all." Ben walked her to a bench along the path and they sat down.

Rachel decided it was time to change to a more neutral topic. "How do you like living in Miami?"

Ben shrugged. "Like any other big city, crowded, noisy, but exciting. You have to be careful because it is a city and there's crime. But Miami has its charm and draws you in, that's the allure. There always something happening."

"I've never lived in a big city. I grew up in a small town where it was safe and everyone knew everyone…and their business." Rachel laughed.

"I think I left out the anonymity of the big city," Ben said, smiling.

"Well small towns certainly don't lend themselves to anonymity. If anything it's the opposite. You can't get away with a lot in a small town," Rachel said, thinking of the accusations and glares of the people where she had once lived such a happy life.

Ben grinned, "I actually know what you mean because I didn't grow up in Miami…I'm a transplant from a medium-size town in Georgia."

Rachel cocked her head. "I thought there was an aura of the southern gentleman about you, Mr. Ben."

"Yes, ma'am, there surely is."

Rachel leaned back and looked up at the stars. "Pretty sky tonight."

Ben leaned over and feathered his fingers down her jaw. "May I…?" He gently kissed her and when she responded, he intensified the kiss. Her mouth opened under his increasing pressure and she closed her eyes. His fingers moved like feathers around her neck and down her bare back. Her body burned like it was in a fiery pit of coals, in places she had forgotten existed. Rachel wanted him more than anything else right now.

Then she pulled back, panting. "Oh, my God!" she said. What was she thinking? This was insane, but his force was like a magnet pulling her in. Was she so needy?

"*Yes*," cried the voice in her head. Rachel couldn't shut it off. Her imagination ran off with reason chasing after it. Imagination ran faster, leaving reason gasping in the sand. This was a dangerous game and Rachel would be a fool to play. What was that about fools rush in…?

He jumped back. "I'm sorry, Rachel; wrong time, wrong place. It's just that you're so beautiful and real and I want to make love to you so badly."

Rachel reached out and took his hand. "I want you, too, Ben, but not right here, right now. It's been a very long time for me and I want it to be just right. Besides, there are the kids."

Ben closed his eyes. "You're right, of course. We could go back to your room or my boat, but chances would be very high that one of the four kids would show up."

"Isn't that what usually happens?"

He laughed and pulled her against his body. "So let's just sit here and stare at the stars and imagine we're in your hotel room, undressing each other...."

Rachel laughed. "Stop, that's cruel."

"Well, we could just drop down on the sand and do it right here."

"I can just see it in tomorrow's paper: Prominent Miami attorney found...um, copulating on a public beach with blonde. They were bailed out of jail this morning by their teenage children, but still face charges of indecent exposure and violating statute, something, something, something of the Florida penal code."

Ben threw back his head and laughed until he began to choke. Rachel patted him on the back.

He turned to her. "I could fall in love with you Rachel Wells."

That brought her up short. Sex was one thing...love was another. She couldn't afford to fall in love, not now, not with him, not ever.

"After only...let's see...." She looked at her watch. "Um...about four and a half hours. You are a fast worker, Ben Ross."

Ben's dimples deepened. "Why waste time? Life is too short."

"You're right about that. What can we do about it?" Rachel quipped.

"We could go to a different hotel."

"Hmm, I hadn't thought of that, but what if the kids needed us?"

"Are you kidding? My daughters are probably buying everything in sight and will be until the stores close in about two hours. Abigail and Danny are…well touring the marina."

"Wait! What does that mean?" Rachel jumped up. "I'm going to look for them, right now. How could I be so dumb?"

Ben grabbed her hand. "Come back here. Abigail is perfectly safe with Danny."

"You were 15 once; raging hormones, libido in high gear, moonlit night by the sea. Oh, my God! My baby!"

"Calm down. Danny is a good boy, a gentleman. He would never do anything inappropriate."

"And you know that because…?"

"Because I've known Danny Winters since he was born, I know his family, and I trust him with my daughters, you should, too."

"There's a difference. Your daughters grew up in a big city. They've been exposed to people since they were born. They're sophisticated compared to Abigail. She's only known our island and me. She has no clue about the realities of life except what she gets from me, books and television."

Ben sighed. "Okay, you may be right; about Abigail, I mean, not about Danny. We'll go find them." He took her hand and they walked toward the marina.

FRAN ORENSTEIN

CHAPTER THIRTY-NINE

After an agonizing twenty minutes, while she imagined every conceivable horror being inflicted on her precious Abigail, Rachel saw them in the distance sitting on the edge of the dock eating ice cream, legs dangling over the side, swinging in unison.

"Don't you say a word, Ben Ross."

Ben put his hand over his heart. "Who me?"

"So maybe I over-reacted a little back there. Mothers do that."

"I understand," he said soberly.

Rachel looked at him suspiciously. "Are you laughing at me?"

He shook his head and bit his bottom lip.

"You're laughing at me."

Ben bit harder and couldn't meet her eyes. Instead he examined his sandals. She glared at him and finally he couldn't keep it in any longer. His shoulders shook and a loud guffaw popped out of his mouth.

Rachel began to laugh, she couldn't help it. The whole situation had run away from her. They were laughing so hard that they didn't see Danny and Abigail until the teens were standing directly in front of them.

"What's going on?" Abigail asked.

"Something must be very funny," Danny said.

Rachel and Ben looked up at them and laughed harder. Tears ran down Rachel's cheeks and Ben held his belly like it was about the fall off.

"Okay, Mom, we'll just sit right here and wait it out." Abigail pulled Danny over the sea wall and they sat, legs swinging in tandem, pretending not to notice the antics of the adults who were acting like a pair of chimpanzees on speed.

Finally, it was over. Gasping for breath, Ben and Rachel tried to breathe normally. Rachel wiped her face with the back of her hand and Ben straightened up.

"So are you going to tell us?" Abigail asked.

"I don't think so," Rachel gasped.

"Private joke," Ben said.

The teens looked at each other and shrugged and Rachel realized that Abigail was quickly learning the unspoken language of adolescence. Where was her little girl?

Surely not this child, wrapped in the burgeoning body of womanhood on the edge of defiance and independence.

"Face facts...she won't be yours much longer," the pragmatist said.

"Shut it, fool! She doesn't need your philosophy right now," hissed the idealist.

"Who's a fool?" countered the pragmatist.

"You are...."

Rachel tuned them out and turned to Ben. "I think we should call it a night."

The kids groaned. Ben laughed. "I think you're right. Come on, Danny, let's go find the girls and get some sleep."

He turned to Rachel. "Will I see you tomorrow? How about breakfast at nine?"

Rachel looked at Abigail who nodded, grinning. "Sounds great."

"We'll come by your hotel and pick you up," Ben said. "Come on, Danny and I will walk you to your hotel."

They waited until Rachel and Abigail had entered the lobby and waved goodbye.

"Wow, Mom, he's the bomb."

"What?"

"He's great, you know, the bomb," Abigail said.

Rachel nodded. "Uh huh," she replied, dreamily.

"I'm talking about Danny, Mom. Who are you talking about?"

"What?" Rachel woke up. "Oh, of course, Danny."
"Uh oh, Mom, I think you meant Ben Ross."
"Don't be ridiculous, Abby, we just met."
"Right!"
"Abigail Wells, come back here...."

But, Abigail was already in the bathroom with the door shut. Rachel considered keeping the conversation going, but realized she would just be arguing a case she has already lost. Abby was right...she felt a strong connection to Ben Ross.

"Go for it!" the idealist rejoiced.

"Not a chance...too dangerous," the pragmatist said.

"What danger? She just wants to have a fling."

"You are such an idealist. What if she falls in love?"

"So what, she deserves some love."

"He was a prosecuting attorney...that's what!" the pragmatist announced.

"Hmm...I'll have to think about that one," the idealist said.

Rachel sat down heavily on the bed and put her pounding head in her hands. She couldn't stand the arguments running like an audio loop in her brain. All she wanted was a few days of happiness and fun with another adult, preferably a male adult. Was that too much to ask? Would she exact punishment for that desire, too?

"Hey, are you okay, Mom?" Abigail asked, concern in her voice.

Rachel raised her head. "I'm sorry, honey. Of course, I'm all right. I just have a headache; probably too much wine at dinner. I'm not used to it."

Abigail bounced on the bed and knelt behind Rachel. "I'll massage it away, Mom, just lean back."

Rachel closed her eyes and let her daughter's magic fingers knead away the stress and ache of worry. She pushed all thought out of her mind and pictured black velvet shimmering in moonlight. Gradually, her headache drifted away and her breathing became calm and steady.

Abigail knew the moment and eased her down on the bed. "You rest, Mom, I'm going to curl up in the other bed and read for a while. I love you," she whispered.

"I love you, too, Abby. Thank you." Rachel drifted into a twilight sleep.

It was dark when she opened her eyes. The lights were off and moonlight peeked around the edges of the drapes. She looked over at the other bed and saw the outline of Abigail, gently moving up and down with the rhythm of her breathing. The clock on the side table said 2:00 a.m.

Rachel slipped out of bed and went to the bathroom. She flushed and washed her hands and face and quietly exchanged her clothes for pajama bottoms and a tank top. She quickly brushed her teeth and rinsed, then tip-toed to the side of Abigail's bed and looked down at the sleeping child.

Abigail's hair, spread across the pillow, had darkened a bit, but still reflected the blonde highlights left over from her childhood days. Rachel listened to her soft breathing. Tears threatened. She moved away and pulled the bedspread off her own bed and opened the French doors to the tiny balcony. There were two plastic chairs and she wrapped herself in the bedspread and sat on one of them. Across the marina, she could see the blue-black ocean and the moon reflecting on the water. Further down, tiny white-caps lapped against the beach. She gazed up at the sky and the myriad of tiny winking lights that filled the firmament. The big dipper stood out and the points of Orion. She could see a small solid light to one side of the moon, perhaps Jupiter or Venus.

"Oh, Gaia, help me. I'm caught in a web of dark secrets and I don't know how to get out of it," she whispered. She thought of Ben Ross and then Jack. "Would you forgive me, Jack, if I had one night of bliss? I know it can't be a lifetime because I've done a terrible thing and deserve to be punished…but just one night."

A gentle breeze wafted across her neck, gently lifting her hair. She breathed in the faint scent of salt water and lemony after-shave and felt an invisible blanket of peace envelop her. "Thank you, Jack," she whispered. "I promise, just one night."

GAIA'S GIFT

Rachel sat outside watching the moonlight and white-caps for a while longer, then went back in and fell into a peaceful sleep.

FRAN ORENSTEIN

CHAPTER FORTY

Abigail was already up and dressed in a two piece bathing suit and shorts by the time Rachel opened one eye to bright daylight. "Oh you evil girl, you opened the curtains in the middle of a lovely dream."

Abigail giggled. "Time to get up, sleepy mom. It's almost nine o'clock."

Rachel rolled off the bed. "Why didn't you wake me earlier? Now we're going to be late."

"Don't worry about it. I'm going to the lobby and I'll tell them you're washing your hair, or something girl-like. They'll understand."

"Ooh, you really are evil. Don't you dare! I'll be ready in ten minutes."

Actually, it was fifteen minutes, but Rachel knew they would be waiting. They were sprawled on couches in the lobby, the twins curled up together on a large armchair, asleep. Ben and Danny jumped up and said at the same time, "Good morning!"

Rachel and Abigail laughed. "Good morning to you, too!" Rachel said. "Sorry we're late."

Ben shrugged. "I have two daughters so I expected it."

Rachel rolled her eyes in mock horror. "Are you stereotyping us?"

Ben smirked. "Absolutely not, my life would be a living hell if I did something like that."

"Did what, Dad?" Mandy yawned and stretched.

"Nothing!" he said.

"What nothing?" Missy asked, rubbing her eyes.

"So, who's famished besides me?" Ben said quickly.

Abigail giggled and Danny covered his smile. Rachel leaned toward Ben and whispered, "Good save."

"Thanks," he whispered back.

Danny said. "I'm starving."

"Hmm, he's always starving," Mandy said, stretching like a cat.

"I'm a teenage boy. We're supposed to be hungry all the time," Danny announced.

"Yeah, well it's a good thing you're not our brother, you eat everything in sight." Missy retorted.

Danny took Abigail's hand. "You see how they abuse me? Must mean they really love me, right?"

"Oh, barf!" Missy gagged.

"Yuck! Let's go, Missy." Mandy said walking out the door to street.

The others followed them down the street to the pancake house, Abigail giggling all the way.

The giggling bothered Abigail, but she didn't know how to stop it. It just flew out of her mouth, uncontrolled and uncontrollable. Sometimes, she felt like an idiot, but there wasn't any on/off switch marked 'stop giggling'. Why today of all days when she was trying to impress Danny? She pinched her lips together so no sound would pop out, but it still shook her chest and shoulders trying to force its way out of her throat. Digging her nails into her palm to cause pain deflected the giggles a bit, but she was afraid that if someone said anything even remotely funny, it would start again even worse than before.

Danny appeared oblivious. He kept up a one-sided conversation about his dream car, never even noticing that Abigail wasn't responding. Please don't say anything funny and please don't let me think anything funny, please. Then she realized he had asked her a question.

"I'm sorry," she said.

"I guess I'm boring you," Danny said.

"No, not at all, cars fascinate me. I mean we don't have any on the island, no roads, you know. I just missed the question," Abigail said, desperate to keep the conversation turned on.

"It's not important."

"Sure it is. Please?"

Danny shrugged. "Okay! I asked you if you liked a Mustang or a Corvette."

"I know what a mustang is…a wild horse, right? But what's a corvette?" Abigail was stumped.

"Wow, you really don't know about cars, do you?"

Abigail shook her head. "I told you, I've never even been in a car, at least I don't think so."

"What do mean, you don't know. Wouldn't you know if you've been in a car?"

"Sometimes I remember things from when I was really little but I'm not sure because the memory is strange."

"Don't you ask your mother?" Danny asked.

Abigail nodded. "I do, and she explains, but it's still a weird feeling."

"What's weird?"

"There are people I remember, but it's foggy, like off in the distance…somebody named Ann and Captain Paul. Then there are these houses, all pink and blue and green, you know all pastel colors, but bright."

"Like the ones down in Miami Beach," Danny said.

"Mom told me that when I first met the twins and they said they came from Miami. I remembered the word, Miami and the bright houses. I asked Mom and she said we had been down there a few times when I was very little."

Danny squeezed her hand. "Everybody has memories of things when they were little. I remember falling off the porch on my head when I was around three."

"Hah! That accounts for it."

"What? Accounts for what?"

"Nothing," Abigail said, giggling again.

"Come on, accounts for what?"

Abigail bit her lip to stop the giggles and said, "Your superior brain. The fall must have rattled some cells."

Danny laughed. "Okay, I'll let you get away with that one."

CHAPTER FORTY-ONE

After breakfast, the four kids decided to go swimming before the daily thunder storm rolled in.

"Do you think we should go with them?" Rachel asked.

"They'll be fine, so unless you have a desperate desire to go into the water or bake in the sun, I have a better idea." He leaned over and whispered a couple of words in her ear.

Blushing, Rachel considered the offer, whatever it might mean and decided that it held better prospects than lying in the hot sand. "Don't forget sunscreen, Abby," she called.

"I know, Mom, it's in my beach bag with the towel."

"Mothers are all the same, aren't they?" Mandy said.

"They think of all the details and then nag you about them," Missy agreed.

Danny laughed. "Let's go swimming."

Rachel watched them run down to the beach. "Are you sure it's safe to leave them alone? What if there are sharks or a rip tide?"

"You worry too much. They're perfectly safe and there's a life guard station just down the beach. They'll be fine. Danny is very trustworthy."

"I know, but he's still only fifteen," she said.

"And raging with hormones," the pragmatist added.

"You again? There are three girls and one boy," the idealist said.

"Yes, but his hormones...."

The idealist shouted, *"Shut up about hormones, he's not a serial killer rapist."*

"And you know that for a fact...?"

Rachel pictured a red stop sign. She would not turn into a paranoid, overbearing mother. Abigail was on a crowded, public beach in the middle of the day with police patrols and a lifeguard station.

"They'll be fine. Missy has a cell phone and we'll check on them regularly if that will make you feel better."

"All right! I'm sorry; this is all new to me. We've lived alone on a secluded island for so long that I've forgotten what the real world is like."

"It's fine, Rachel. I understand." Ben looked down at her and ran his finger across her lips.

Rachel shivered. She hadn't felt this way in a very long time, not since...*don't go there, not today*, she told herself.

"Come on, we're going sailing," Ben said taking her hand.

Rachel willed her mind not to react to this announcement. It was perfectly safe. They were not going out in the middle of the ocean. The sky was clear and she refused to go beyond the moment. "Let me tell Abigail."

Before he could stop her, Rachel rushed to the beach and knelt down in front of her daughter. He saw Abigail look up at the sky and nod. Missy turned toward him and waved. He raised his hand in response. Rachel walked back and smiled. "Thank you, Captain Ben."

"You're quite welcome, Miss Rachel," Ben drawled in his best southern gentleman accent. She laughed and walked beside him toward the pier. Rachel almost glanced back once more at the beach...almost. Enjoy the moment, Rachel...just enjoy the moment. She closed her eyes and silently said, *"Forgive me, Jack, my forever love."*

***

Ben turned the boat into a secluded cove out of sight of the boat traffic and the marina, but not too far, intuitively sensing that Rachel would not venture more than a few miles from her daughter. He wondered at her obsessive behavior about Abigail, but in this day and age of child kidnappings and violence, he couldn't blame her. He was careful about his daughters and had seen too much as a prosecutor to blithely toss the fears aside. But that was in Miami.

This time, though, they were together as a group on a public beach in full sight of security patrols and a lifeguard station. Perhaps Rachel was just an overprotective mother. He wondered what she would do as Abigail grew into her teen-age years, wanting more and more independence. It had been tough when Tara had started dating and then went off to college. He remembered sweating the hours until she came home safely, imagining all kinds of scenarios, each one worse than the one before. Then finally, the click of the front door and the expulsion of pent up stress in one huge breath, until finally, falling into a dream-riddled sleep.

It had taken a while for Ben to allow himself to think in terms of a relationship or even allowing himself to be attracted to anyone again. He looked down at the woman sunning on the deck, her golden cap of hair blowing like a wild, curly halo around her head. Rachel Wells was as different from his tall, dark wife, well...his ex-wife, as the sunflower from the black tulip.

Carolyn was the quintessential career woman who had walked away one day, but unlike Lot's wife she had never looked back. Not that she ignored the girls; they spent two weekends a month with her and vacations. She attended their school events when she wasn't too busy and talked to them during the week. It was just that something was missing, like the empty chair opposite him at the table and the cold, untouched pillow on the other side of the bed.

His feeling of abandonment was fueled by the loss of this woman he had thought would be his companion and his love until one or another of them died, far off in the future. Now, he faced a bleak and lonely life unless someone came along, someone he could trust, if he ever fully trusted anyone again. Perhaps it was time to move on, time to take that leap of faith.

***

From the deck chair, Rachel watched Ben lower the anchor. His body was tanned, and firm above the swim trunks and his muscular legs…control yourself she commanded, but her hungry libido forced her gaze once more to his swim trunks. She closed her eyes and suddenly there he was beside her, shedding his trunks. His arms circled her and he kissed her, gently opening her lips. She responded in starving desperation, like a lost traveler in a parched desert finding a lush oasis and lapping up the life-giving water. He unhooked her bra and tossed it aside, moving his lips down her body, slowly exploring every inch, until she nearly screamed. She could feel the hardness of him pressing against her thigh and when he finally tore off her bikini bottom Rachel moaned and gave herself over to the moment.

CHAPTER FORTY-TWO

They lay on the deck, lulled by gentle rocking of the boat and the rhythmic lapping of the wavelets against the hull. Ben's fingers moved leisurely over her body and he nuzzled her neck. She rolled toward him. The second time was slower and longer as they savored each other and explored with new awareness. When they were sated, Rachel sighed and opened her eyes to the sight of black clouds hovering just to her left.

She shot up, pushing Ben to the side. "Oh my God! Get us out of here. Now!" Rachel jumped up and threw Ben's swim trunks and tee shirt at him. She pushed him toward the bridge and pulled on her own clothes, hopping around the deck half in and out of her shorts, like a demented stork.

"What? What's the matter with you?" Ben dressed as fast as he could and grabbed her by the shoulders. "Rachel, talk to me...what's wrong?"

Incoherent, Rachel babbled something about a storm and pointed up to the sky. Ben looked up at the threatening clouds. In the distance, lightning flickered and muted sounds of thunder echoed across the water. "Okay, storm's heading our way, but there's plenty of time to get back to the marina."

Rachel shook her head, "No, no...right now...we have to go right now."

Ben inhaled. "We are going right now. You haul up the anchor...the winch is over there and I'll start the engine. We're going to be fine, Rachel." He looked at her for a moment wondering what he had gotten himself into. Obviously this woman had issues.

With the anchor secured, Ben turned the boat toward the marina. The dark clouds hovered overhead now, but the marina was in sight. Rachel sat on the deck in the corner shivering, even though it was hot and humid. Once Ben docked, Rachel jumped up and off the side of the boat onto the dock, and raced in the direction of the waterfront without even stopping to help tie off the boat. He shrugged and shook his head. "Crazy woman afraid of a little thunder," he mumbled, stepping off the deck and looping the rope around the stanchion.

When Ben finished tying down the boat and fastening everything for the storm, the thunder was louder, closer and fat rain drops pelted the dock. Lightning flashed out in the bay telling him to get off the dock and under cover. This was the lightning capital of the world and too many people had been struck by lightning, even standing by windows in their own homes. Not wanting to add to the statistics, Ben ran toward the nearest building and pushed his way through the doors. It happened to be a pizza parlor and he saw his daughters sitting at a table with Danny playing cards.

He breathed a sigh of relief and joined them. "Hey Dad, want to join the poker game?" Missy asked.

"Penny ante," Mandy added.

"Sure." Ben emptied his pockets and separated all the pennies in a pile, putting the rest back in his pocket. "Is anyone here hungry besides me?"

"Sure," Danny said.

"You're always hungry," Mandy said, laughing.

Danny opened his mouth, but Missy interjected, "We all know about "the growing boy" syndrome."

Ben smiled and waved at the server. After he had ordered a large pie and two calzones, and she had walked away, he said, "I don't see Rachel or Abigail."

The twins looked at each other and then at Danny. "Well...," Missy said, as though reluctant to talk.

Ben's patience was dying quickly. "Well what?"

The girls looked down at their cards. Danny counted his pennies.

Ben's voice grew louder. "Will one of you please tell me what is going on?" Head turned at the other tables. Ben lowered his voice, "Speak, now!"

They all spoke at once…

"Abby had a meltdown…"

"She got hysterical…"

"Something about boats and storms and…"

"She kept screaming 'may day, may day'…"

"Then Rachel got there and grabbed her…"

"They ran up the street to the hotel…"

Ben swallowed. "Let me get this straight. Abigail had a meltdown over the storm and started screaming 'may day'. Rachel found her and took her to the hotel. Is that the story?"

Danny nodded. "Yes, sir…it was so weird. One minute she was lying on the sand laughing at my dumb joke and then she pointed at the sky and started screaming."

"Yeah, Dad, we didn't know what to do," Missy said.

"Then Rachel came flying onto the sand and held her. She kept saying it was okay, she was safe and not on a boat," Mandy added.

"Right! Then she practically carried her off the beach and to the hotel."

"It was like, really weird, Dad."

Ben was silent. They both had issues with boats and storms, so maybe Rachel's behavior wasn't so hard to explain. She might have known how Abigail would react knowing Rachel was out on a boat and a storm was coming and that's why she was in such a rush to get to her. It made sense; a mother would do something like that. Wouldn't she?

Ben thought about his ex-wife, the uninvolved dermatologist, whose career was more important than her daughters, the woman whose passion for wielding a scalpel far outweighed her passion for sex. He used to visualize her having an orgasm with the first cut into a malignant skin lesion.

That was unfair, she was a dedicated doctor who gave free clinic hours helping kids with hideous birthmarks live a normal life, but in truth, the dedication didn't extend to family. Perhaps that's why he was now the custodial parent of twins and the parent of choice for Tara.

Not every woman was Dr. Carolyn Davis-Ross...excuse me, Dr. Carolyn Davis, minus the Ross, now. He didn't really know Rachel or her story. An hour or so of good sex...well, great sex...something he hadn't had in a long time, didn't make a relationship, but it had been a start and he had hoped....

Thunder rolled overhead and lightning touched down on the water out in the Gulf. Further thoughts in that direction fled as the server delivered the pizza and they all dug in.

The next morning, Ben woke early to a world of clean, fresh sea air, a world washed clean by yesterday's storm. He dressed and jogged down to the marina to check the boat. *Four Gals* bobbed gently in the calm water, none the worse for wear after the storm. He started down the walkway toward the slip where Rachel's boat, *Gaia* had been docked. It was empty.

Ben stopped short and caught his breath. That was it? She disappeared like they had never met or connected. No note, no message and he had no clue where to begin looking for her. Maybe this was his fate; women leaving him.

"Stop the pity party, Bennett Ross, shit happens all the time. You're not being singled out," he mumbled. "At least the sex was great. Consider it a one-night stand and suck it up." He turned and walked slowly back to the hotel, head down.

"What do you mean, they're gone?" Missy shouted.

"People don't just leave without saying good-bye." Mandy stomped around the room.

Danny just sat on the edge of the bed, staring at nothing.

"Girls, their boat is gone. They must have left as soon as the sun came up. I'm sorry you're upset, but there's nothing we can do about it," Ben said.

"We have to find them," Mandy announced, turning at the far end of the room to pace in the other direction.

"How would you suggest I do that?" Ben asked.

"I don't know, Dad. You have all those connections, you used to find criminals, right?"

"Yes, Missy, but Rachel and Abigail aren't criminals. Rachel probably never even got a speeding ticket. They won't be in the system." Ben swung around. "Mandy, stop marching around the room, you're making me dizzy."

She sat down on a chair. "Sorry, I'm just so mad. It was rude to disappear like that."

Ben turned to Danny. "Son, are you okay?"

Danny shrugged. "I guess I just can't believe they're gone like that. It's like weird, you know?"

Ben knew just what Danny meant. It was very weird. He intended to do a search when they got back, but he wasn't about to tell the kids. They would just pester him non-stop until they got an answer.

Danny said, "Maybe they'll answer the radio."

"Great idea, Danny. Come on Dad, let's go to the boat and try to call them." Missy grabbed her father's arm.

"Okay, but first we pack and take everything down to the boat, so we can leave after breakfast."

"But, Dad that's going to take too long," Mandy said.

"Then stop whining and get packing," Ben told her.

Had his mood been lighter, Ben would have laughed at the speed with which the kids packed up and lined up in the hall while he checked the rooms for forgotten items. Carrying his duffel, he found them by the elevator, Missy's finger on the button. "Good job, everyone. Let's check out and…."

The elevator door opened and they rushed in before he could finish the sentence. Ten minutes later they were on the boat crowded around the radio. "Does anybody know the call numbers?"

Silence.

Then: "I never even looked;" "F something and numbers, I think;" And one shaken head.

Ben shrugged. "Sorry, kids. No numbers, no call." He felt as dejected as Danny looked, but wasn't about to let them see that.

"Okay, we'll just have to wait until we get home and then use the short-wave radio," Danny said, brightening.

"You're so smart, Danny Winters," Mandy said.

Danny blushed and looked out toward the horizon.

Ben wondered if they would even answer the radio call. There was something very strange about Rachel's behavior and sudden disappearance. He wasn't sure about anything any more. Perhaps a thorough search would shed some light on the mystery of Rachel and Abigail Wells. Otherwise....

CHAPTER FORTY-THREE

Rachel, hands on the wheel, surreptitiously glanced at Abigail every few minutes, but the girl sat rigid on the deck staring out at the water rushing by, back straight as if a brace had been clamped on her spine. She hadn't spoken at all and rejected the suggestion of breakfast, downing a glass of orange juice in one long swallow. Rachel had tried to talk to her while they were dressing, but Abigail pressed her lips together and refused to meet Rachel's eyes.

Intuitively, Rachel understood that Abigail was drowning in a deep well of shame over her breakdown on the beach in front of the other kids, especially Danny. She also knew that unless Abigail faced it now, she would forever be haunted by what happened and the feelings would resurface again and again.

"Abby, please look at me," Rachel pleaded.

Abigail turned her back and Rachel sighed. "This may seem like the end of the world to you, sweetheart, but it really isn't that bad. If they're really your friends, they'll understand, especially if you explain to them that storms, especially storms on the water freak you out."

Abigail spun around, her face a mask of fury. "I'll never ever see them or talk to them again. I hate them all," she screamed.

"Why? Did they say something mean?"

Abigail turned her back. "I don't want to talk about it any more and don't ask me again."

Whew! Rachel blew out her breath. Oh boy, welcome to the teen years.

The pragmatist laughed. *"What did you expect, the perfect child until she turned 18?"*

"Do you always have to be so negative?" the idealist complained.

"The truth is the truth is the truth," the pragmatist stated imperiously.

The idealist sneered. *"So now you're a learned philosopher."*

Rachel shut them off and sighed. Perhaps it was too good to be true. Abigail had been the perfect child, well almost perfect, perhaps a bit headstrong…but in a lovable way. Now…the outside world had intruded and the snake of reality had reared its ugly head, exposing lethal fangs. She turned back to steering the boat to their secluded island sanctuary, but was it really a safe harbor, or a beautiful prison of her own creation. Did she have the right to lock this glorious child away?

The pragmatist surfaced. *"Feeling guilty are you?"*

"She has a right to be happy," the idealist answered.

"At whose expense?" the pragmatist countered.

Silence….

***

Angry and embarrassed, Abigail sat rigidly on the deck and stared at the wake of the boat, her thoughts churning like the water under the propellers, unanswered questions, and unexplained emotions roiling in her brain.

A shroud of shame covered her, cutting off her breath. How could she be so dumb, like some little kid freaking out at a stupid storm? She'd lived through a hundred storms like that one and hadn't freaked, but she knew why this one was different. Rachel wasn't there next to her…she was out in a boat on the water; a boat that could splinter on the rocks and take her mother away. She knew Ben's boat was fiberglass and not wood and that it couldn't fall apart like…like a boat she remembered lurking in the dark recesses of her memory. She didn't understand her memory of this boat caught in a storm and a hodge-podge of words…*Ann, I need you, mayday, mayday, mayday, whiskey….*

She had asked her mom but never got a satisfactory answer. "It's a dream you're having, Abby, just a dream and dreams aren't real."

Abigail knew it wasn't just a dream because now she knew dreams were experiences or wishes, and why would she ever want to be caught on a boat in a storm that would fall apart. And who was Ann and the man saying mayday, mayday? Abigail was convinced they were memories, not dreams.

A mass of unanswered questions built up over the years haunted Abigail. The father named Paul, who never came back from the sea, a mystery woman named Ann, and the biggest puzzle, Emma, her mom's first child, the one who died...how, when and where? All unanswered questions that Rachel managed to explain but with answers Abigail believed were lies, or at least not the whole truth. She had thought about doing a computer search on the mainland, but there had never been an opportunity when Rachel wasn't around and she just didn't feel right sneaking behind her back.

Now it didn't matter because she was never going back there. Forget about moving to the mainland and down to Miami, she could never face the twins or Danny again. The shroud of shame pulled tighter and tighter around her body and tears squeezed out of her scrunched-closed eyes. We'll just keep on living our lives on the island where it's safe and any trips to the mainland would be purely business and shopping, no more meeting other kids for ice cream and swimming.

She thought of Sandy, lying these long, long months under the ground and wished she could lie down beside him and cuddle against his soft fur body and sleep forever. He was her friend, her companion, her protector and she missed him so much. She would have told him how she was feeling and he would have understood and accepted without question, not like her mom who had to solve the problem and make it better, like kissing an owie when you were a kid and didn't know any better. Now there was just loneliness and longing for something that she couldn't explain and believed she would never, ever have.

FRAN ORENSTEIN

CHAPTER FORTY-FOUR

Caught up in a difficult court case for the next several weeks, Ben had only time for fleeting thoughts of Rachel and Abigail. Finally, he could sit down at the computer and do a search. He entered Rachel Wells, Florida and found reference to a boating accident 17 years ago, which mentioned the deaths of Jack Wells, 26 and Emma Wells, 3. Rachel Wells, 23 was the sole survivor.

The next hit showed a picture of the family on the boat; Rachel, young and vibrant, sunlit hair blowing in the wind holding a laughing toddler with blonde curls. A handsome young man grinned, his arm around Rachel's shoulder; Jack and Emma.

Ben pushed his chair back. It made no sense. How did she come to have a fifteen-year-old daughter? If Abigail was her child she would have been born at least three to four years later and who was the father?

"Stop!" he said to the empty room. "It's none of your business. Maybe she remarried or decided to have a baby some other way, like adoption or artificial insemination."

Ben put his hands in his lap and stared at the computer screen. He couldn't let it go. Curiosity aced his self-control. He scrolled the cursor to the Google box and placed his fingers on the keypad.

Ben still hesitated. *Not your business.* His fingers had a mind of their own and he entered Abigail Wells, Florida. No hits, well nothing that made sense. Besides, if there had been a surviving child, the articles would have mentioned it.

The memory of Abigail's fear of storms and Rachel's panicked reaction to being on a boat during a storm gave him an idea. Driven by an unseen force, Ben keyed in a search of boating incidents in Florida approximately six years following the Wells' accident.

He wondered why this compulsion to know the truth had possessed him like some unholy spirit. Rachel was beautiful and kind and loved her child. Perhaps that was the draw...her mothering of Abigail. This wasn't a woman who took parenting lightly. Rachel would never walk away from her child for a career. The bitterness bit deeply into his soul. He had enjoyed her company and the sex had been...well...let's face it, great. It was the trust factor. He needed to trust Rachel and believe that he had not made another mistake.

That was still no excuse to pry into someone's life like a voyeur. This wasn't a criminal or a witness he was researching, it was a woman he admired and wanted to see again. The need to know the truth drove him on, though. The screen flashed a number of hits and he scrolled down until he saw a name that caught his breath. *The Sweet Abigail* out of Miami, lost at sea during a sudden storm.... He opened the site and read the entry with rising trepidation.

"Ann and Paul Stern, 26 and 27 respectively, and their three-year-old daughter, Abigail are missing and presumed dead off the coast of Florida in the Gulf of Mexico south of Tampa Bay. On July 3rd, the Sterns sailed up the intercoastal waterway and out into the Gulf on a two week vacation. Mr. Stern's parents last heard from them shortly before they disappeared and were told that they were having a wonderful time.

After a week, the search has been called off after no signs of wreckage or bodies were sighted. Paul Stern, a partner in his family's real estate development company and his wife, Ann, a stay-at-home mom are residents of Miami. A spokesman for the family said they have not given up hope that they will all be found alive and well."

A family snapshot appeared on the screen and Ben sat back, stunned. Could it be the same Abigail? The age was right and the coloring matched. Ann Stern even resembled Rachel. What the hell was going on? He printed the article and picture and then backed up to the article about the Wells family and printed that out. Placing the pictures side-by-side, he exhaled. The likeness between the families was astonishing. Rachel Wells and Ann Stern could be sisters and the babies might have been twins, like his girls, alike but not quite.

His legal mind kicked in and scenarios coursed through his brain. It made no sense. Why would Rachel lie about Abigail being her daughter? He couldn't believe he might have been duped again by a beautiful woman. *"Leave yourself out of the equation,"* he thought. *"Stick to the facts."*

What facts? He didn't have enough information. Should he go forward with an investigation? Ben knew he was too close to the situation. He could give it to an assistant district attorney. He still had friends in the department or perhaps hire an investigator, but something blocked his thinking. The decision was benched by a knock on his study door. "Come in."

Mandy and Missy danced into the room. They never just walked serenely or gracefully, they bounded like gazelles. Ben shut the laptop.

"Hey, Dad, can we go over to Danny's house. He's going to try to contact Abigail," Mandy asked rubbing her father's head.

Ben brushed her hand away. "Don't mess with the few hairs I have left."

The girls laughed. "Soon we'll have to call you Baldy instead of Daddy,"

Missy said.

Ben growled, jumped out of the chair and lunged. The girls darted out of his reach. "You ever call me that I'll talk to the hairdresser and make sure he gives you a buzz cut the next time you go there."

"What do you think, Missy? It might be interesting with long hoop earrings."

"Very funny, girls," Ben shouted after them, grinning. He stared at the door, his heart filling with love until he thought it would burst. *Ben Ross, you have to be the luckiest man in the world with three gorgeous and wonderful daughters, but....* Ben pushed the memory of his wife to the background and sat back down at his desk.

He tried to concentrate on the information before him and the fateful decision he was reluctant to make, but visions of Rachel, her lithe, naked body arching under his caresses intruded. His head filled with her laughter and the clever quips that seemed to dart from her lips. Oh, those lips….

"Stop!" he said aloud. He might have fallen in love with this woman had a sudden Florida thunderstorm not blasted him into a reality filled with unanswered questions and devastating scenarios.

Ben made a decision; he needed more information and an explanation that could only come from Rachel Wells herself, but where was she hiding? If she was guilty of kidnapping, then she wasn't going to go back to the mainland at the same location where they had met. If they truly lived on an isolated island by themselves, then he would never find her.

How did she survive? She had to have money for gas and necessities. Was it buried under some rock in the garden or inside her mattress, or did she have an account somewhere in a bank with a branch at the marina? No, too traceable. Perhaps someone sent her money on a regular basis. It would have to be impersonal, like a post office box. Would she have rented it under her own name or an alias?

"Give it a break," he muttered. "She's not a master criminal."

Or was she? A resourceful, clever woman, Rachel had survived alone on an island, raising a young child and making periodic forays to the mainland for money and supplies. What did he really know about Rachel Wells, other than she was a good mother, needy for male companionship, beautiful, and sexy as all hell.

"Don't go there," he said to calm his rising libido. He switched gears and became the hardened attorney. "I need more information." He turned off the computer and went out of the house, locking the door behind him.

CHAPTER FORTY-FIVE

Ben strode down the street to Danny's house and knocked on the door. A battle raged in him fueled by desire and conscience. The father, the lover, the man, and the lawyer fought an internal war that predicted no clear winner; its conclusion might end in tragedy. For a moment, he considered turning away, but Danny opened the door, grinning when he saw Ben.

"Did you make contact with Abby?" Ben asked.

"We've been trying, but I don't think their radio is turned on," he answered.

"Danny, hurry, somebody's on the radio," Missy yelled from somewhere in the back of the house.

Ben followed Danny down the hall and into a small study that looked out onto the backyard garden. Mandy waved the microphone at Danny and he slid into the chair. They all gathered around.

"Abby, is that you? Abby…," Danny said into the mike, his voice rising.

The radio remained on, but silence filled the room against a background of static.

"Abby, come in, please. It's Danny."

A tiny, tinny voice floated across the airwaves. "Danny."

Mandy opened her mouth to say something, but Ben shook his head and put his finger on his lips.

"Hey, Abby, you okay?" Danny asked

The room was silent for a minute, then, "I'm sorry, Danny."

"It's okay, Abby, nobody's mad at you," Danny said.

"I'm mad at me. I acted like a little kid afraid of the dark or something."

"So what, everybody does that. My mother shrieks at spiders and locks herself in the bathroom until we get rid of it."

A faint giggle came through the speaker. "Really?"

"Uh, huh, I swear on my sister's life," Danny said.

"You don't have a sister," Abigail said.

"Well, if I had one, I would swear on her life."

Abigail giggled again. "Are the twins there?"

Mandy looked at her father, who nodded. "We're here, Abby."

"Dad's here, too," Missy added.

"Hi M's, Mr. Ross. I hope you're not mad at me for going off like that. I feel like such a jerk," Abigail said. "And, please don't blame, Mom, she did…well, she did what she had to do."

Ben smiled. "Please call me Ben, Mr. Ross is my father. One day I'll tell you some of the dumb stuff I did as a kid."

Missy grinned at her sister. "You did stupid stuff?"

"I thought you were the perfect child, Dad," Mandy said.

"Never mind, I shouldn't have said anything. Now they'll make me crazy until I tell them some of my childhood escapades."

"You could just tell me, Mr. Ross, I won't tell them."

"Hmm, Abby, that is a possibility."

"Da-ad," the girls said making it a two syllable word.

Ben asked, "Abby is your mom there?"

"She's in the herb garden. I don't think she wants to talk, now."

"Well, please tell her this; I understand that parents do what they need to do, she'll understand."

The twins looked at each other in silence. *Some parents*, Mandy mouthed.

Missy glanced down at her shoes. Ben sensed a shift of balance in the air and said, "Listen, Abby. The kids want to visit you. Can you give me the coordinates of your island?" The girls' faces brightened.

Ben could practically hear Abby thinking through the radio. "I don't know; we've never had visitors. I'd have to ask my mom."

Ben put on his most persuasive voice, the one he used to beguile juries. "We could surprise her, I know she'd like that, she told me so when we were out on the boat."

"She did?" Abigail asked.

Ben crossed his fingers behind his back and hoped his kids never found out about this blatant lie. "Absolutely, but the storm came up before she could give me the information."

Abigail paused and then gave them the coordinates.

"Thank you, Abby. Now don't tell her because we want to surprise you both."

"You mean you'll just show up?" Abigail asked nervously.

"You never know. One day our boat will land at your island and we'll come calling at your door."

Abigail giggled again. "You are so funny, Mr...uh Ben, but I don't know how my mom will feel about that."

Ben took a deep breath. "She'll be just fine with it, Abby, don't you worry your pretty little head. Everyone loves surprises. Now I'm going home and leave you with your friends."

Ben let himself out and leaned against the trunk of a tall palm. He exhaled and felt a bit sick at fooling a child into giving him the information. *"As an officer of the court, I need to find out the truth,"* he rationalized. *"And as a man."*

It briefly crossed his mind that some things were best left 'interred with their bones', as, Shakespeare once said. Perhaps this time he should bury the pragmatic attorney and go with his gut...and his heart. *"We'll see,"* he thought.

FRAN ORENSTEIN

CHAPTER FORTY-SIX

In the weeks that followed, Abigail spoke to Danny and the twins several times a week, this time it was on the satellite phone.

"We may be sailing into your cove, one day soon," Missy said.

"School's letting out for the summer and Dad says it's time for a vacation," Mandy added.

Danny voice interrupted them. "I'm invited, too."

"Well of course you are, silly. You're part of the family," Missy told him.

Mandy whispered loudly into the speaker phone, "Besides, if we don't take him to see you, he'll just waste away pining for you."

Abigail heard Missy giggling in the background as Danny growled, "I'll get you for that, Mandy, don't think I won't."

"Come on, big guy, let's see you try." Mandy taunted.

"Hey, you two, save it for when you get here, then I can be part of the fun," Abigail shouted.

"I can wait, revenge will be sweeter when she doesn't expect it," Danny announced.

Abigail could hear the smirk in his voice. Missy laughed, "I want to see this, too. We're going to have a great time, Abby."

Abigail turned off the phone and stared at it, smiling. In all these weeks, no one had been angry or laughed at her. They had accepted her initial explanation and apology without making her feel embarrassed. Best of all, they still wanted to be her friends and

Danny wanted to see her again. What better plan than a visit? She hoped her mom would appreciate the surprise.

Abigail grew excited at the prospect until a light lavender-scented wisp of air touched her ear and a sudden feeling that she had made a grave mistake smothered her happy mood. Something was very wrong in her safe, tidy universe and that a very bad something was coming to destroy it. Should she tell her mother, would she even believe her?

It's nothing, she decided, just the jitters. There was no way Abigail was going to spoil Ben's surprise. She had never kept a secret from Rachel before, but then the outside world had never intruded either.

The flicker of air touched her ear. "What have I done?" she said, wishing that Sandy were here. She had told things to Sandy that she never told Rachel, hopes and dreams of the future that might upset their carefully planned life. Sandy had calmed her and made her feel that everything would work out.

Abigail stood up and left the house. Glancing toward the garden, she saw her mother kneeling with her back turned, weeding. Abigail broke into a run until she reached the pet cemetery and sat down by Sandy's grave. She placed her hand on the mound that covered the beloved dog and cat. "I don't know what to do, Sandy. I feel like something bad is coming our way, like somehow I made a mistake today, but I don't know what I did. I don't know how to fix something I don't understand. It's just…this awful feeling."

The air around her was empty and Abigail didn't sense the presence of her companion. "Are you gone, Sandy. Have you and Charm moved on? Are you running together, playing without me? I'm so lonely, Sandy."

Abigail lay down on the grave and sobbed until there were no more tears to shed and fell asleep. The dream engulfed her.

She was alone on the Gaia. Thundering black clouds rolled in overhead and lightning forked down on the water. The boat rolled in the raging sea and Abigail clung to the helm trying to keep the boat on a straight heading toward land, a tiny speck in the distance. Off to the south she saw a tiny boat bobbing violently in the turbulent water. A figure lay in the boat and she knew it was Rachel. Abigail struggled with the helm to turn the ship toward the boat, but it kept bouncing up and down on the waves, moving further and further away and she knew she would never reach it in time. "Mama," she screamed. "Don't leave me, Mama."

Abigail sat up and sprang to her feet. For a moment she didn't know where she was. Then she remembered the dream. What did it mean? Was she going to lose her mother? Whatever happened, it would be her fault. She would never make it in time. She would never be able to save her mother.

Abigail doubled over from a sudden cramp in her belly and threw up.

"Abby, honey, are you all right?" Rachel leaned down and felt Abigail's forehead.

"I'm fine, Mom. Probably shouldn't have run so soon after lunch." Wiping her mouth on her shirt, she threw dirt over the vomit to hide it.

"Are you sure? Maybe, I should make some chamomile tea to settle your stomach." Rachel stood and took her daughter's hand. "We'll have an old-fashioned tea party."

"I'm too old for that, Mom."

"You are never too old to have tea and cakes, the British do it all the time."

Abigail knew when she was beaten and let Rachel lead her back to the house. The atmosphere imperceptibly shifted, and a tiny bubble of lavender-scented air bounced along unnoticed behind them.

FRAN ORENSTEIN

CHAPTER FORTY-SEVEN

Abigail sat at the table eyeing the small crumb cakes on the plate. The kettle whistled and Rachel poured boiling water over the tea leaves in the mugs. The scent of chamomile drifted in the steam wafting over the table. Abigail inhaled and her body relaxed. Rachel set the teapot back on the stove and sat down across the table. "I bet you feel better, already."

Abigail pressed her lips together, the hint of a smile lifting the corners of her mouth.

"You're allowed to smile, Abby. There is no commandment that states 'Thou shalt not smile at your parents between the ages of 13 and 19.'"

Abigail giggled. "Mom, you are bizarre sometimes. You come up with the craziest things. Maybe you should have been a writer."

"Perhaps one day when I'm old and all alone, rocking on my front porch contemplating the rest of my life, I'll consider it."

"You'll never be alone, Mom. I'll always be there for you."

Suddenly, Rachel's throat constricted around a lump in her throat and tears swelled behind her lids.

"Come on, Mom. You're not going to go all mushy on me, are you?"

Rachel took a sip of tea and swallowed the lump. "Me? I'm stoic and devoid of all emotion."

"Uh huh, like a limp dishcloth, a wet, limp dishcloth, a mushy, wet, limp dishcloth," Abigail said.

"Okay, that's enough, I get it. You think I'm emotional goo."

Abigail nodded. "Exactly."

"Eat your cake!"

They sat in companionable silence, chewing and sipping, while the imperceptible rift in the air lingered at the edge of their vision.

"She's here, isn't she?" Rachel finally asked.

Abigail nodded. "Emma loves tea parties."

Rachel sighed.

"Who is she, Mom? She can't be you, because she's dead and you're alive."

Rachel sighed more heavily. Had the moment finally come? Nearly 12 wonderful years with Abigail and in the next few moments it could all crumble like the edge of an ancient cliff and tumble down the mountain in an avalanche of pain and remorse.

Abigail saw the uncertainty and pain in Rachel's eyes and regretted ever bringing up the subject. Never would she ever want to hurt her mother. Despite her fits of anger and nastiness, Abigail loved Rachel totally, but her stubborn streak won out and she clamped her lips together. This time she was going to find out the truth, whatever the cost.

Rachel watched the myriad of emotions pass across Abigail's face, like old silent movies that flickered on the screen in disjointed movements. In the end, the girl clenched her teeth and Rachel knew that the moment she had dreaded all these years had finally caught up. Her chest constricted. Perhaps her heart would give out right now and she could pass on without ever destroying their love.

A puff of breath in her ear and a faint whisper, and Rachel knew that her time had not come. Death would not save her, not yet. Lie after lie flew through her brain like a flock of birds leaving on their northern pilgrimage, but none resonated true enough, not this time. Time had loosened the web of deceit she had so carefully constructed. It floated on the breeze drifting further and further away from its anchor. Perhaps she had finally reached apex of the confrontation that had warred in her mind all these years.

Rachel opened her mouth, but no sound emerged. Instead tears fell over her eyelids like first crack in a dam breach, until the floodgates opened and coursed down her cheeks. She pushed the words out of her throat in a hoarse whisper. "Emma is, was my baby."

Once released, the story poured out. "She would have been a woman by now had she survived, but Gaia pulled her out of my arms and took her away on that horrible black sea, her tiny body in an orange life vest crashing against the rocks...." Rachel screamed, "**AND I COULDN'T SAVE HER**." softly now..."I couldn't save her, I couldn't save her."

Abigail jumped up and threw her arms around Rachel, "Oh, Mom, I'm so sorry. Please don't cry any more. Please." Abigail held her until Rachel's sobs subsided and she had calmed down. "Just sit, I'll make another cup of tea. It'll make you feel better, Mom."

Despite her pain, Rachel couldn't help but smile at her own words echoing from Abigail's lips. Chamomile tea, the cure for everything. She sniffed and said, "Thank you, Abby, that will be good."

The girl fussed at the stove until putting fresh tea leaves in the caddy and waited impatiently for the kettle to whistle, casting furtive glances at her mother. But Rachel seemed in control, now and sat staring at the far wall, hands clasped on the table. Finally, after what seemed an interminable time, the whistle squeaked once and Abigail snatched it from the burner pouring the steaming water into the mug. She put it carefully down in front of Rachel and then moved her chair so she was next to her.

Putting her arm around her mother, she said, "Come on, Mom. It's okay, well it's not okay, but then you had me and I'm not going anywhere. Drink your tea and you'll feel better."

Rachel shuddered, but picked up the mug obediently and inhaled the fragrant steam. The child thought she knew everything, but the entire the story could still remain Rachel's secret, locked away in a small leather pouch hidden under the floor in the chicken coop and buried in a sandy grave two miles west.

"Thank you, Abby, I feel better already."

Abigail believed this was only part of the story and she knew it was stupid to ask any more questions right now, but she had this incessantly growing need to finally know everything. It had been gnawing at her for a long time, fueled by the images of people and places she vaguely remembered that appeared in foggy glimpses with no foundation. Images of people like a woman named Ann and a man named Paul and someone singing to her about a bird. Scary memories floated in and out of a storm and a boat and the sound of woodpeckers on the roof and cracking wood. Words stuck in her mind...mayday, tango, whisky, Miami.

She glimpsed images of dolphins, cars, pastel-colored houses and tall buildings with bright lights that lurked in the corners of her memory. Now she knew the words were boat talk...call letters and the boat's locale and mayday meant danger. Had she been on that boat, too, when Emma had died? How was it possible, when she wasn't even born, yet? And—who were Ann and Paul? These were the questions that forced themselves out of her mouth and she knew it was a mistake as soon as the first words escaped.

"Mom, was my father named Paul?" Abigail twisted her hands on her lap and couldn't meet Rachel's eyes. She wanted to take back the question, but it was too late.

Time stopped and Rachel forgot to breathe. Finally, she nodded, the lie hiding inside truth, like the pit in an olive, invisible until an unsuspecting tooth bit into it, cracking from the impact.

"Was he Emma's father, too?"

Rachel closed her eyes, 'to lie or not to lie, that is the question?' A parody on the Bard's words filled in her mind, triggering the usual warring dialogue.

"The truth always surfaces," the idealist intoned.

"Nonsense, she has to protect herself," countered the pragmatist.

"She can't hide it from the child, forever," said the idealist.

"I disagree...."

Rachel shut them off with her internal switch. The truth, then, or at least partial truth, she decided. "No, Emma's father was named Jack, he died with her."

Abigail was relentless. "So, then you met my father, Paul and had me?"

Rachel bit her lip. The answer was tricky. Yes, would be an outright lie, but no, would trigger more questions. Rachel thought quickly and an answer popped out of her mouth. "I got you, Abby"

Seemingly satisfied with that ambiguous answer, Abigail sat back her mind churning. Rachel exhaled, but watched Abigail closely, waiting for the next question. She felt like a felon under interrogation for a crime she had committed out of need and love, like Jean Valjean in *Les Miserables*. He had paid dearly for the theft of a loaf of bread. Would she, too, pay for her crime, a crime far worse than stealing a loaf of bread? Would someone hound her through eternity and destroy everything she had? Not that she needed a hunter. Rachel hounded herself with guilt and fear.

"Mom, who was Ann? Why do I keep remembering her on a boat?" Abigail looked expectantly at her mother, her eyes trusting and filled with love.

Rachel stood up and began to clear the table. A delaying tactic while she frantically tried to think of an answer that would suffice, but not split them apart. That's what parent's did, right? They told half-truths to keep the peace and spare the child. Children don't need to know everything until they are old enough to handle the truth. Stupid platitude! This wasn't a five-year-old asking how the cat got the kittens in her belly.

A surge of guilt pressured her to tell Abigail everything, but the realization of the consequences stunned her. Their world would shift and the life she had constructed could tumble into the rift of a catastrophic earthquake.

"Mo-om?" Abigail extended the word into multi-syllables.

"Hold on that thought, Abby. I need the bathroom. Be right back." Rachel rushed out of the kitchen and into the bathroom, shutting the door behind her. She sat on the toilet seat lid and put her hands over her face. "What am I going to do?" she moaned.

Rocking back and forth, Rachel prayed for an answer. "Just a few more years, until she turns 18, that's all I ever wanted. Please, help me."

Abby knocked softly on the bathroom door. "Mom, are you okay?"

Rachel stood up and opened the door. "I'm sorry, honey. I must have a slight touch of whatever you have."

"I'm sorry, Mom, I shouldn't have pestered you with questions. Why don't you go lie down and rest."

Rachel nodded and crept off to her bed, wishing she could break into a wild dance and twirl around the house. Thank you, Gaia, she wanted to shriek; another delay of the inevitable.

"Just a coward's way out," the pragmatist muttered.

"You just don't know when to shut up, do you," the idealist scolded.

Silence!

CHAPTER FORTY-EIGHT

Several weeks later, as was her habit, Rachel sat cross-legged on the floor of her bedroom, meditating. Abigail knew never to disturb her during this daily routine unless it was an emergency. Two blasts of a boat's horn startled Rachel out of her trance. "What the hell!" She jumped out and ran out of the house onto the porch. Abigail was racing down the path to the beach. "Abby, come back."

Abigail stopped and turned. "They're here, Mom. Go make yourself beautiful."

"Who's here? Abby?" Rachel called.

"Ben and the kids…it's a surprise. Go on, Mom comb your hair and put on some make-up or something."

"You knew, you little brat. I'll get you for this."

Abigail laughed and turned away.

"Wait, stall them…I stink."

Abigail half-turned. "Don't worry; I'll give them a tour."

The last words faded as Abigail turned and continued down the path toward the inlet. Rachel stared after her, horrified. What surprise? What visit? "Oh my God, I'm such a mess, the house is a disaster. I'll kill her for this." Rachel ran back into the house and looked around the kitchen. It was immaculate. Abigail must have cleaned it while she was meditating. Rachel checked the living room and threw a fallen pillow back on the sofa.

In the bathroom, she stripped and showered, shoving the offending clothes in the hamper. As the soil and sweat from gardening swirled down the drain, she shampooed her hair, drawing up a mental list of the worst punishments she could think of a payback for the 'surprise'. She pulled on clean clothes and combed the tangles out of her hair. Adding some gloss to her lips, Rachel checked herself in the mirror and shrugged.

They were already tramping up the steps onto the porch. She raced into her bedroom and threw the blanket over the bed in a semblance of bed-making and shoved her sleep shirt under the bed with her foot. She stared for a moment at the bed and remembered Ben's beautiful naked body and his kisses…. What would it be like to have him in her bed? Stop! Remember who he is, Rachel, keep your wits about you. This could all come flaming down around you and all of Abigail's questions would be answered. But still, those gentle hands caressing her body….she ached to feel them again.

Then she remembered her prayer for deliverance, just 15 minutes ago. "Thank you," she whispered to the Universe.

She met them on the front porch holding on to the railing with whitened knuckles, so she would not race down the steps into Ben's arms as she ached to do.

"She's out of control," the pragmatist noted.

The idealist snorted. *"What do you know about love, automaton."*

"Hey, who are you calling an automaton?"

"I tell it as I see it," the idealist said.

Rachel turned off the voices spouting nonsense, of course it wasn't love after only two days; it was need. Well, perhaps a little lust thrown in, that's all. Besides, after her behavior and disappearance, she was surprised he even showed up on her doorstep. She extended her hand. "Hello, Ben, girls, Danny. This is certainly a surprise." She glanced at Abigail, who had the grace to look ashamed, behind the smirk.

Ben took her hand and held it. Rachel felt the blood rushing to the roots of her hair, but didn't sever the connection. Their eyes met and Rachel felt herself falling into their depths.

"Uh, Da-ad?" Missy said, smothering a grin behind her hand.

Ben dropped Rachel's hand as if scorched and turned to his daughter. "What!"

Missy stepped back. "Sorry, Dad, I didn't mean to interrupt." Mandy and Abigail giggled and Danny suddenly found something fascinating to explore under his nails.

"Um, right, sorry. I didn't mean to yell at you," Ben said.

"That's okay, Dad. We're going to check out the animals and stuff, we'll see you later." The kids all trooped off, heading behind the house.

Mandy turned back. "We'll be gone for a while, Dad." Her shoulders shook as she followed the others.

Rachel looked at Ben and they both started laughing. "I guess we fooled them," Rachel said between gasps.

"Were we that obvious?" Ben asked.

"God, I hope not. Do you want to come in?"

Ben raised his eyebrows and grinned.

"Behave yourself, Bennett Ross."

"Me? I'm the picture of decorum and yes, I would like to come inside."

Rachel held the door open and gestured inside. "Welcome to Chez Wells." Rachel shut the door and stood still staring at this male invader in her home, her sanctuary.

They looked at each other for several seconds, until Ben took two steps toward Rachel and clasped her to him. He bent down and found her lips, his hands gently snaking under her shirt, caressing her back, then inching around toward the front. Rachel shuddered, suddenly overcome with longing. She pulled him toward the bedroom and closed the door. Pulling the shades down over the windows, Rachel turned and pulled her shirt up over her head. Ben took a deep breath as he moved toward her. He reached out and Rachel gasped, then she unzipped his shorts, pulling them slowly down. Ben ran his hands down over her hips and pushed her shorts off. They stepped out of the discarded clothes and he yanked his shirt off tossing it on the pile. They fell on the bed. Rachel pushed the thought of four kids roaming around somewhere outside and submitted her body to the tantalizing lips and hands of her lover.

FRAN ORENSTEIN

CHAPTER FORTY-NINE

An hour later, Rachel and Ben were dressed and outside on the porch. As if cued by a director, the kids turned the corner of the house and spread out across the steps. They all sat in silence for ten seconds and everyone spoke at once. Then giggling and renewed silence.

Rachel finally interrupted the awkward moment. "What do you think of our little island oasis?"

Danny spoke first. "It's a cool place, but awful quiet; no cars, people, noise."

"I think it's beautiful...," Mandy started to say.

"Like a tropical island...," Missy added.

"It is a tropical island...," Mandy interrupted.

"I mean like a movie set, you know, like Blue Lagoon or something like that," Missy explained.

Danny grinned.

"What are you grinning about," Abigail said.

Danny shrugged. "Nothing!"

"Right!" laughed Mandy.

"He's probably thinking about skinny dipping in the ocean at night with Brooke Shields when the moon is out...," Missy began.

"Okay, okay, that's enough, kids," Ben said.

Rachel hid a grin, thinking that Ben probably had the same idea. An image flashed across her mind of them swimming together, nude, in the cove under the moonlight. She glanced at him and he met her eyes with a dreamy smile on his face as if reading her mind. She shut that thought off quickly and said, "So who's hungry?"

The voices all shouted at once until Ben intervened. "Everyone to the boat and bring the picnic lunch." The four teens turned and ran toward the water.

Rachel looked at Ben. "You didn't have to bring food."

He watched the foursome as they disappeared around the curve of the inlet and then leaned over and kissed Rachel, his lips growing more insistent with each second. She gently pushed him away and glanced at his shorts. "You won't be able to stand up when they get back."

He laughed. "You're right, and it's your fault, Rachel Wells. I can't keep my hands off you. Even when I'm not touching you, I'm touching you. I've thought a lot about you these past few months. I've never felt this way about a woman, well not for a long time."

Rachel looked down at her hands twisting in her lap. "Let's go slow, Ben. It's been a long time, so please don't rush me."

He raised his hands and leaned back against the railing. "I'm cool, as the kids would say. Take however long you need, but know this, I could easily fall in love with you, Rachel. In fact, I'm not sure I haven't already."

"Now that's not slow, Ben Ross. We've only been together about 12 hours, total. I think we need a little more time than that to decide if it's love or lust." As Rachel said the words, she knew she was fooling herself. She felt the same way...this was a man she could love, but there was still the lies dangling over her like a hangman's noose. How could she even consider falling in love with anyone, especially an attorney? Fear and guilt washed over her and she shivered.

Noticing the emotion, Ben moved closer and put his arm around her, pulling her into his embrace. "It's fine, Rachel. Please don't get upset. Everything will work out the way it's supposed to happen. I believe that."

Ben's words niggled at her brain like a feather tickling her ear, but Rachel leaned into him, anyway and felt his strength infuse her body. She knew a wonderful life could exist, because she had seen one possible future with Ben, but she also knew that the alternative was also possible and more than likely probable. Lying to Abigail and Mary Cross and of course herself was one thing, but lying to Ben was a whole other story and Rachel knew she wasn't capable of loving this man, any man in a world of deception. There were too many variables to cover up, especially Abigail's identity. No, she would endure this visit and then when Ben was gone with the kids, she would leave here and find someplace on the mainland, far from south Florida and begin the next phase of their lives. Abigail would go to school and meet new friends and eventually forget Danny and the twins.

Rachel pulled away from Ben and stood up. "Would you like to help me set the table? At Chez Wells, we dine alfresco," Rachel quipped, knowing that she was speaking too fast. She breathed deeply and willed her nerves to calm down.

Ben shrugged and followed her into the house, carrying out the dishes and cutlery to a long table under the trellis. Rachel draped a bright red plaid cloth over the table and together they set out the place settings. This foreshadowing of domesticity frightened Rachel and she rushed back into the house for glasses and napkins.

He was right behind her when she turned to go back outside. He took both her arms and stopped her. "You're like a terrified bird, flying back and forth in its cage, flapping its wings and hitting the bars. I'm not going to force anything, Rachel. Well, maybe later...." He leaned over and whispered in her ear.

"I don't think so, Romeo. There are three very nosy girls and one horny teenage boy and I'm only feeding them food, not fodder for their imaginations."

Ben smiled. "Moonlight shining on the water, you and me in the altogether gliding through the water...."

"Shush, they're coming back." Rachel pushed him away. "Over here," she called.

FRAN ORENSTEIN

CHAPTER FIFTY

Abigail was so excited she could barely sit still long enough to chew and swallow the delicious sandwiches and salad her friends had brought with them. She didn't want to think about the contents of the sandwich because it was so good. Drinking the iced sun tea, Abigail realized that she liked having friends her own age and lively conversation around the table. Rachel was a wonderful mother and her best friend, but it just wasn't the same. She suddenly knew that all along the feeling that dragged her down and reduced her to tears was loneliness. Out of the corner of her eye, she saw the swing moving higher and higher and knew that Emma was here and angry. Abigail hoped no one would notice the swing moving on a wind-free day.

That wish was not to be. "Hey look at that," Danny said, pointing toward the swing. Everyone swiveled and stared.

"How can it be moving like that?" Mandy asked.

"There's no wind," Missy said.

Abigail looked at Rachel in horror. Her eyes implored her mother to say something, explain it away somehow. She could practically hear Rachel's mind working for a logical answer.

"Look," Ben said pointing to the tree. "The swing is attached to that branch and an animal, probably a squirrel must have run across it and started the swing going, then it just picked up on it's own momentum."

Abigail let out the breath she hadn't realized was locked in her lungs. She wanted to leap at Ben and hug him. She caught Rachel's eye and they both nodded imperceptibly.

"Uh huh," Danny said, taking a huge bite of his second sandwich. "This chicken salad is delicious."

Abigail gulped and looked down at the remains of her sandwich. A vision of Charlie the Rooster and his wives and children flashed across her mind. This is not my chicken family; this is not my chicken family. She swallowed back the bile that threatened to rise into her mouth and took a gulp of tea. When her stomach had settled she glanced at the others, but no one had noticed her discomfort, except her mother.

Rachel nodded in understanding and said, "I have a surprise for dessert, everyone."

Abigail brightened and they all looked up, expectantly. "Brownies," Rachel said inclining her head. "Freshly baked this morning by Chef Rachel."

"That's why the house smelled so good," Abigail said. "Um, not that it doesn't always smell good, I meant…never mind." Startled by her own words, Abigail looked at Rachel who laughed and the girl relaxed.

"Did you know we were coming?" Danny asked, wiping his mouth.

"No, but I was overcome by a chocolate sensation when I got up earlier than usual and couldn't fall back to sleep. So, while Abigail slept in, I baked a batch of brownies."

Missy giggled. "I get that, too, a chocolate feeling."

"Missy's addicted to candy bars," Mandy said.

Missy gave her a dirty look. "Oh, and you hate them, I suppose."

Mandy shrugged and both girls laughed.

"Well, don't cry when your clothes stop fitting and you want money to go shopping. Oh, and don't forget your teeth rotting and falling out," Ben said, smiling at Rachel.

"Da-ad," Mandy dragged out the word.

Ben just shrugged. "I'm only suggesting that you think about it."

Abigail giggled and watched the bi-play. For the first time, she wished she had a father to tease her, someone like Ben. Maybe….

She looked at her mother watching Ben banter with his daughters and saw the sad expression in her eyes. She understood that her mother realized Abigail's life was missing something important. Abigail looked at Ben and wondered what it would be like to have him for a father. She had no one to compare him to and she wondered if all fathers were like this or were there some who were mean, rotten fathers. There was so much she didn't know and so much she wanted to know, needed to know. Television wasn't real, this was.

After dessert, the teens cleared the table and cleaned up in the kitchen. "What are you planning for this afternoon?" Rachel asked.

"I thought we could all go on a hike along the beach. Danny collects shells," Abigail answered. "So do you and Ben want to come along?"

Rachel looked at Ben who imperceptibly shook his head. "I think we elderly folk will stay here, maybe rock on the porch or something geriatric like that."

Everyone laughed. "Right," Mandy said. "That's just Dad's thing."

"When he's not running a marathon or swimming…," Missy said.

"Or biking and hiking," Mandy finished.

"We might just go swimming this afternoon," Ben announced, meeting Rachel's eyes with a twinkle.

"Okay, that's settled," Abigail said, wiping her hands on the dishtowel. They all trooped off to change into socks and sneakers.

"I'm going down to the boat to change," Ben said.

"Let me grab a suit and I'll meet you there." Rachel's heart raced as Ben leaned into her and kissed her long and hard. Every inch of her body tingled in anticipation and all rational thoughts fled her mind, including the warning to Abigail to hike east and not west. By the time she remembered, they were gone and she had no idea in which direction. Please Gaia; keep them away from the wreckage. There was nothing she could do now but have faith that all would end well and their world would not burn up in the harsh light of truth.

She grabbed a towel and walked out the door, down the path. Rachel could see Ben standing on the deck of the boat in skimpy red trunks. Surely he didn't wear that when his daughters were around. Then again her bikini wasn't exactly safe around Danny, either. She could see him swelling as she walked along the dock and approached the boat, marveling at the power women had over men. He took her hand and hauled her up on deck, leading her to the cabin below. It was a while before they came up on deck again and jumped into the water.

CHAPTER FIFTY-ONE

Abigail and her friends hiked along the shoreline heading into the afternoon sun. She had never been here before and the delicious sense of rebellion tickled her. Perhaps she would finally find out why her mother was so adamant about her not going in this direction. It was probably some adult thing that kids never thought about. Every now and then, Danny would stop and pick up an interesting shell for examination. It would either go into the bag dangling from his waist, or get thrown back into the sea. The three girls walked behind, every so often running through the surf and kicking water at Danny who would chase them.

Once or twice, Abigail glimpsed a shadow out of the corner of her eye that wasn't human. She knew that Sandy was nearby running in and out of the surf. A lump formed in her throat, but she swallowed it and realized that Sandy was a spirit guide and protector and would always be with her. She wiped her eyes. How could she ever think that he would leave her? Charm was probably sleeping on the porch railing, too. *I'm sorry, dear puppy. Thank you for being with me."* Abigail felt a shift in the breeze and something brushed her leg.

Danny put his arm around her shoulder. "Hey, you okay?"

Abigail nodded. "Just some spray in my eyes." His arm felt good, strong and sturdy. The twins were up ahead when Danny stopped, leaned down and kissed her. She felt the pressure of his mouth and her own lips parted and pressed back. Oh God, this was her first kiss and it was amazing. She wanted more, but Danny pulled away and started walking again, his arm still around her shoulder. For a moment, she felt abandoned, but then his hand rubbed her arm and Abigail realized that he was as shocked as she with the sensations the kiss had caused.

The sisters had stopped and waited for them to catch up. Mandy was grinning. "Don't say anything, or I'll throw you in the surf," Danny growled.

"Me? My lips are sealed." Mandy said prancing away. "Right, Missy? We didn't see a thing."

Missy nodded, smothering a giggle. "Not a thing. Eyes closed the whole time."

Abigail laughed and pulled away from Danny. "See that tree all the way down there. Race you." She broke into a run and the others followed yelling that it was unfair; she'd got a head start.

Abigail reached the tree just ahead of Danny and collapsed on a piece of driftwood, strangely shaped, like the curved side of a boat. When she could breathe normally, Abigail looked around. Old wreckage littered the beach, pieces of wood, some still showing faint streaks of white paint and a tattered, leathery chair.

Nearly out of breath, Danny dropped down beside her with the twins right behind him, huffing and puffing. "Look at this place…it's a shipwreck."

"An old one," Missy said, picking up a piece of rotting wood.

A life preserver ring hung on a sturdy stick that had been pushed into the sand, now tilted at an angle like a tired old man leaning on his cane. Abigail stood up and lifted the ring off the stick, peering at the faded lettering. She could just make out enough letters to guess the first word, Sweet and then Abi-a-l then a space and M---mi. Sweet Abigail? Miami? The boat's name was Sweet Abigail and it had originated in Miami. She shivered as icy fingers touched her back and traveled up her spine into her skull. It was weird that this boat would have her name?

Mandy looked over Abigail's shoulder. "That's so weird; it's like your name."

"Let me see," Missy said, pushing her way in.

Danny joined them. "That is so cool. It probably says Sweet Abigail, Miami. I wonder what happened to the crew."

Abigail stared at the Sweet Abigail...the words lit a tiny flame in her mind...a man's voice singing a song about a little girl named Sweet Abigail. A song he made up, a story song. She remembered the rough feel of his cheeks and his strong hands lifting her high into the air, while she shrieked in delight. "Up, up daddy," a childlike voice echoed from the distant past.

Abigail dropped the ring and knelt down running her hand over the sand in front of the stick.

Danny knelt beside her. "Hey, you okay?"

Abigail couldn't speak; she had a bad feeling about this place. Was this why her mother had forbidden her to ever go in this direction? She thought she heard a faint bark, like an alarm. "Did you hear that?"

"Hear what?" Mandy asked.

"A dog barking."

Mandy looked at her sister and then at Danny. "Nope, I didn't hear anything. Did you guys hear a dog barking?"

"Not me," Missy answered.

Danny shook his head and grabbed Abigail's arms. "Abby, why don't we go back to the house?"

Abigail pulled away. "No I want to see what's here." She felt the slight hump of the sand that ran in a ridge from the stick to about six feet away from it. She shivered and sat back.

"I think this is a grave. Someone buried something or someone here." Abigail looked around and spotted a rusty metal plate, probably from the galley. She picked it up and returned to the mound. For a moment she stared at it and wondered if she was doing the right thing. If it was a grave, should she violate it? Curiosity relentlessly kneaded her like a persistent cat's claws and she plunged the plate into the sand. "Come on, help me."

They each found something they could use to dig and in a few minutes they had dug a hole deep enough to yield part of a skeletal hand with a gold band on one of the remaining fingers.

Mandy and Missy jumped back in horror. "Oh my God, there's a body buried under here," someone shouted.

Abigail reached toward the finger, but shied back in revulsion and fear. "Don't touch it, Abby. You could get some disease or something," Mandy said.

Danny tried to pull Abigail back from the grave, but she shrugged him off. Her thoughts flew in chaotic circles. This had been a living person, someone with hopes and dreams, who loved and was loved. Abigail somehow knew it was a wedding ring. She wiped her hand on her shorts, then without touching the bones, delicately slipped the ring off and dropped it in the palm of her other hand. She gingerly turned it and saw writing around the inside of the ring. *"Ann and Paul, forever"*

The words came rushing in like a runaway train… *"Mayday, mayday this is Sweet Abigail… Ann, I need you"* Abigail gasped. She looked around for the thunder clouds and pelting rain, like a hundred woodpeckers, but the sun blazed down on her head and the sky was blue and cloud-free. Where had these memories come from and why in her mind? What was her psychic connection to this Ann and Paul and why did the boat have her name? She shoved the ring on her own finger as myriad questions galloped through her mind. No answers appeared.

A strange sensation tickled the back of her neck. Abigail raised her head and looked across the sand. There, by a tall palm stood the vague outline of a young couple. They were barely visible, just an alteration in the light pattern of the air around them. They smiled at Abigail and the woman nodded. They faded and disappeared. The world went black.

CHAPTER FIFTY-TWO

Abigail opened her eyes and squinted against the blazing sun. Her mother's face swam into view, concern written in the three deep lines between her eyes and the tears dried on her cheeks. She closed her eyes against the light and snuggled into her mother's arms.

Rachel clasped her tightly, rocking gently back and forth and speaking aloud to herself. "Oh, Abby, Abby, why did you go here? I told you not to go west."

Abigail whispered, "I'm sorry, Mommy, I'm so sorry. I should have listened to you."

"That's not important, Rachel. Let's get her back to the house and we'll sort everything out there."

Abigail turned her head and stared into Ben's worried eyes. She felt him lift her up into his arms and saw Danny and the twins standing in a circle around them. They started back along the beach, but Abigail pushed against Ben's chest and said, "I'm fine, I can walk."

"But honey, please let...." Rachel never finished the sentence because Abigail struggled until Ben stood her on her feet. She wobbled a bit, then found her strength and walked defiantly ahead. Danny caught up and put his arm around her. She shook it off but didn't move away.

"I'm fine, Danny, I just need to walk on my own."

"Okay, but I'm here if you need me."

Abigail nodded and marched defiantly on, her brain churning with unspoken questions and answers she feared, yet needed to understand. The gentle waves lapped the sand and gulls screamed in the distance, black silhouettes against a brilliant blue sky. Abigail, so wrapped up in her own shame and misery, heard none of this. She had never fainted in her life and she had to go and do it in front of her friends. How dumb was that?

She felt a light touch of air against her leg and dropped her hand so it dangled just above the ghostly essence of Sandy. Whatever happened, he would not leave her; their spirits were forever united, just as Emma and Rachel were joined for eternity. Abigail suddenly felt a hole open in her belly, an emptiness that left her soul lonely and alone. She didn't belong to anyone; she knew that as well as she knew her face in the mirror. She looked like Rachel and once looked like Emma, but she wasn't of them, she was an outsider, an interloper. Now Abigail understood why Emma often got so angry. Emma must have hated her because she was alive, here with Rachel and taking her place as Rachel's child.

So who was she? Where did she come from? Did it have anything to do with the Sweet Abigail from Miami and the woman Ann, buried in the sand? So many questions churned in her head and no answers. A wave of nausea threatened to overtake her, but she fought it off swallowing hard and breathing through her nose. She wouldn't embarrass herself any more in front of Danny.

Danny leaned close. "Are you okay, Abby? At least let me hold your hand."

Abigail took a deep breath and then placed her hand in Danny's. He squeezed it and they continued walking.

"I'm sorry I was such a baby. I don't know what came over me," Abigail said, softly.

"Don't worry about it, Mandy had to sit on the sand with her head between her knees and Missy threw up. But don't tell them I told you, they'll kill me."

Abigail smiled, despite her despair. "I won't tell. So did you go get my mother and Ben?"

"Oh yeah, I think I'm going out for track next year. I beat the world's record in sprinting."

GAIA'S GIFT

Despite her feelings, Abby giggled. "I bet you did, thank you, Danny."

"No problema!" Danny said.

"Huh?"

"Oh, it's from an old movie, Terminator 2. This kid, who supposed to save the world when he grows up, is being hunted by this robot from the future, who's a terminator and wants to kill him so he can't save the world, and another terminator robot, who really isn't one any more, is sent to protect him and the kid teaches him the expression."

"Right!" Abigail said.

"Well, you have to see the first movie to understand the second and third."

"There were three movies?"

"Oh, yeah!" Danny answered. "Good, too! Maybe one day we can rent the movies and watch them together. We'll have a Terminator marathon."

"Popcorn?"

"Absolutely! What's a movie marathon without popcorn? Maybe we'll even invite Mandy and Missy and the old folks," Danny quipped.

"My mother would just love to be called old folks." Abigail realized what she had just said and her mind froze. Danny was still talking, but Abigail had shut off all sound.

Horrific visions of a skeletal hand reaching up through the sand, beckoning. No! The skeleton wasn't calling her from the grave. *Shut up!* Suddenly she remembered why she fainted. The man and woman she saw, they had to be spirits, there was no one else on the island. Why had they smiled at her? Were they Ann and Paul? Had she worn this wedding band once upon a time, a living time?

Was Rachel really her mother? Who was Abigail Wells and was that really her name? The stupid movie marathon and popcorn receded into the depths of her memory as the terror that her life might change in a very short time and not in a good way, pushed a sour taste into her throat.

"Abby? We're here at your house. Abby?" Danny was shaking her shoulder.

Abby looked up at him, tears running down her cheeks. She broke away and ran around the house and down to the pet cemetery. Lying down on the grave of her two best friends, Abigail pried the wedding band off her finger and stared at the inscription. "Oh, Sandy, I don't know what to do. I'm so scared."

Rachel found her there, weeping. She turned her around and held her, rocking back and forth. "My sweet baby, please don't cry. I love you and I always will." Rachel took out a tissue and wiped Abigail's face. Then she held the tissue to her nose and said, "Blow."

Abigail sat up and took the tissue. "I can blow my own nose."

Rachel sat back on her heels and willed herself to be calm. She knew their world had shifted and they were about the fall off, but she had to make the landing as soft as possible. "Come with me and I'll explain."

Abigail shuddered. She shoved the ring in her pocket, but stood up and followed Rachel to the chicken coop.

Rachel paused outside, amid the squawking of the few remaining chickens. She stood at the crossroads of right and wrong, tamping down any argument between her idealist and pragmatist. This was the moment to take the step in one direction or the other and Rachel wavered, trapped at the corner of free will. The idealist pushed her way through the barrier, *"No more lies!"*

"You have the right to protect yourself," the pragmatist stated.

"You don't know what you're talking about, fool. Abby is the one she has to protect...."

Rachel tamped down on the voices and stepped across the threshold of the coop.

Abigail watched, as Rachel lifted a loose floor board and extracted a plastic bag. She opened it and pulled out a leather pouch. Hesitating, she held it tightly in her hand; the moment of truth and the moment of change. How could she be so naïve to think this life could last forever? Nothing good goes on forever, fate always intervenes and Gaia always wins in the end.

CHAPTER FIFTY-THREE

Outside, Ben crouched against the wall by the opening to the chicken coop. He had sent the kids to pack the boat and get it ready to sail as soon as he returned. They had argued, but he was adamant and finally they obeyed, walking off in full teenage-sulk mode. It hurt Ben to eavesdrop, but he had to know if this beautiful, sexy woman pulling him into the vulnerable web of love could be trusted, or would she turn out to be another female failure in his life, like his ex-wife.

Ben also felt the pull of his profession and his beliefs. Could he betray the law because his libido and emotions were out of control, or could he disassociate himself and do what he had always believed was the 'right' thing to do? *"What was the 'right' thing to do, anyway?"* He thought, *"You're not a prosecutor any more, Ben Ross. You defend people and you don't question their guilt, just give them the best defense. Is Rachel any different?"* Still bewildered by indecision, Ben settled in and listened.

Rachel and Abigail sat cross-legged facing each other on the floor of the dusty coop, ignoring the angry chickens that finally stalked out the door. Breathing deeply as though it were her last breath of free air, Rachel opened the pouch and pulled out a packet of papers. She held them out to Abigail. The girl hesitantly reached for them and stared at them before placing them on the floor by her feet. She picked up a passport and opened it, reading the name intently. Then she opened the next passport and read that one. Finally, Abigail opened the third one and stared at her baby self, then at the name, Abigail Jane Stern and the date of birth. Her birthday was in October and she was three years old in this photo. That made her almost 15, now.

Biting her lip, Abigail set them aside and picked up the next packet, photos of the Stern family, Ann, Paul and Abigail, a happy couple and their adorable child, always with a furry bear. Abigail gasped when she realized it was Jon Bear, clasped close to the little girl's chest. One was a picture of an old couple, probably somebody's parents, or grandparents. She had family somewhere in the world, if they were still alive and she was really this Abigail.

Tears flowed and she brushed the back of her hand across her face. There were two Florida driver's licenses with the same Miami address, Ann's and Paul's. She gently laid them down and opened the captain's log, but she couldn't read it because the words blurred. Finally, she sobbed, "This is me, isn't it? This was my life. I lost so much. How could you never tell me?"

Rachel stared down at her hands that had at once saved, stolen, loved, and nurtured this child. Now they were reforming as claws, grasping and greedy. Finally she spoke, "I lost my mind after Jack and Emma died. I tried to die, too, for a year, but I was too much of a coward. I came here and made a life for myself, for five years, with only Charm as company. I healed, but never forgot.

"One night in July, a storm sent a boat onto the rocks. I couldn't save them because they never saw my lantern through the dark rain. I found them the next day, your parents and buried them. Your mother, Ann looked so much like me, it was scary. I was suddenly hurled into the past with the memory of a tiny girl holding my hand.

"But then I lost the image when I heard a cry and I found you alive in a little house-cave you had built from a piece of hull and some palm fronds. I also found a starving puppy with you, determined to protect you from a pack of feral dogs that were following him. I chased them off and took you both home. Although I knew somewhere deep in my conscience it was wrong, my desperate need took control. I believed Gaia had returned my child to me and I could never let you go."

Abigail refused to meet Rachel's eyes. "Were you ever going to tell me the truth?"

Rachel nodded. "A lot of your memories surfaced over the years, especially when you met the twins and Danny; memories of Miami. I was going to move us to the mainland this year so you could go to school, but I hadn't thought it through yet, I mean about inoculations and a birth certificate. I was hoping to wait until you turned 18 and were old enough to be on your own, in case you decided to leave me...couldn't forgive me, for what I had done. Then...." Rachel's voice choked and faded and she stared into space.

"Then what?"

Rachel sighed. "I would pay the consequences."

"Consequences for what?" she yelled. "You saved my life. You raised me and loved me. You're my mother." Abigail panicked; terrified of losing Rachel even though she was still furious with her.

"Abby, in the eyes of the law, I kidnapped you."

"How could you kidnap me? My parents were dead!" Abby shouted.

"But you may have had family. I didn't want to know. I needed you and I kept you."

Abigail pulled the picture of the old couple from the pile of pictures and turned it over. The words, Grandma and Grandpa Stern, 1966 jumped out at her. "Look at this, Mom. They're old in 1966. They must be Paul Stern's grandparents and they're dead by now." She still couldn't bring her head around to the conclusion that Paul Stern was her father and these might be her grandparents or great-grandparents.

Rachel gathered up the papers and tucked them back in the pouch, which she placed inside the plastic bag. Then she stood and pulled Abigail up. "We'll just have to find out, won't we?"

Abigail threw her arms around her mother. "No, I won't let you do that. I can't lose you. We'll run away, change our names or something. They'll never find us."

Rachel held the girl and smelled the salty sea air in her hair, smoothing the dark blonde curls. Her tears wet the back of Abigail's tee shirt.

Ben stood and silently turned away, still unnoticed. He walked down the path and around the house, his head hanging down in despair.

At some point, Rachel heard a motor start and froze. Every inch of her wanted to race down to the dock and stop him, to try and explain, but how could she ever make anyone understand; maybe Ben the man, but never Ben the lawyer. This brief, happy episode in her life was over, the future looming bleak and dark like black storm clouds on the horizon moving inexorably toward the tiny wooden boat on which she was trapped.

CHAPTER FIFTY-FOUR

Three days later, an argument resulted from a simple question. Abigail was preparing salad and Rachel was sautéing vegetables for pita sandwiches. Mundane activities performed in a household besieged by fear and an invading army of unanswered questions.

"Mom, why can't I even speak to Danny or the twins?"

Rachel stirred faster. "We've been over this, Abby. Until I figure out what we are going to do, we have to stay to ourselves."

"But they're just kids, Mom. They can't hurt us?"

Rachel gritted her teeth, but willed her voice to be calm. "Ben Ross is an attorney. He was a prosecutor and that means he put people in jail."

Abigail slammed down the pepper mill. "I know what a prosecutor is. Stop treating me like a baby."

Rachel spun around. "What don't you understand about this situation, Abigail?"

Abigail knew it was time to back off when her mother used her full name, but she was propelled by her stubborn streak right into the war zone. "He's not going to send you to jail."

"He's an attorney; he's sworn to uphold the law."

Abigail refused to eat dinner and slammed out of the house. She sat on the swing, moving backward and forward, Jon Bear clenched tightly against her chest. Her fists were so tight around the ropes that the nails dug painfully into her palms. The more her hands hurt the less pain she felt inside. She concentrated on the physical discomfort and for a brief moment felt a respite from the horrors of the day.

Abigail could still see the curled bones of the hand, the wedding band shining in the sunlight. Her mother's hand that once fed her brushed her hair and helped her dress. Hands that had comforted her when she was sick, held her when she was scared, because that's what mothers did, didn't they? She tried hard to remember the touch, any touch, but the feelings eluded her. All she could see were the bony fingers, a picture she would see until the day she died.

She stopped the thought before it overwhelmed her and thought of her father, her real father. Paul Stern, the smiling, blonde man looking out from the photo, a stranger except for the memory of his voice calling "Ann, I need you." Who was this man? A million questions assaulted her brain, none of which she could answer.

Abigail tried to focus on the image of the ghostly couple standing by the palm, but it was too vague and she couldn't recall their faces. Had her real parents been here all this time and she never saw them? Maybe they had to wait for the right time to appear to her, when she would understand.

It was all so lopsided. Abigail loved Rachel more than anything in the world, well except Sandy and he was gone forever. Rachel was her anchor. What would happen to her now? What if she had to leave Rachel, or she was taken away. Where would she go? Who would take care of her? Tears dribbled down her cheeks as terror gripped her. She couldn't lose Rachel, the only mother she had really ever known. In a panic, Abigail jumped from the swing and ran to the house.

"Mom, Mom, where are you?" she cried, racing up the porch steps.

Rachel turned from the sink at the sound of the door slamming open and hitting the wall. She nearly lost her balance as Abigail hurtled into her and threw her arms around her, taking her breath away.

"Don't let them take me away, Mom, please." Abigail turned her tear-stained face up to Rachel. "I'm so scared."

Rachel wrapped her arms around the shaking child. "I won't let anything happen to you, Abby. I promise." Rachel marveled at how easily the lie flew from her mouth. She had no idea what was going to happen in the next few weeks, or even days. Next week at this time, she could be in jail and Abby in foster care. It's a mother's prerogative to lie if it's for the good of her child, she reasoned. It was also a mother's responsibility to change the course of events if necessary for her child's welfare.

FRAN ORENSTEIN

CHAPTER FIFTY-FIVE

After arguments and angry exchanges about their abrupt departure, the girls were mostly silent on the trip across the bay. Danny, lost in his own private world, shut them all out, sullenly doing what he was told and not speaking to anyone except for typical fifteen-year-old grunts in response to direct questions. Ben headed south along the coast to get as far away from the key as possible. Finally they found a marina and checked into a hotel. Knowing that dinner would be a total loss, Ben ordered pizza and drinks delivered to their rooms and left them to their own devices. When the kids were finally settled in their own rooms at the hotel, Ben locked both the hallway door and the adjoining door to the girls' room and sat down at the desk.

While the laptop powered up, he opened a manila envelope and spread the articles and pictures of the Stern and Wells family out across the desk. Then he began to Google names. Two hours later he stretched and opened the tiny refrigerator, popping the cap on a cranberry juice cocktail and opening a packet of chips to go with his cold slices of pizza. He chewed automatically, tasting nothing, thinking miserable thoughts.

Finally, he sat back down and researched some more, until he could no longer see the screen clearly. Ben now had the possible scenarios and he would have to decide what he was going to do about it.

He reached into his backpack and pulled out a pair of latex gloves, which he put on. Then he withdrew two plastic bags. Each contained a piece of paper with initials, a sample of hair pulled from a brush; a couple of used tissues, and an empty water bottle, things no one would notice were missing. After the episode at the chicken coop, Ben hadn't gone right back to the boat, but had invaded Rachel's house, like a thief in the night.

Shuddering, he withdrew a third bag and placed it on the desk. His stomach lurched and he instantly regretted eating the cold pizza. Inside were some strands of dry, brittle hair, a small piece of fabric with a dark, almost black stain, and a skeletal finger.

While everyone was focused on Abigail, Ben had dug into the sand and found the skull, which still had some tufts of hair attached. Wrapping his shirt tail around his hand, he had managed to pull some hair off the skull, quickly re-burying it so the kids wouldn't see. There were fragments of stained cloth and he took one of those. Then he steeled himself and broke off a finger, rolling it and the hair in the cloth and stuffed it into an empty zippered pouch in his backpack.

Sure, it was tainted, and he didn't even know if the sample would be useful, but he wasn't trying to follow police procedure, just hoping they would yield DNA, the chromosomes that made up the human body. It was the element that determined the genetic link between people in the same family, or conversely, proved the opposite. First he had to figure out how to get a lab to examine them without giving anything away.

Ben knew that he was treading on the edge of a crumbling precipice and his world could collapse around him, but he had to know the truth of what he suspected before he acted. It was easier because it was his law firm and no one would openly question his actions. They might wonder, but he could easily explain the new client; an inheritance or custody case involving DNA from a deceased relative. He just hoped no one questioned how the samples were obtained. It was close enough to the truth to believe it himself, making it that much easier to convince his staff. Ben carefully pulled up his files and opened a blank document to create a new client file, a fictitious file.

An hour later, he pressed send and the file flew through cyberspace to become just one of many emails in his computer at work. Tomorrow, his secretary would sort through the emails and create a paper file under the names Wilson/Stone: Custodial Case. Ben would maintain a separate file in his locked drawer with the articles and on-line information he had collected.

When he returned to Miami in a few days, he would send the samples to a lab outside the city where he wasn't known and personally hire a private investigator not connected to the firm, perhaps from Fort Lauderdale or Palm Beach to find out more about the women's histories and if any of Abby's relatives still existed.

Yawning, Ben barely managed to take off his clothes and crawl under the covers, wondering if his hunch was correct and if so, how he could manipulate the information to save Rachel and Abigail. As tired as he felt physically and psychically, Ben's mind ran in circles; each scenario creating ever increasing anxiety. Before falling into a troubled sleep, his last thought was Rachel's beautiful body as she swam naked toward him in the lagoon.

Ben finally gave up on a sound sleep at 5 a.m. and sat by the window watching the black ocean slowly turn blue as dawn awoke in the night sky. At six, he took a long hot, then cold shower, trying to scrub away the myriad of conflicting feelings that had bombarded him during the night, to no avail. They clung to him the way parasitic moss hangs on old live oaks.

The kids were still too angry to bombard him with questions and breakfast was a blessedly silent affair. They checked out of the hotel and were on their way to the inter-coastal waterway heading back to Miami; the adventure that had been so happily planned, aborted by unexplained events.

Ben spent the next few days in isolation, while the kids talked among themselves, ignoring him. He shrugged it off, recalling his own sullen, angry adolescence. They would just have to wait for an explanation until he had all the facts and could present them coherently.

"You sound like they're a jury and you're an attorney at the rail giving a summation. These are your kids." Ben shut off the words even though he knew he was probably treating this like a

trial. He just couldn't handle their questions without more information. That wasn't the whole truth; he still hadn't come to terms with his own feelings and his role in this melodramatic soap opera.

GAIA'S GIFT

CHAPTER FIFTY-SIX

The spirits watched and waited for the final act. For weeks, the horizon flamed red-orange twice a day, the backdrop for a perfect Florida postcard, the eternal turning of the Earth. Three times, thunder clouds formed and exploded with a sound and light show surpassing a Fourth of July celebration and still they waited. The living plotted and planned, dreamed and paced, agonized and compared scenarios, while a myriad of possible futures passed before their eyes. Each dwelled in a lonely, unconnected world filled with frustration and indecision and the spirits bided their time.

Rachel, torn between right and wrong, sin and redemption, wasted precious hours researching possible relocation situations. Facing a dilemma of infinite proportions that would impact their lives forever, she could not make any decision. She felt herself slipping again into the miserable morass of dark self-pity that had crushed her nearly 18 years ago. She thought of calling Mary Cross just to unburden her soul, but never acted on it.

Rachel's dreams became nightmares of iron bars and razor wire. She reached through the bars toward the receding figure of Abigail growing smaller and fainter in a thick fog.

Then she was on a dingy in the middle of the ocean watching the oars drifting further and further away until she could not reach them. In the distance she could see a tiny orange speck, but could no longer retrieve the oars and save her baby.

She awoke from these dreams shaking, her heart pounding in her ears. Emma and Abigail, Abigail and Emma, intertwined in her mind. Was it her destiny to lose her children?

***

Abigail, frightened and alone, watched her mother drift further and further away. She agonized over the consequences of losing Rachel or finding her birth family. After talking for hours to Sandy's spirit in a one-way dialogue, she never came to any conclusion as to which was the scarier scenario. Abigail knew that whatever happened, she would lose Rachel. Then she would be alone in the world without anyone if all her birth family was gone and Rachel was in jail or worse.

Abigail often woke in the night from nightmare visions of skeletons rising from the sand, reaching toward her to pull her down into the grave. She wanted to be a little girl again and run to Rachel's bed, where she could snuggle under the covers and pull the warmth from her mother's living body. Instead, she hugged Jon Bear and pretended that Sandy's warm body protected her.

***

Danny wavered between trying to contact Abigail and keeping his promise to Ben Ross to wait just a few weeks. He didn't know why he had been asked to wait, but understood it must be important. At fifteen, though, his waiting ability was close to the breaking point. He wanted to burst through the gates like a thoroughbred plunging ahead before the gun. Sometimes he sat by the short-wave radio running his fingers over the call letters and numbers to the Wells' radio, but never keyed them in or pushed the button.

At night he dreamed of Abigail, but sometimes his dreams included a bony hand reaching up out of the sand beckoning. He heard a disembodied voice calling for help and woke, sweating and shivering in the air-conditioned room.

***

The twins, frustrated and angry plotted rebellion against their father for his stubborn refusal to discuss anything to do with Abigail and Rachel. First they threatened to go live with their mother, which Ben knew was a fruitless gesture because she had abandoned them in the first place. Then they put their older sister, Tara up to getting the answers out of him and that only left Tara curious and frustrated.

They tried unlocking the study door before he came home, but their lock-picking skills were not up to the task. The study window remained locked, too. Short of breaking and entering, which their father would figure out in a minute, they could only stand outside the door and fume.

In their similar nightmares, graves opened and skeletal hands reached up from the sand. They felt the bony fingers grasp their legs and arms pulling them down into the darkness. The twins took to sleeping with each other to ward off the terror waking alone from all too frequent nightmares. It never occurred to them to tell their father or Tara. They had always relied on each other.

***

Ben immersed himself in work and disappeared into his study when he finally did get home. He did acquiesce to dinner each night, but refused to talk of anything but ordinary daily events. He depended on summer camp and Tara, home from college for the summer, to supervise the girls. When the twins confronted him, he promised them it would be over very soon and to please have patience, although he knew asking teens to have patience was like asking the rain to pour up and not down.

***

And so the weeks passed and the spirits waited for the conclusion, like an audience watching a psychodrama series on television and knowing that after a set number of episodes the end would play itself out with a cliff-hanger dangling until next season. At last the spirits sat up, alert to the delivery of a pair of thick envelopes by Federal Express.

FRAN ORENSTEIN

CHAPTER FIFTY-SEVEN

At last Rachel marked the map; Virginia Beach the home of the Edgar Cayce Foundation, surely the sanctuary she sought, where otherworldly abilities and beliefs would not be challenged or condemned as witchcraft. At least she hoped this would prove to be so, that she would be welcomed there. She could continue to home-school Abigail without the paperwork required by the bureaucracy and Abigail could participate in activities like sports, clubs, music and art lessons, perhaps dance classes, where she would meet other teens her age. It wouldn't take long before she forgot about her friends in Miami and moved on to new safer interests.

Rachel had packaged a tidy life for them both, until Abigail turned 18 and was ready for college. Then she could use her own birth certificate without any questions. Indeed, Rachel had it all figured out, except for a pair of Fed-Ex packages that had just arrived on Ben Ross' doorstep, which she knew nothing about.

Rachel presented the idea to Abigail after dinner. "So, Abby, what do you think?"

Abigail shrugged her shoulders in a teen gesture of sullen confirmation that she had heard but wasn't ready to commit so easily.

"Come on, Abby. Give me a break here. I'm trying to keep us together as a family."

Abigail knew exactly what Rachel was doing and agreed in her head, but felt an unnatural urge to punish, fueled by unanswered questions. She still had a driving force pushing her to find out if she had a family out there, despite the consequences. "Sure, whatever you want, Mom."

"A tiny bit of enthusiasm would help, here," Rachel said, exasperated by the sporadic vibes of anger flowing off Abigail.

The girl took a deep breath to calm her heaving stomach. "I'm sure you have it all figured out, Mom and it's probably the best solution. So if I enthusiastically agree, will you do one thing for me?"

Suspicion reared up on hind legs, pawing the air, heavy with sarcasm. Rachel looked closely at Abigail, who wouldn't meet her eyes. "What?"

"We'll leave here, then you have to swear you'll help me find my family, if there's anyone left. I won't make contact. I just want to know," Abigail said.

Rachel expelled the breath she had been holding. "Deal!"

"Really, you'll do that?" Abigail seemed surprised that it had been so easy. Could she really trust Rachel after all the years of lies? *"Never mind,"* she thought. *"Once I'm off this island I can do it myself."*

Rachel nodded and waited, for she knew there was something else on Abigail's mind.

Abigail chewed her upper lip. "We have to take Daisy and Buttercup and the chickens with us."

Rachel nearly laughed, but caught herself at the last moment. This was not what she expected. She thought Abigail would want her parents reburied on the mainland, but perhaps they weren't real to her as parents, as family. Rachel owned the land and in the future when Abigail was an adult, she could always have the bodies relocated.

She wanted to whoop for joy, instead she said, "The animals will go with us. We'll find a place where we can keep them, maybe get another dog and cat, and I can have my herb and vegetable gardens."

Rachel scanned Abigail's face for a response. Taking a chance she held out her arms. "Can we hug on that?"

GAIA'S GIFT

Abigail ventured a slight smile and slid into Rachel's arms. She had her own agenda and to make it happen, she had to escape this tropical paradise that had become a graveyard of memories.

FRAN ORENSTEIN

CHAPTER FIFTY-EIGHT

The evening, following the delivery from Fed-Ex, Ben came home from work and found two envelopes waiting on the hall table. The anticipation of weeks turned sour in the moment of revelation. He took them into his study and placed them side-by-side on the desk and sat down heavily in his chair. His hands remained tight fists in his lap, pressing into his thighs and he stared at the envelopes with dread, as if they would burst into flame if he touched them. He could still walk away and let Rachel and Abigail go on with their lives, never knowing the truth. On the other hand, perhaps the information could save them, save Rachel, the woman he believed he might love.

Do something! Ben lifted the thinner of the envelopes, the one from the detective he had hired and slit it open with a silver-handled paper knife. Moving aside the other packet, he removed the papers and spread them across the desk. Then he read and reread until he was sure he understood everything. Abigail Stern and her parents had no living relatives, except.... Ben froze. His heart pounding like a deep kettle drum, Ben set that piece of paper aside and with shaking hands, picked up the next sheet of information.

Paul Stern's grandparents had raised him and they had died fifteen years ago, six months apart. Ann Stern, birth name Ann Lawrence, had been a foster child from age two. Her parents had died in an automobile accident, leaving no relatives willing to take her.

Ben considered the cruelty of people. Ann Lawrence had to have been a beautiful child, blonde, blue-eyed, the dream of childless parents. Why had no one ever adopted her? He read on and found the explanation. She was never adopted because there was a sister and no one wanted to adopt two girls. With no one to advocate, the sisters had finally been separated and placed in foster care. For 17 years, Ann had been shuttled from home to home, never remaining more than a year or two at any one place. Finally, Ann had run away, probably to get out of a difficult foster situation. Her activities during the years until she met and married Paul Stern were blank and Ben didn't want to consider the implications of what her life might have been like.

He set aside the packet of papers on Ann Lawrence Stern and picked up the next set of pages. Ben stared at the file name and wanted to leap for joy. He picked up the paper he had set aside and placed them side-by-side on the desk. He swallowed and took a deep breath. Rachel Wells was born Rachel Lawrence. Ben actually laughed, for if fate had a warped sense of humor this had to be the classic coincidence of all time.

Rachel's life-story read as fairy-tale compared to Ann Lawrence. She had several foster homes, but finally at age six had settled into a good home with a family of five boys, some of whom were already out of the house and on their own. The older parents desperately wanted a daughter and adopted Rachel. They never knew about Rachel's sister for her four-year-old mind had forgotten in the confusion of the years as a foster child, except for memories of a tiny hand clutched in her own and the name Annie. The adopting parents would surely have searched for Ann and perhaps adopted her, too. Ben considered what life would have been like for the two sisters, had Ann's existence been known. He shook off the sadness for there was no undoing in the timeline of life, it just kept marching onward.

The detective discovered that the parents had died, for they were older when they adopted Rachel and her much older brothers had scattered all over the world. Rachel must have lost touch with them and any other family members who still lived.

GAIA'S GIFT

There was more information about the sisters after they married and many of the same articles about the tragic boat accidents. Ben was astounded at the similarities in the women's lives, and the survival and subsequent connection of Rachel and Abigail. Was Rachel Wells actually Abigail's biological aunt or was it another joke of fate, a coincidence of names. Ben could not believe that such a cruel resolution was possible.

Ben put the reports back in the first envelope and lifted the second. He closed his eyes and for the first time since childhood, he prayed. Would the proof be in this envelope? He pushed the thought of a decision far from his mind. That was for later. Slitting the envelope, Ben pulled out the lab report and turned the page. His breath caught in the swelling lump in his throat and the words blurred.

… FRAN ORENSTEIN

CHAPTER FIFTY-NINE

Abigail sat beside the grave of Ann and Paul Stern, clutching the leather pouch that marked her life. She knew by now that living life meant making choices and right now she could go in lots of directions.

Lies, her whole life was based on lies. You're supposed to trust your mother, but then Rachel wasn't really her mother, so what did it matter, anyway. The hot anger that raged inside her aimed its arrows at Rachel, but also at the skeletons buried under the sand. "Why did you desert me? I hate you both," she cried to the wind.

Rationally she understood that they hadn't planned for the storm or for the boat to hit the rocks and leave them dead and her still alive. She was grateful she had lived and had all this time on a tropical island with Rachel who she knew loved her. Still, Abigail wondered what her life would have been like living with her real parents in Miami, going to school, making friends, having a whole family and maybe brothers or sisters.

She had other family. Sandy and Charm would always be remembered, especially Sandy. Charlie Chicken and his six wives, and the two goats, Clover and Billy also hovered on the edges of her memory. They had all been her earliest friends, the ones she grew up with; silly Charlie cock-a-doodling at his wives scurrying around, pecking at grain, and sweet Clover, who had tried to eat her dress…no, Emma's dress. Emma, who knew all along, but couldn't communicate except through a poltergeist's childish tantrums.

Abigail squinted as though she could see Ann and Paul Stern through a filmy, gauze curtain. "Are you here? Have you been here all along, but I didn't know?" The wind picked up and the palm fronds rattled. A whisper of something different, a tear in the weave of the ether, brushed Abigail's ear. She touched her ear and whispered, "You are here with me, you've always been here, but couldn't reach me until I found you again."

How could she hear them when she didn't know about them? All these years her parent's spirits must have lingered, unable to communicate because Abigail was lost in another life that did not include them in her memories, except for the name Ann and a storm that so frightened her as a child. Did the spirit of Ann Stern ache to hold her when she screamed from nightmares of rain like woodpeckers on the roof or thunder booms crashing down upon her? Did Paul Stern, locked away forever on this island wait in terror for her return when she and Rachel sailed to the mainland?

"I'm sorry we missed a life together. I can't call you Mom and Dad because I never knew you, well only for a few years, but you are my mom and dad and well…I wish we had been a family." Tears coursed down Abigail's cheeks and she watched them drop by drop, darken the sand-covered graves. The gentle breeze continued to caress her.

Abigail looked around at the wreckage of the life that might have been and made a decision. At fourteen, decisions are not made with wisdom and forethought, but instantly in emotional turmoil. Still clutching the leather pouch, she rose and turned her back on the sun, her course of action set in stone.

GAIA'S GIFT

CHAPTER SIXTY

Rachel carried the cooler down the dock and hauled it into the boat. She stowed it away out of the sun and adjusted the tarp, tying it down. Annoyed that Abigail had disappeared and she had to do all the work herself, Rachel's mood grew grumpier as the time passed. *Where was that girl?*

The idealist wasted no time jumping into the conversation. *"No doubt she is exercising her adolescent angst somewhere."*

"*Know-it-all,*" the pragmatist grumbled.

"*She has every right to act her age,*" his opponent declared.

"*Hmm, there is such a thing as respecting your parents or in this case, parent.*"

"*It's today's generation. They just go their own way.*" the idealist declared.

The pragmatist harrumphed. "*Yes, with no regard to anyone but themselves.*"

"*It's all part of growing up, which they all do eventually.*"

"*Indeed, if their parents don't murder them first....*"

Rachel shook her head to shut off the dialogue. Why couldn't her brain just be still for a few minutes? She couldn't even summon the peace and quiet necessary to meditate any more, decisions and more decisions got in the way. Her mind churned in a whirlpool of constant activity sucking in ideas, plots and consequences in this complicated script. "It's your own fault," she grouched to herself. "You set this in motion 12 years ago when you made the decision to keep her. So you can't pass it off on anything or anyone else. Live with it Rachel Wells."

Just three more years and Abigail would be old enough to go it alone. There was a college fund and a trust to keep her financially secure for the rest of her life if she was wise about spending. Rachel knew Abigail had good common sense, so she didn't worry about her financial future. If she could just hold off her need to find out everything for three years...

"Mom," Abigail called from the end of the dock. "Need any help?"

Rachel stared at her and pointed to the bulging tarp. "I managed. Where were you?"

Abigail shrugged and stepped off the dock, turning toward the goat pen and chicken coop. "I'll just make sure the animals have everything they need for a week."

Rachel closed her eyes and shook her head. Calm, she ordered, calm. "Give them some extra in case we stay longer, especially water." Although she knew that rain was inevitable this time of year, just in case of an unlikely drought this week, she wanted to return to healthy, living goats and chickens.

Rachel went up to the house to throw some last minute items in a backpack. Abigail's backpack sat on the floor by the door, where it hadn't been earlier. Abigail must have been in the house packing it while she was loading the boat. *"I will not lose my temper,"* although visions of reaming her out danced in her head. Rachel's guilt hung like an albatross around her neck, choking her, preventing her from voicing her true feelings, her anger.

"She's had enough pain in the past few weeks to last a lifetime and I will not add any more," Rachel reasoned aloud. "She'll come around." But Rachel wasn't sure of anything; she had no experience with teenagers.

Abigail petted Daisy and Buttercup, who nuzzled her palm for treats. She had raided the vegetable garden and gave them each a stalk of celery. The rest of the vegetables were piled high in their trough. She wouldn't be back to eat them anyway and the whole vegetable garden would flower and go to seed. Giving the nanny goats each one last hug, Abigail let herself out the gate of their large enclosure, but didn't close it all the way. She hoped Rachel wouldn't double check and shut it. Abigail wanted to give the goats a fighting chance to survive. "Bye chickens, sorry I never named you. Bye Daisy, bye Buttercup, be good goats."

She dumped the entire bag of feed onto the ground outside the chicken coop and spread it around with her feet. "Eat hearty, chickies and listen every morning for Charlie's crowing. It comes on the morning wind, but you have to listen really, really hard."

Finally, Abigail visited the pet cemetery and sat at the foot of their grave. "I have to leave now Sandy. I'm sorry. You will always be my best friend and I'll never forget you, brave puppy. Goodbye, Charm, you were the best kitty ever. You and Sandy are together forever and one day we'll meet again." She sniffed and swiped her eyes. The breeze picked up and Abigail thought she heard a distant, muffled bark. "I know sweet puppy, but I have to say goodbye now. I love you, Sandy."

Abigail rose and stared into the distance. For a moment, space shifted and she saw a yellow dog and a black cat running along the beach and then the image faded and they disappeared. "Goodbye," she whispered and turned away.

FRAN ORENSTEIN

CHAPTER SIXTY-ONE

Ben's excitement must have spurted from every pore because the twins bombarded him with questions at dinner. Tara was out on a date with the "nerd-monster', Mandy and Missy epithet for their sister's latest boyfriend.

"You look too happy, Dad," Mandy exclaimed.

"Are you plotting something?" Missy stared at him suspiciously.

Ben smiled and shrugged.

"Come on, Dad," Mandy whined. "Tell us."

Ben shook his head and refused to talk.

Missy reached over and tickled him. Ben squirmed away. "We'll overpower you and tickle-torture you until you confess," Missy said.

"You're in love," Mandy stated.

Missy turned to her sister and frowned. "Are you crazy?" she shrieked.

Mandy ignored her. "Well, are you…in love, I mean?"

Ben continued to eat ignoring their pleas. The twins glared at him, but Ben refused to meet their eyes. At last, he finished the last crumb still paying no attention to his now sullen daughters. "I'm going down the street to Danny's house." He stood up and cleared his dishes. "You will stay here and clean up the kitchen."

"But Dad…," they both said.

"No buts…stay here." Then he amended the order with "please."

As he opened the back door, Ben turned and said, "If you stay here and do what I ask, I might just tell you what's going on when I get back."

He grinned as the clatter of dishes hitting the sink followed him out the door.

Ben cut through the backyards until he reached Danny's house. The garage was open and the car was missing, but someone was home, because he could hear a loud base beat shaking the house, which meant Danny was inside, destroying his hearing.

He knocked on the door, but no one came. He knocked harder, then shouted. Still no one came. How could anyone inside hear through that noise, well music such as it was. He turned the knob and entered. "DANNY!" Ben yelled as loud as he could and still keep his vocal chords intact.

Danny appeared in the hall still bouncing to the beat. "Hey, Mr. Ross, I didn't hear you knock."

"Of course you didn't," Ben thought. He pointed to his ear and gestured for Danny to turn down the music.

"Oh, yeah, sorry, Mr. Ross," Danny said bouncing back into the family room. In a few seconds the music dropped to a tolerable level and Danny returned.

"Uh, my mom and dad aren't here. They went shopping with my brothers."

"That's fine, Danny. I wasn't looking for them. I was hoping you would be here and help me call Rachel Wells on your short-wave radio."

"Oh, sure, I can do that. Come on down." Danny led the way to the basement door and bounced down the stairs. "Do you think she'll talk to you? I mean, after what happened when we were there?"

"That's what I'm hoping, Danny. Can I ask you a big favor? Just make the connection and then go back upstairs so I can talk to her privately."

Danny blushed. "Uh huh, I guess so."

Ben suspected a potential drama unfolding in Danny's head. He said nothing to dispel Danny's imagination because then he would have to explain his reason for calling Rachel.

Danny fiddled with the set and static came out of the speaker. He turned to Ben. "I'm sorry, Mr. Ross, nobody is answering. I don't think it's even turned on. Maybe later?"

Ben mood hit rock bottom. Damn luck! They must be out of the house, somewhere. Then he remembered the cell phone. "Danny, do you have their cell phone number?"

"Yeah, it's here somewhere." He pushed around scraps of paper on the table and shook his head. "Stupid," he said, then fished a small wallet from his pocket. He poked around and pulled out a scrap of paper. He wrote the number on another scrap of paper floating around in the paper mess on the desk and handed it to Ben. "Sorry, I guess I learned my organization skills from my dad," he said gesturing at the paper-strewn desk.

"Don't worry about it, Danny. I used to be the same way until I went to law school. Then I learned to organize or lose the case. Besides, my secretary would kill me if I left so much as a shred of un-filed paper on my desk." He leaned closer to Danny and said softly, "Don't ever tell anyone, but behind her back, I call her The Organizer Bunny."

Danny laughed and followed Ben to the stairs. As the front door closed behind him, Ben felt the house shake again with the booming bass beat.

Back in his own yard, Ben sat down at the patio table and flipped open his phone. He keyed in the numbers for Rachel's phone and hesitated, his finger poised over the send button. He needed to control his excitement first and figure out what he was going to say to her. As an attorney, he would never address the court in this state without having it all worked out in his mind. What had he been thinking? Fingering the phone, his thoughts tumbled through his brain in chaotic disorder. *Be calm and put it in sequence,* he thought. *Organize, organize.*

FRAN ORENSTEIN

CHAPTER SIXTY-TWO

Rachel entered the house and called, "Abby, are you here?" The silent house had an abandoned feeling to it, as though the life force that made it home had faded and left this shell behind. She ran through the house, calling, but the empty rooms echoed only her voice. A sudden sense of doom came down like a cloud as Rachel slowly looked around Abigail's room, searching for anything out of place. Then she found it, the anomaly. Jon Bear was no longer sitting in his place of honor on the bed.

The muffled sound of the boat's engine suddenly hit Rachel like a mallet in the gut. She spun around and out of the house, jumping the porch steps and running down the path toward the dock, but the boat was already moving away toward the open sea. She raced up the dock screaming, "Abby, Abby, come back. Abyyyyyyy!" Abigail turned once to glance behind her, but the boat sailed on, moving faster and growing smaller by the minute.

Rachel sank down on the dock and hysteria battered her. She railed at Gaia screaming and raising her fists. "Take me, take me, I don't deserve to live. She's innocent. Take me...." The breeze picked up, rattling the palm fronds and swirling little sand tornadoes. "Please, take me," she sobbed. Enveloped in a lavender scented breeze, Rachel lay on the wood planks watching the boat, now a tiny speck on the vast ocean until it disappeared over the horizon.

The sun moved overhead and Rachel sat up. "You win, Gaia." She rose and walked back along the dock and down onto the sand. Slowly, with forced, deliberate steps, she went into the shed and lifted the ax from its shelf on the wall. She stared at the blade, as if hoping to see a revelation in its metal surface. Nothing!

She turned and without closing the door behind her, walked robot-like to the old wooden dingy once used for fishing. Tossing the ax into the boat, Rachel untied the mooring line and pushed it off the sand into the water. Wading out a few feet, she climbed in and put the ax on the seat next to her. She stared at it like an object from another world that she had never seen before. Then she locked the oars into place and began to row, pushing at the bottom sand until the water was deep enough to float the boat.

Soon she could no longer see her island, just the relentless sun blazing overhead from the cerulean sky and puffy white cloud shapes floating on a celestial sea. The ocean loomed before her, an endless seascape of blue dotted with small whitecaps. Rachel felt like a bug trapped between twin worlds, not quite identical. An image of Missy and Mandy flashed across her mind and then their father. "Don't go there," she said. Rachel lifted the ax and raised it in salute. "Here's to you, Gaia, as we destroy you, so you destroy us."

Between the first breath and the last there exists a lifetime, perhaps one minute or 100 years, but for each soul that walks in the world of the living, the souls of the dead linger, patiently waiting to connect or reconnect. A hint of essence floats on a gentle breeze to tantalize the nostrils. A shadow drifts by in the corner of an eye or a whispered word, familiar, yet it lies just beyond comprehension. To some the barrier is a gossamer veil, to others a stone wall.

Spirits watched and waited as the dingy swayed gently on the waves, a wooden cradle rocked by a giant hand reaching up from the depths. Now drifting westward toward the horizon, the golden sun glared down at the seascape, oblivious of the drama unfolding below. Below the surface of the water sea creatures continued their life and death struggles unaware of the curtain rising on the final act in the small dingy above them.

Alone, bereft, burdened with guilt, Rachel tensed her arm to swing the ax downward. Suddenly, the wild strains of a Mozart sonata jolted her and she dropped the ax. It hit the edge of the dingy and bounced off into the water. Rachel desperately reached for it, rocking the boat until it nearly capsized. Grasping the dripping handle, she managed to slide to the other side of the seat and reset balance. The boat wobbled then righted itself, while the violins played on in the pocket of her shorts.

A ridiculous thought crossed her mind. *"Saved by the bell, or in this case Mozart on a cell phone. Wolfie, you may have saved a life today."* Rachel reached into her pocket and pulled out the cell phone. She looked at the incoming name…Ben Ross. Her face fell. She knew it was impossible, but she hoped for a fleeting moment that it might be Abigail.

Stupid! Abigail didn't have a cell phone and she couldn't have reached the mainland, yet. Startled, Rachel wondered how such a rational thought could invade her brain, pushing aside the other horrors and rise to the surface. Perhaps the power of a mother's fear for her child superseded everything else, except she wasn't really Abigail's mother. She was an imitation, a usurper.

Rachel looked from the ringing phone to the dripping ax. She would never understand why she flipped open the phone and pressed the green button, but she would always wonder if some otherworldly being had intervened and altered her fate.

FRAN ORENSTEIN

CHAPTER SIXTY-THREE

"Hello?" Her small voice tentative as if unsure, but pushed by an unseen source.

"Rachel, thank God. I've been so worried about you. Where are you? You didn't answer the short-wave and I still never got the call letters for your boat. Are you all right?"

Silence as Rachel held back.

"Rachel, are you there? Say something, please."

"She's gone, my Abby is gone."

"What? Gone where?"

Rachel sighed. "She took the boat and ran away."

"Oh my God! You mean she's all alone out there on the boat?"

Rachel nodded and then realized Ben couldn't see her through the phone. "Yes, but she knows how to sail. I taught her and she's sailed it before, with me.

"Where would she go?"

"The only place we've ever been is the marina where we met. I expect she'll go there." Rachel rubbed her head; the sun was beating down on it mercilessly. Why didn't she bring a hat? *Stupid, you should have been with Emma and Jack by now. Why would you need a hat?*

"I'm sorry, Ben, I'm so sorry."

Ben could barely hear her. "There's nothing to be sorry about. I understand."

Rachel shook her head and looked in wonder at the tiny phone. "How could you understand what you know nothing about?"

"Rachel, listen to me. I know everything and more."

She jumped. "What do mean, you know everything?"

"Please don't get angry and hang up, but I've been investigating and I learned some things you need to know," Ben spoke quickly to keep her from hanging up the phone.

"You investigated me? Oh, of course, I forgot you're an attorney first, a man second," Rachel said in a tone edged in bitterness.

"That's not true." Ben took a deep breath. "I love you, Rachel."

The anger faded. The same words echoed from the past; another man's voice, Jack's voice. Rachel caught her breath. She almost called his name. "You love me?"

"Yes, Rachel, I love you."

Jack? Wake up, Rachel it isn't Jack. He was long dead, swept away in the Gulf Stream so many years ago. This was a either a GB Shaw farce or an ancient Greek tragedy. Rachel actually smiled for a brief second, then sorrow etched lines in her face again. "It's too late for help, Ben, 12 years too late."

"No, Rachel, listen to me. This is not what you think, I want to help you. There's a way out. Please hear me! I can help you. I can save you and Abigail."

"Maybe I don't want to be saved, Ben. I can't live with the lies and guilt any more."

Ben shouted into the phone. "Rachel, please don't talk like that. You don't understand. Give me a chance to explain. I'll drive up, four hours tops. I'll leave right now. I'll drive straight to the marina and bring Abigail back in the boat."

Rachel looked at the ax and then around at the vast and empty water. "I'm sitting in the middle of the Gulf, Ben in an old wooden dingy with an ax. I was about to scuttle the boat when a Mozart violin sonata called out from my pocket. You'll never find me before the sharks."

GAIA'S GIFT

"No, Rachel, please. I want to spend the rest of my life with you. Please throw the ax overboard. Start rowing back the way you came."

"And which way is that, Ben? What is the direction to happiness?"

"Oh my God, Rachel, don't do this, please, don't do this."

"I'm sorry, Ben. I can't go on living a lie."

Ben softened his voice. "Abigail needs you."

Silence.

"Rachel?"

Desperation strangled him like a vise around his heart. He saw no other solution. "Abigail is your niece. Her mother, Ann was your little sister. That's why you all look so much alike, you're one family. Do you hear me, Rachel?"

Stunned, Rachel sat in silence rocking on the lapping waves.

"Rachel? Are you there, Rachel?" Ben screamed into the phone.

"M-my niece?"

Ben breathed in relief. His imagination had run amok. "Yes, I swear. DNA never lies. You and Ann Stern are sisters and Abigail is her daughter. I have all the social service records, her foster homes and your adoption. You raised your sister's child."

Rachel started to shake her head. It was impossible. Such things just didn't happen in the real world. Maybe it was all a dream and she would wake up still lying on the deck of the boat with Jack at the wheel and her precious Emma still napping below. That's what this was, just a long bad dream. Then she smelled lavender and felt her heart constrict. This was real.

"How could that be?"

"Just stupidity on the part of social services, one hand not knowing what the other was doing. Who knows? I have the whole story, Rachel. You are Abigail's only living relative. Do you understand what I'm saying?"

Rachel nodded so hard her neck hurt.

"Rachel did you hear me?"

She found her voice. "Yes, Ben, I hear you."

He heard a splash. "Rachel, what was that? Please tell me you threw the ax overboard."

"Yes, Ben."

"All right, now pick up the oars and start rowing back to the island."

Tears clouded Rachel's eyes. She cleared her throat. "I'm going to head west. I'm not that far off the island. If I'm going in the right direction, I should see it soon."

"Give me the call letters to the *Gaia* and I'll notify the Coast Guard. We'll find Abigail and you. I'm on my way. Hang up to conserve the battery. I'll call you back as soon as I hear anything."

Rachel gave him the information and powered down the phone. She picked up the oars. "Gaia, you've given me back my life. Please show me the way home."

CHAPTER SIXTY-FOUR

Rachel's shoulders ached from pulling the oars and her head pounded from the hot sun. She hadn't even brought water. Why bring water when you're going to die? Where the hell was the key? She hadn't gone this far when she started her journey, had she? Would she pass it by and never know? Turning her head, she glanced behind her and there in the distance was a small black dot on the horizon.

Rachel ignored the pain and pulled harder, the blisters on her palm beginning to sting. She kept turning around to keep the image alive. It grew larger, finally becoming a land mass. Then she could make out trees and a beach. Not her beach, but sand nevertheless, sand strewn with the old wreckage of a boat and white life preserver hanging on a stick. Rachel laughed hysterically; had the sun and thirst finally driven her mad? Was this a mirage? Had she really landed 2 miles from her own house? She rowed into shallow water and crawled out, using the last of her strength to pull the boat onto the beach.

Falling down by the graves, she pressed her hand into the sand. "Oh, Annie, I didn't know it was you. I didn't even remember you, but in the end we found each other and I found your Abigail." Rachel lay down atop her sister's sandy grave; her final thought, *did you guide me back here to our island?*

The music of the cell phone woke her. She ran her tongue around her mouth trying to get some moisture, but she was parched and her lips were cracked. She took the phone from her pocket and flipped it open.

"Rachel, it's me, Ben. "They found her, Rachel. They found Abigail. She was almost at the marina; Abigail is safe."

Rachel tried to speak, but her mouth was so dry she could barely whisper. "Ben," she croaked.

"Where are you, Rachel?"

She tried again. "On land, by the wreck and grave. So dry, no water, can't speak."

"Shit! We're on our way back, half-way there. Can you get to the house?"

"Don't know." Rachel pushed herself up and lurched onto her feet. She looked at the dingy and then at her bleeding hands. She squinted up at the sun and knew she would never be able to walk two miles without water or shade. She tottered down to the dingy and pushed it into the water, rolling over the side onto the seat. She laid the open phone on the seat. There was only one bar on the phone.

Taking off her shirt, Rachel painfully tore off two squares and wrapped her hands. She draped the remaining shirt around her shoulders and tucked the ends under her bra. Then she grasped the oars and began to pull toward the dock. She bit her lip and pushed the pain to the back of her consciousness. She could hear Ben's tinny voice yelling into the phone. She leaned down and whispered, "In the dingy. Abigail?"

"Hold on, Rachel. You can make it," Ben said. "Here's Abigail."

"Mom, oh God, Mom, I'm so sorry. I was so stupid. I love you."

"Love you," Rachel whispered and saw the dock in the distance. She could barely pull the dingy up on the beach and make it to the house. She crawled up the porch steps and into the kitchen. She got on her knees and pulled the handle of the refrigerator and gasped at the cold air rushing at her. There was an open bottle of water in the door and she twisted off the cap, grateful that it was already loose because she didn't think she would have been able to remove the cap, otherwise. She fell back on the floor and rolled the bottle on her burning forehead.

They found her there, beside the open door of the refrigerator, the empty bottle of water clutched in her hands. Ben lifted her in his arms and took her into the bathroom. "Run a bath, Abby, not hot, okay? I'll get her undressed."

Abigail didn't question him, but did as directed. Ben carried Rachel to the tub and laid her gently in the water. "I can take care of her now," Abigail said.

Blushing, Ben backed out of the bathroom and went back into the kitchen. He closed the refrigerator door and threw away the empty bottle. He found the cell phone on the floor and turned it off. He didn't know where the charger was, so he put the phone on the counter. In the freezer, he found some containers marked soup and brought them outside in the heat to defrost. He paced up and down on the porch, too wired to relax. Maybe he should take Rachel to the mainland to a doctor. Then he told himself to stay calm and wait.

After an interminable wait, Abigail called, "It's okay now, Ben, you can come back in. Mom's awake and in bed."

Ben rushed to Rachel's room and found her sitting up against the pillows. "Hi," she said in a small voice.

"Hi, yourself. Where's Abigail?"

"She went to my workshop to get some herbal salve for my hands and lips."

"Are you sure? Maybe we should go to the mainland to a doctor?" Ben's forehead wrinkled.

"I'm fine, now. Just a bit dehydrated and sunburned."

Ben let out the breath he was holding. He sat down on the side of the bed and gently smoothed back her damp hair. "I'm defrosting some soup…you know that penicillin kind."

Rachel smiled. "No chicken soup in this house. We're vegetarians; can't eat your friends."

A quizzical look came over Ben's face. "I'm lost."

"Later, I'm too tired and my throat hurts."

"I'm sorry. I talk too much," Ben said.

She took his hand. "It's all right, Ben. Talk all you want." She closed her eyes.

Ben smoothed her hair and pulled up the blanket. He leaned over and kissed her forehead. It was still too warm. He went back into the bathroom and wet a cloth with cool water. He placed it on her forehead and sat beside the bed holding her hand.

CHAPTER SIXTY-FIVE

Abigail watched them tableau from the doorway and backed away. She put the jar of cream on the counter and quietly let herself out of the house. The goats had gotten out and found the vegetable garden. Most of the lettuce was gone. She shooed them back inside their enclosure and locked the gate. Then she walked slowly toward the pet cemetery behind the shed.

Settling down beside Sandy's grave she said, "I almost lost my mom today, Sandy. I'm such a stupid kid. I didn't think." Abigail felt a subtle shift in the breeze and reached to where the feathery air brushed her leg. She could almost feel his rough fur ripple under her hand.

"I don't know what I was doing. I had no place to go. And, Mom, she could have died out there on the ocean and…." Abigail put her head on her arms and sobbed.

Ben found her asleep on the grave a couple of hours later. He gently woke her. "Come on, Abby; let's go see if your mom is up to some soup."

She looked up at him. "Is she okay?"

He nodded and helped her stand up. Together they walked back to the house. "I bet you could use some soup, too right about now."

Abigail nodded.

"Your mother said something about no chicken soup?"

Abigail smiled. "When I was little, we had a rooster she named Charlie, who had six wives, Lara, Dara, Sara, Lora, Dora, and Cora, rather like King Henry VIII, except nobody lobbed off their heads. They became our family, along with Charm, the cat and Sandy, the dog. Oh, and the two goats, not the ones we have now, but their parents, Clover and Billy. We were a menagerie."

Ben's whole body shook with laughter. When he could speak he said, "That's quite a story."

"It's not a story, it's true." Abigail stood in the doorway looking askance at Ben.

"I'm sorry, Abby; I didn't mean to imply that it wasn't true. It's just an unusual family, that's all."

Abigail regarded him, then said, "A family is a family as long as they care about each other. Sandy was my very best friend. He was my brother." The girl bit her lip to stave off the tears.

Rachel came up behind her and put her arms around the girl. Abigail leaned back into her mother. "You are a very wise young lady," Rachel said, looking over her head at Ben.

"Not that wise, Mom. I was very dumb today."

"I was dumb, too, Abby. Maybe we could have a 'who was dumber contest'."

Abigail giggled.

Ben cleared his throat. "Why don't we have a soup eating contest, instead? I'm starved."

"First I have to take care of Mom," Abigail said. She opened the jar of cream on the counter. Rachel held out her hands and Abigail gently smoothed the cream over the blisters on her palms and finger pads. Then she put some on Rachel's lips and her forehead.

Ben was almost afraid to speak in the squirrelly atmosphere of teenage moodiness. He had lots of experience in this situation and often found it best to keep his mouth shut. Curiosity won over and he opened his mouth to speak.

Rachel saw his discomfort and said, "It's an herbal salve that I make for burns and abrasions."

"I didn't know you were an herbalist." Ben said.

"It's what I did before…well a long time ago. I used to sell my teas and herbal mixtures to health stores and shops. They were well known."

"What was the label?" Ben asked.

"*Gift of Gaia*," Rachel said.

"Wait a minute that sounds familiar. I remember seeing something with that name in the health food store." His voice trailed off and he blushed. "I'm sorry."

Rachel smiled. "Don't be. I stopped selling herbs after.... Well, a long time ago."

"*Gift of Gaia* products are still sold, though," Ben said.

"I also sold the name to the company that had been buying my herbs. They are very reputable."

Ben smiled. "You are a very smart business woman."

"Um, excuse me, but my mother needs to eat." Abigail interrupted, hands on hips.

Ben looked at Rachel and raised his eyebrows. "Of course, the nurse knows best. Let's heat up the soup."

They ate dinner together at the table. Rachel was much stronger after resting and the salve had relieved the pain in her hands. After ice cream for dessert Abigail cleared the table. Ben offered to help with the dishes, but the girl shook her head and left them soaking in the sink.

Rachel said, "Ben, I think you have something to share with us."

"Right! Are you sure you're up to it?" he asked.

"Yes, please. We're anxious, aren't we, Abby?"

Abigail nodded. "I want to know what's going on."

Ben's stomach churned. He desperately wanted this to work out for everyone, but especially for Rachel and Abigail.

FRAN ORENSTEIN

CHAPTER SIXTY-SIX

They went into the living room and Ben took the two envelopes out of his briefcase that he had left by the sofa. He pulled up a chair and spread everything out on the long wooden coffee table facing Rachel and Abigail. Then he told them the story of two sisters, orphaned as young children, then separated by tragic circumstances, but whose lives had taken similar paths. He showed them the DNA reports and the confirmation of their blood ties. He apologized for taking the samples, but it was the only way to confirm his suspicions.

Rachel already knew some of this, but Abigail was shocked. Rachel put her arms around her and held Abigail while she cried for her lost family. She looked up and nodded at Ben, who left them and went outside to watch the darkening over the Gulf.

Finally, Rachel joined him on the porch.

"Where's Abigail? Is she okay?" Ben asked.

"She's looking at the pictures of her family and trying to make sense of the whole business. She's a survivor. I'm curious though, what are you going to do?"

Ben looked at her. "Do, do about what?"

"Me, about what I did? I broke the law Ben. I kept a child who wasn't mine."

"In reality she was yours because you were her only living relative."

"That's ridiculous, Ben. I didn't know it at the time. I should have taken her to the mainland and told the authorities."

"And that would have accomplished what? She would have been made a ward of the state and placed in foster care while they searched for family. They probably never would have found you in the family tree and she would have had the same fate as her mother, spending years shuttled around in foster homes until she aged out. Is that what you wanted for Abby?" Ben was vehement.

Rachel sighed. "I've felt so guilty all these years. It was like a gift of my child back from Gaia and I kept her."

"And you raised her to become a terrific and beautiful young lady. She's your daughter, Rachel, make no mistake about that. Can you live with what you've done for Abby...with what you did for your sister?"

Tears fell and Rachel brushed them away with the back of her hand. Overcome, she nodded and whispered, "Thank you, Ben."

"This will be our secret, yours, mine and Abigail's. No one ever has to know. Her parents died in a boating accident and you raised her all this time. The truth is always best."

"What about legal papers for school?" Rachel asked, still overwhelmed by Ben's acceptance.

"Leave it to me. I'll figure it out. It's what I do." Ben said.

Abigail stood in the doorway. Her brain was tired from trying to figure out how she felt. She just wanted to go to sleep and forget the horrors of the past month. Looking again at the pictures, Abigail realized what she had missed, but it was not Rachel's fault; she didn't cause the storm or the boat accident that killed her parents. She still couldn't get around the fact that the skeleton in the sand and the other one she hadn't seen were her mother and father. That skeletal hand had held her, washed her, fed her...given her life. Abigail shuddered. She looked at Rachel...this was her living, breathing mother, not the woman in the grave and pictures. "*I have had two mothers,*" she thought.

Stepping onto the porch she asked, "Figure what out?"

"How we are going to get you into school?" Ben said.

"School? Where, when, how?"

Rachel had no clue about the agonizing chaos churning in Abigail's brain as she tried to put everything in its place. Instead, she wondered how children were able to bounce back so quickly. Rachel was still processing all the information, but Abigail had moved onto the mainland already and was starting school. Rachel knew, though, that the tears and questions would surface many times over the next years and she had to deal with them, but truthfully from now on. No more lies. Then there was Ben, another piece in the puzzle of her life and it fit right into place.

"In Miami, Abby, the same school my daughters and Danny attend. How does that sound?"

"Oh my God. That's so awesome! Mom can we buy a pink house? You know we can come here for vacations. We'll make this house bigger so everybody can come. Wait, what about the goats and chickens. We can't just abandon them."

"We'll find a nice farm for them, Abby, don't worry." Rachel said.

Abigail danced down the porch steps and ran down the path around the house. Rachel heard her voice in the distance, "Come on Sandy, I have to go tell Daisy and Buttercup and the chickens. You too, Charm. Oh, Charlie, there you are, come along."

Ben put his arm around Rachel and pulled her against him. "Why is she talking to the dog and the cat? I thought they died. And who is Charlie again?"

Abigail's chatter faded. Through the window, Rachel watched the swing move in the still air, now saturated with the scent of lavender. Rachel snuggled closer. "Charlie was our rooster, remember? Well, Ben, there are things about us that you still need to know."

Rachel trembled at the words she was about to say, but from now on only the truth would tumble from her lips, and Ben could accept or not. She looked up into his beautiful eyes and saw love. Palm fronds swayed in the gentle breeze, and the foamy blue-green sea lapped at the sand. Gaia and her sons rested for now. The air rippled and the spirits smiled, fading into the landscape with the scent of lavender.

FRAN ORENSTEIN

About the Author

Fran Orenstein, Ed.D., award-winning author and poet, wrote her first poem at age eight and received her first rejection for a short story at age twelve. Her published credits include a 'tween mystery series, *The Mystery Under Third Base* and *The Mystery of the Green Goblin*, a fantasy series for 'tweens, *The Wizard of Balalac* and *The Gargoyles of Blackthorne*, a 'tween fiction novel dealing with childhood obesity and bullying, *Fat Girls From Outer Space,* two young adult historical romances, *The Spice Merchant's Daughter* and *The Calling of the Flute*. Her poetry book for young children is out-of-print, but she plans to reissue it with additional poems in summer 2012.

Moving into literature for adults, prize-winning short stories and poetry have appeared in various anthologies. A book of poetry for adults is currently in the works for publication in spring 2012.

Fran has been a teacher, written professionally as a magazine editor/writer, and also wrote political speeches, newsletters, legislation, and promotional material while working for New Jersey State Government for fourteen years. She produced professional papers on gender equity and violence prevention, which were presented at national and international conferences.

She has a BA in Early Childhood Education, a MEd in Counseling Psychology, and an Ed.D. in Child and Youth Studies.

Fran is currently writing the third book in the 'tween fantasy series, *The Centaurs of Spyr*, and has more YA and adult books in the works.

FRAN ORENSTEIN

Visit Fran's World at www.franorenstein.weebly.com